ALL THAT
GLISTERS
IS NOT
SILVER

The third 'Little Wychwell Mystery' novel

1

following *Did Anyone Die?*

and *A Very Quiet Guest*

Disclaimer

The characters in this book are not based on any real people, living or dead. The activities of the secret service personnel in this book are also entirely fictional and bear no relationship to the activities of any real secret service personnel.

All That Glisters is Not Silver

Executive Summary: Priscilla is pleased to have devised a suitable word for the effect the combined Smith family have on her.

Summary

The third 'Little Wychwell Mystery', following 'Did Anyone Die?' and 'A Very Quiet Guest'.

Priscilla becomes the temporary and unwilling landlady of Walls, Barnabus' playboy friend. Shortly afterwards Antholian (Tony), Boris the Great Dane, Priscilla and Walls all accidentally become involved in an Undercover Operation.

Those who have been wondering about when they will encounter Charles, Priscilla's elusive husband, and Felicity, Walls' similarly absent fiancée, in person will be glad to hear that this is the book in which they both finally appear.

The author would like to emphasise that the events described in this book are entirely fictional, as are all the human characters, although most of the places exist. Coromandel and Kings Colleges are fictional as is the village of Little Wychwell itself. Pippy and Isambard are both based on real animals.

Chapter 1

Priscilla abandoned continuing her work and gave an annoyed exclamation. She rose to her feet, somewhat more unsteadily than she expected due to the discovery that her kneeling position on the lounge carpet had made one of her feet go completely to sleep. Using some rather strong Latin words she stamped her foot on the carpet a few times, wiggled her toes, and emitted a few restrained and quiet screams.

It could only be her un-nephew Barnabus, the youngest son of her old college friend Elodea. Anyone else would have respected the idea that if you ring a front doorbell six times without a reply then either the person concerned is out or that they wish you to believe they are out. Barnabus was either incapable of understanding this convention, or so absolutely convinced that he was entirely welcome at all times that he felt it did not apply to him. In fact Priscilla wondered what he did when both she and Angel were out and no one answered the door. How many times did he ring before actually giving up and going away? Angel must be out or she would have already crashed down the stairs and answered the door.

It couldn't be Angel herself. If Angel had locked herself out she would never ring the bell; she would just sit on the pavement in floods of silent tears until Priscilla happened to open the door in order to either enter or exit.

Angel was Barnabus' fiancée, who had been deposited in Priscilla's house by Barnabus so that she could lodge free of charge with Priscilla. Priscilla really could not account for the fact that she had agreed to this arrangement, unless it was because she was so thrilled when she discovered that Angel was accompanied by a hamster, a pet which Priscilla's own mother had never allowed her to own. After making longer and closer acquaintance with Isambard the hamster, whom Priscilla had renamed Amadeus because of his musical ability, Priscilla now felt that her mother may have had a good point.

After a happy year of loudly twanging melodies on his cage bars in the very early hours of the morning Isambard had, sadly, died at the ripe old age of four – quite venerably ancient for a hamster. Priscilla hoped that he had an angelic harp now as he would so much enjoy playing music in the Aeolian Fields. She thought he would also very much enjoy having wings as he would be able to *fly* towards human angels in order to bite them instead of having to jump in the air to reach them with his teeth. Isambard was now buried in Priscilla's back garden.

On the day that the hamster had died Angel had rung work and told them that she was unable to come in as she had suffered a bereavement. This was deceptive since it suggested the death of a human rather than a hamster, but she was in far too much distress to be a waitress that day. Together Angel and Priscilla had searched through the earth in Priscilla's tiny garden for a suitably sized flat stone. This task was impeded by the fact that both Angel, who was often in tears, and Priscilla, who hardly ever cried, could hardly see what they were doing for tears. Then, between sobs, they had carefully written *Eheu fugaces labuntur anni* followed by *Eram quod es, Eris quod sum*, onto the stone in permanent black ink. The pathos of both these phrases had caused them to weep even more. Angel had insisted on adding the hamster's name and the date of his death. Priscilla felt that this rather spoilt the Latin but she had to give way as Isambard was technically Angel's hamster. After the solemn little funeral they had been in such floods of tears that they had had to go back into the kitchen and down a whole bottle of Moet et Chandon to get over it. The champagne seemed terribly inappropriate for a funeral but they felt it would cheer them. It did.

Barnabus was considerably startled when he called round later to offer deep and sincere condolences. He was completely dressed in black so that he would look appropriately sympathetic, and was bearing a tiny wreath that had been painstakingly constructed by Elodea with the tiniest fresh flowers from their own garden. He had expected to find Angel in a miserable heap, drowning in tears and being grateful for his sympathy, and Priscilla being as bracing as possible while choking back the occasional sob. He was, therefore, somewhat surprised when, in actuality, Angel and Priscilla were singing bawdy folk songs at top volume in the kitchen and giggling in between each ditty.

Priscilla felt her eyes fill again just thinking about little Amadeus, aka Isambard. Dear me, she was turning into Angel! She remembered hearing you were supposed to become like your pets, but not like your lodgers, surely? *Est quaedam fiere voluptas*!

Jolted back to the present by another violent peal from her doorbell, she began to hurry towards the door. But she did not want to get caught crying in front of a visitor, not even Barnabus! She blew her nose loudly, wiped her eyes hastily, checked her white manuscript gloves were still pristine, took them off to keep them clean, couldn't find anywhere to put them, returned them to her hands, assumed what she hoped was an "I am very busy and Angel is out" expression, and then flung the front door wide open.

It was not Barnabus. It was Elodea, his mother.

Although Priscilla and Elodea had been friends for such a long time they generally avoided incommoding each other by visiting each other's houses, and met in neutral cafés where they could both relax since neither of them were at home. Their general lack of actual intrusion into each other's domesticity kept their friendship closer. Of course this rule was broken sometimes. Priscilla had had an over-exciting time when she was co-opted into house-and-dog sitting for Elodea eighteen months earlier. When Elodea's children were younger she had also been known to deposit some of them with Priscilla for 'babysitting'. But this *totally unannounced arrival* was unprecedented. Elodea had not even warned her in an email or text or phone call. Then Priscilla remembered that she had her phone and computer turned off for the morning.

Priscilla recovered from her surprise.

"I haven't forgotten to meet you for coffee, have I? I am so sorry! I have my phone and emails switched off this morning because I am proofreading my latest book!"

"No," said Elodea, "you haven't forgotten. You weren't expecting me. I have run away from home!"

Then, looking more closely at Priscilla, she added hastily, "I say, are you all right?"

"Run away from home?" said Priscilla, playing for time while she thought what to do about this unexpected visitor, and then adding, equally hastily, realising that Elodea might be able to detect her recent tears for Amadeus, "I'm fine. I have a slight cold. Nothing more!"

It was not that she did not like Elodea or that she would not usually let her into the house, but right now she had printed off the proofs of a whole chapter of her latest book, and had them carefully arranged on her lounge floor in exactly the right position and order so that she could proofread them carefully and exactly. It would be just like Elodea to ignore the sofa and both the chairs and sit on the floor on top of the proofs.

"Can I come in?" asked Elodea, smiling, inwardly, rather wickedly. She had heard the phrase

11

'proofreading' and knew what Priscilla was thinking. Priscilla had never, ever got over Elodea's visit to Priscilla's flat when Priscilla was proofreading her D. Phil. dissertation. Elodea was pregnant and suffering from queasiness and had developed a theory that she felt less sick if she sat on the floor rather than on chairs. She had accidentally crushed several vital dissertation pages by sitting heavily on them without realising they were there. She had apologised and explained to Priscilla that it was difficult to see the floor below her pregnant bump, but Priscilla had remained frigidly unamused. This lack of amusement seemed likely to persist through the rest of eternity, thought Elodea, as she felt her own lips begin to curve upwards in a visible smile and tried to get them under control. It was much harder to produce typed pages then – computers had made things so much easier now – but Priscilla would still not want Elodea to repeat the dreadful crime. Elodea felt that Priscilla ought to be able to proofread at a table these days, since she owned a large enough one, but Priscilla had persisted in crawling around the floor. At least the proofreading explained why Priscilla was wearing white manuscript gloves. Elodea thought this was a completely ludicrous affectation: suppose a page should become marred, Priscilla could reprint the pages from her computer any time! Elodea was also sure that Priscilla's hands were pristinely scrubbed in the first place. But Priscilla was so uptight when she was proofreading! One might have thought the pages were something *really* precious, like a baby!

"Run away *with* me, Priscilla! We could take a fortnight in Greece. Last-minute booking. Very good offers at present! Or Rome if you prefer!" cried Elodea.

"What?" said Priscilla.

"I told you, I'm running away! You can run away *too*; it's out of term!" explained Elodea.

Priscilla sighed inwardly about the attitude of people who did not have paid employment towards people who did. She realised it was 'out of term' but that meant that she did not have to fit tutorials and lectures in and could devote her whole time to the more important pursuits of research, writing learned articles and books, submitting to journals and publishers, and proofreading. Other 'out of term' hard work involved the arduous business of attending conferences providing academic fellowship, shared learning, and fine living in five-star hotels. De facto, she worked *all* the time. Priscilla felt virtuous and pleased with this version of her own life. She swivelled her thoughts back to the current situation. What *was* Elodea up to today? She reviewed her memory for any examples of similar previous aberrant behaviour by Elodea. Ah ha! This could explain it!

"Is John away somewhere remote, by any chance?" Priscilla asked.

"He's in Japan for the whole month. It's impossible. The time change. Can't even speak on the phone and even emails are a sort of delayed-response affair. I don't see why I can't run away as well. Then he would understand what it was like to have someone who isn't where you want them to be!" Elodea replied.

"You *can't* run away because you are in sole charge of a dog and a pig, let alone all your duties with the church and the village," said Priscilla firmly.

"Pippy's in the car. I've got her little passport with me. She's had her rabies injections, you know. Cyril can always look after Mr Poggles. Oh, *do* say you'll come with us, Priscilla! Pippy and I need a *holiday*!" begged Elodea.

Priscilla had a momentary vision of travelling around Greece with a very awkward, strong-minded and frequently incontinent, if utterly cute and adorable Yorkshire terrier. She closed her eyes for a fraction of a second, and an expression of deep pain flickered across her face. Fortunately she had an excuse readily available.

"I've told you, I'm proofreading!" she said, *very* firmly this time. She looked at Elodea's desolately disappointed expression and relented. "I can compromise on a trip to the Ashmolean for a visit to the café, and that is *it*!"

Elodea brightened up at once. She generously endowed Priscilla with her best smile.

"I knew you would say that, Priscilla, I knew you would! I knew if I asked you to come away for a fortnight you would be able to fit me in for coffee!"

Priscilla glared at her friend. But Elodea's radiant smile was always irresistible. Priscilla had to smile back.

"You and your children! Deceptive persuaders! You all need locking up for the purposes of public safety! You do realise this proofreading is *important*? I need to finish the whole chapter *today*!" Priscilla pronounced.

"Yes, yes, but it's not *that* urgent. You can always sit up all night and finish it!" said Elodea, airily.

Priscilla reluctantly cleared her mind of references, authors, quotations and discoveries, and abandoned all hope of renewing acquaintance with any of them before the afternoon. She was not so easily convinced that sitting up all night proofreading would be a pleasure but Elodea was always so persuasive that there was no denying her anything. Barnabus was just as bad!

Underneath her compliance Priscilla was feeling vaguely annoyed. Elodea had no idea, no idea *at all*, how much effort was involved in getting one's mind into the right zone for academic proofreading. It would take hours to return to her former mental position of total organisation and accuracy. In fact Priscilla might just as well give the whole thing up until tomorrow now. Perhaps they could go for a wander along the Cherwell after lunch, or even punt?

But Priscilla did hope Elodea wasn't going to turn up on her doorstep every day for the next month till John got home. She really would have to refuse to answer the door and hide upstairs if Elodea did that!

"You can come in while I sort myself out and get my bag. But *don't* enter the lounge! My proofs are laid out on the floor. I don't want to find you *sitting* on them again!"

"I'll go straight into the kitchen without even approaching the lounge!" said Elodea, apparently humbly but with a secret giggle bubbling up inside her.

Priscilla found Elodea sitting meekly on one of the kitchen stools when Priscilla came back downstairs having changed her clothes and shoes and redone her make-up. Elodea was holding Priscilla's little silver laughing buddha in her hands and pulling a matching face back at it. Priscilla looked at Elodea and sighed. What was Elodea wearing? She considered Elodea's ensemble – red skirt, thick blue knee socks. Priscilla wondered from where in the world you *bought* blue knee socks, pink trainers – admittedly from a brand encouraging the study of the Classics by having a gold tribute to a Greek goddess on the side – a blue T-shirt with a strange slogan on it, a pink designer hoodie and, to top everything off, a formal black jacket. Priscilla reflected sadly that, despite the fact she appeared to have dressed in the dark from the random contents of the clean laundry basket, it never really mattered what Elodea wore. Even at this age Elodea got wolf whistles from builders with disturbing frequency. She was one of the fortunately endowed who would look, most unfairly, as if she was in designer clothes if she was wearing a plastic bin liner and, even more unfairly, would always look as lovely as she had done in her twenties. Priscilla made

18

considerable effort and outlaid a high proportion of her salary in order to dress fashionably, smartly and suitably, and felt this was unjust. She tried to ignore Elodea's whole gaudy ensemble but could not stop herself from asking, "What *exactly* does your T-shirt slogan *mean*?"

"It's not my T-shirt; it's one of Barnabus'. I found it after I had packed my cases. I couldn't find any more of mine."

That figured, thought Priscilla, although that speech did suggest that Elodea really *had* got packed suitcases in the car. How very odd she was being today!

Priscilla decided to persist in finding out what the T-shirt meant, as the strange slogan just might explain the whole mystery of Elodea's behaviour. "And the slogan means…?"

"Rowing!"

"Ah!" said Priscilla vaguely. "There are a million ways to die but only one way to live" had not struck her immediately as referring to *rowing* but she supposed it might make some kind of sense if you were Barnabus. This was no help in deciphering the meaning of Elodea's behaviour, as the choice of T-shirt had clearly been entirely random

"Aren't you a little overdressed for the temperature?" Priscilla enquired.

"Yes, but I had already packed and closed the cases and then I thought it might be cold on the journey so I put the hoodie on and then I remembered that I once went on holiday with no jacket and it can be really cold at the top of mountains and things so I grabbed the jacket as I left and put it on as well. I could take something off while we have coffee, I suppose?"

There she went again, thought Priscilla. Elodea really did seem serious about taking a sudden and unplanned holiday. But why? At least it might be possible to get *one* layer removed and thus improve the tone of the whole startling outfit slightly.

"Shall I take the jacket off?" asked Elodea. "That would be easiest – it's on top!"

"Good idea," Priscilla agreed, and then realised her error. Once the jacket was removed the hoodie displayed large gold letters that formed a misspelt obscene word.

"I think it's a little too hot for the hoodie as well!" said Priscilla, trying not to look too pained at the sight of the lettering, which *she* did not find at all amusing.

"It's French Connection UK, you know!" giggled Elodea. "I saw it and I simply couldn't resist it. Don't you think it's hilarious? I bought it specially to wear for a formal Physics Department 'do' that I didn't want to attend. It was one of those things where 'wives', or rather 'partners', are expected to turn up as well and it was all going to be very boring and I suddenly felt like a handbag! Well, not a handbag, because John doesn't have a handbag, naturally, but that sort of thing, you know, an accessory, not a human! But John noticed what I was wearing before we left the house, which was surprising actually, and he said he thought it would cause a lot of upset and I realised how distressed he would feel if I was *quite* so outrageous, so I took it off and wore a proper evening stole instead. Only today I had packed all my other hoodies in the suitcase and already fastened it and so I thought I might as well wear this one since there was no one else around to notice, except Pippy, of course, and she doesn't care!"

"Quite!" said Priscilla, feeling this was a suitably non-committal answer. She was actually thinking that the only suitable place for that particular hoodie would be the nearest clothes recycling bin, and at the same time wondering if Elodea thought that her dog could read. Hopefully not!

"I suppose it bothers *you* now!" said Elodea, with a sigh, looking at Priscilla's expression. "I'll take it off!"

She removed the hoodie to reveal a very gaudy cartoon of a rowing eight above the slogan on her T-shirt. The effect of this T-shirt design in combination with Elodea's skirt, which featured a classic fabric design of red roses, was, Priscilla felt, not at all desirable.

"Zeus!" Priscilla exclaimed, before she could stop herself. "Maybe you should put the jacket back *on!*" She then added, as a hasty afterthought, in case Elodea needed a reason to adjust her outfit *other* than the fact that it looked quite extraordinary, "You might be cold without it: the Ashmolean café air conditioning, you know!"

"I say," said Elodea, completely ignoring Priscilla since she had never been perturbed by any comments on her fashion sense, and picking the buddha back up from the work surface, "is this the buddha that Barnabus and Angel bought for you?"

She looked into the buddha's face and jiggled it absent-mindedly on her knee, as if it was a restive baby.

"Yes," replied Priscilla. "I keep it by the biscuit barrel to remind me not to overeat."

"It is perfectly *gross* in the *obesity* stakes," agreed Elodea. "I suppose it's not really your taste in ornaments! But it serves you right for pretending to Barnabus that you were upset when he got the buddha that Charles sent to you blown up. Otherwise you would have neatly disposed of the original and not been lumbered with this replacement afterwards."

A bicycle bell tinkled. It must be someone just outside in the street.

"I know it's my own fault!" said Priscilla, honestly. "I could hardly admit to Barnabus and Angel that I had only been *pretending* to be angry at losing the ghastly thing after they had gone to all the effort to get me another."

"Priscilla?" queried Elodea.

"What now?"

"You haven't noticed anything strange about it, have you?" asked Elodea.

"Why?"

"Well, because, because…" Elodea stopped for a few moments. Should she admit what she thought she had seen, even to a best friend? "Because I could have sworn it winked at me just now, very slowly and in a kind of rather leery way. I really must be seeing things!"

"You need coffee and you need it now!" said Priscilla, taking the buddha out of Elodea's hands and putting it back by the biscuit barrel. She swept her friend up from the stool as she passed, and propelled her towards the front door. "Just a trick of the light!"

They left by the front door. The buddha remained in the kitchen, silent and apparently immobile. There was no one left to see whether the little silver statuette repeated its performance of winking or not.

"I am so tired of conferences and workshops and meetings all summer!" said Elodea.

They had paced swiftly up the road and out of Jericho and had now turned down towards the centre of Oxford.

Elodea continued, "John is either at a conference or a workshop or a meeting or in between conferences and workshops and meetings and trying to catch up with work in the department and prepare for the next c, w or m, for the whole of July and August and September and then it's term again. I don't know why everyone always thinks academics get long holidays! I am really, really tired of taking my annual fortnight's holiday in *January*. It's so much worse these days as we have to be careful of our carbon footprints and Cornwall in January is *not* cheerful whatever the advertisements may say. John never seems to worry about *his* carbon footprint when he jets off on holiday abroad on his own!"

"He isn't on *holiday*, Elodea," corrected Priscilla. "Conferences and workshops and meetings are *serious work*! Anyway, you *like* Cornwall and you know you don't like flying very much!"

"I can *cope* with flying! I *can* so! I fly to visit Elizabeth! I wish *I* had a job that involved having to pig it in *expensive* hotels in *glamorous* places!" wailed Elodea.

She really did seem down in the dumps, thought Priscilla. She considered reminding her that if she had wanted a career she shouldn't have got married straight from university, had four children and never returned to the world of work, but decided that might not help the current situation. Priscilla rifled through her mind for ideas. She reconsidered what Elodea had just said and had some inspiration.

"Couldn't you go and visit Elizabeth?" she suggested.

"No. They have a *baby*; well, he's a toddler now, don't you remember? He *screams*. A lot!" Elodea wailed.

"But, Elodea, dear, you *adore* babies and toddlers; you had four of your own *on purpose*!" protested Priscilla.

"I *used* to adore babies and toddlers! I don't have to *always* adore babies and toddlers."

Priscilla gave up. It was just not like Elodea to be so mumpish. Doubtless she would find out the reason eventually. Priscilla knew that Elodea absolutely adored Elodeus, her little grandson. She had had him to stay for a whole fortnight at the Old Vicarage quite recently.

"In any case, I *couldn't* hop off with you for a fortnight right now because Charles is coming here the week after next!" said Priscilla.

"Charles! Why didn't you *tell* me?" demanded Elodea.

"Didn't I? Oh well! I must have forgotten!" Mainly, Priscilla added to herself, because I was hoping to achieve a visit from Charles, who would most likely only stop in Oxford for a few days, without Elodea and John coming to visit him and taking up a lot of his time. Having discovered that John, who was a great friend of Charles, was away in Japan Priscilla had just begun to feel some hope of achieving this aim. But now that she had told Elodea that Charles was visiting, Elodea was bound to feel she *had* to come and see Charles while he was here. Priscilla knew that Elodea did even not really like Charles but she would feel she had to make a social call to see him because it was the polite thing to do.

"He wasn't upset about his buddha being blown up, was he?" asked Elodea.

"No, not at all, not at all!" replied Priscilla, rather too hastily.

"You haven't told him about it, have you?" accused Elodea.

"Well, he was hopping about up Mount Everest at the time, if you remember, and by the time he got back it would have taken too long to explain in an email, and much too long in a text, and we keep our phone conversations for, you know, other things!" Priscilla prevaricated.

"*Other* things?" queried Elodea.

"Saying 'I love you' and things like that. *You* know! *Amantes sunt amentes!*" replied Priscilla, with sudden brilliance, after spending a few seconds trying to hastily think what else she could possibly have been talking to Charles about.

Elodea was amazed, although she tried not to show it, how wonderful that they were still *so in love*. She had not thought it! Charles was Priscilla's husband; they had married while taking their doctorates. Then, shortly afterwards, Charles had gone off to work in a Canadian university, when he was not mountaineering, and Priscilla had stayed in Oxford. They met very infrequently but nonetheless they remained *apparently* happily married. Elodea wondered for the umpteenth time if Charles was actually gay or, if not, whether he had a secret second wife or mistress in Canada. She did not wonder about Priscilla's sexual preferences: Priscilla preferred academic study to sex and always had done.

"He might have seen a piece about the explosions on the news?" suggested Elodea.

"Unlikely. He never really looks at the news – certainly not the *court cases*. I suppose if my picture had been on the *front* page he might have noticed. Not otherwise. But there will never be a trial now, so that's not likely to happen."

"Very true," said Elodea. "*Poor* Frank! Thank goodness that *dear* Fran is being properly cared for now!"

Priscilla wondered, yet again, if Elodea's extensive and generous charitable feelings, which were extended towards friends who cared for her and people who had damaged her alike, were actually *real*, or if she was a very convincing *actress*. On the whole, she concluded, these feelings had to be real: nobody could keep this front up as persistently as Elodea did otherwise, could they?

Big Frank's liver had finally, after years of drug and alcohol abuse, succumbed to a particularly lethal brew of prison hooch at Christmas while he was detained on remand. Several other prisoners had spent the festive season handcuffed to hospital beds but only Big Frank had died.

Priscilla did not think he was much of a loss to the world. Priscilla also felt that Fran should have remained in jail and been appropriately punished for trying first to blow Elodea up and next trying to drown her. But Fran's parents, who had turned out to inhabit an unexpectedly high place in society, seemed to have finally decided to take action to save their delinquent daughter. Priscilla suspected that Lady Wilmington, the lady of the Little Wychwell Manor, had also been active in preventing the case reaching court in order to preserve her own family from scandal. Priscilla suspected that Elodea might have been adding her efforts to this cause, because she was so sorry for Fran and Big Frank. Whatever might have been happening behind the scenes with high level string pulling, the result had been that Fran had been deemed mentally incompetent to stand trial and was removed from prison to take up residence in a psychiatric institution. Without any remaining defendants, since Ustin's status was still missing, presumed drowned, the whole case had been dropped.

"And here we are!" said Elodea as they turned down Beaumont Street. They mounted the steps to the Ashmolean and solemnly and slowly revolved, one at a time, according to the instructions, through the new continuous-movement revolving door.

The steps outside had been quite elegantly empty but once inside they found the refurbished museum was still suffering from over-popularity. Before it had been renovated one had been able to wander quietly around in refined, peaceful and largely empty galleries. Now the whole of the ground floor,

32

renamed the first floor, was packed with tourists and families with small children.

"How splendid that it is so popular now!" said Elodea, trying to be enthusiastic, but her tone wobbled towards an unconvincingly sad note.

"I preferred it before," said Priscilla with complete honesty. "I don't believe any of these people are *looking* at *anything*. They just seem to be occupying the space for no reason at all. I liked the space."

"Well, I'm sure it must be good that it's this popular. It's excellent to see so much interest in history."

"Humph!" said Priscilla, adding, "The basement or the top floor?" She realised that she had been crawling round her own lounge floor for far too long without a break, and was now becoming grumpily thirsty.

"The basement, I suppose," said Elodea faintly. She was never very happy in large crowds and was beginning to feel insecure.

They headed for the stairs and descended to what used to be the basement and was now labelled 'ground floor'. It was just as crowded. They peered into the café.

"It's very busy, even in here," said Elodea, doubtfully.

Priscilla looked at her friend. Elodea had the frantic look that she always wore in crowded places, like a wild animal which was being herded into a trap. She had better rescue her.

"Let's try the *top* floor! It should be quieter up there!"

They headed back for the stairs. Elodea dashed up them as if escaping from pursuing hunters, and continued on past the entrance and up to the first floor, now labelled the second floor.

"I can't *get* these storey names!" said Elodea. "Can you?"

"Just add one on to where you think you are, silly!" said Priscilla.

They puffed up to the top of the stately staircase and found the milling crowds had thinned to pre-redesign levels.

Elodea looked round at all the space and felt happy and relaxed again. Priscilla, her mind firmly on coffee, headed through the second floor to find the next set of stairs and then discovered that she was alone. She hurried back to Early Italian Paintings and found Elodea still there, studying one of the exhibits carefully.

"Look, Priscilla, at this lovely marriage picture! I love this one! Isn't it wonderful? Look at the details! And look at the gold leaf and lapis lazuli on that one over there!"

"Yes, but, *coffee!*" said Priscilla, somewhat desperately, as she tried to entice Elodea back on to the right track. Priscilla set off again but when she glanced back she discovered that Elodea had escaped again. She was just in time to glimpse her vanishing through entirely the wrong door. Priscilla sighed, retraced her steps, and followed Elodea through the automatic door that opened into 'East Meets West'.

"Look, look, Priscilla! A boat, made entirely from cloves! Oh, no, cloves *and bamboo*. Well, whatever it is, I *love* that boat! Look at the tiny little details! And see the netsuke over there! Oh, but see, the labels are wrong; the dog is on the cat's number and the cat is on the dog's."

"Possibly someone was distracted from what they should have been doing when they put them in the cabinet," said Priscilla, with entirely wasted sarcasm, as she hooked her arm through Elodea's and steered her back on to the correct route. By dint of keeping hold of her friend's arm they managed to achieve a seat in the top floor café only half an hour later. Priscilla resolved to take Elodea to the Ashmolean every time they met for coffee in Oxford for the next year. If she had sufficient exposure surely she would stop getting so over-stimulated by the whole experience in future? It all came of living in Little Wychwell most of the time, Priscilla reflected. This fate seemed to Priscilla to be similar to being buried alive: the village was far too distant from decent cultural experiences!

Chapter 2

When they reached the dizzy heights of the rooftop and the ordered peace of the Ashmolean dining room, Elodea discovered that this venue was serving 'brunch' rather than anything involving many different sorts of cake. The lack of copious cake varieties, as far as she was concerned, was unsupportable at *any* time of day. Priscilla, abandoning any hope of at least accessing a cup of coffee *before* descending to the ground floor again, agreed to a change of venue. They renegotiated the Ashmolean, Priscilla only having to retrieve Elodea from forays into Renaissance Paintings and Greek Architecture before finally steering her out of the revolving door again.

"Where shall we *try* now?" asked Elodea.

Priscilla, feeling she had experienced quite enough stairs for one day and wishing that she had offered Elodea coffee in her own house in the first place, even if it had meant endangering her proofs, did not like the sound of the word 'try'. "*Cogita anti salis!*" she said. "Somewhere guaranteed to have coffee and cake!"

"Waterstone's café is only just round the corner but you can read the funny notices on the walls at Puccinos, and then there is always Blackwells. Blackwells and Waterstone's have all those glorious books to browse through on the way in and out too!" replied Elodea.

Priscilla momentarily considered screaming, "Why restrict yourself to considering those three? Why not consider all five billion cafés that are available in Oxford?" or, even worse, yelling, "I don't care! Anywhere that has *coffee!*"

Instead she heard her own voice say, very mildly, "I favour the *closest*", while vaguely gesturing towards the Randolph, which was opposite them. Then she remembered Elodea's eccentric garb and changed her gesture to point up the street, adding helpfully, "All three of those have cake at all times of day, to the best of my knowledge!"

Only after she had completed this speech did Priscilla remember that Waterstone's café was on the second floor. Since the lift took hours to arrive and Elodea would certainly refuse to wait for it, this would mean climbing up four more flights of steep stairs. It was too late to change their plan. Elodea, cake sensors in full operation, had immediately cried "I'll go ahead and grab a table!" and was already vanishing towards their goal.

Elodea was completely out of sight by the time Priscilla entered the ground floor of Waterstone's, so Priscilla decided to take a leisurely trip up in the lift. She caught Elodea up while she was still standing in the slow-moving queue for service and trying to crane around the people in front of her to see inside the cake cabinet.

"There are plenty of free tables!" Elodea announced and then continued, in a satisfied voice, "They still have lots of different cakes at this time of day. No brunch nonsense here! I'll have to have *two* pieces because they have two sorts I haven't tried before and I want to test them *both* out. But I simply *must* have some mini-muffins as well because Pippy likes them and I can save *one* of them for her!"

Priscilla tried not to be annoyed by her slim friend's eating habits, fully intending to order an espresso and a glass of water. However, by the time they were actually served she had also had leisure to study the cake selection and had decided to have a large slice of chocolate cake as well. After all, it would be *very* unsociable to sit there without eating!

"You know," said Elodea, as they squeezed themselves around a tiny table for two, balancing the food and drinks precariously on the small top, "I really worry that I am beginning to go a little senile. Pippy and I are addicted to *Bargain Hunt*."

"The senile bit is *possibly* true," thought Priscilla to herself, "since you have not only forgotten the rules of English grammar but think that a dog helps you shop!"

"Bargain hun*ting*," Priscilla responded, slightly accentuating the 'ing' to help her friend regain her grammatic precision. "Should at least save you money."

Elodea had taken far too large a bite of cake, and the start of her reply was consequently somewhat muffled.

"No, no, not bargain hunting," she said, in a very indistinct way.

Then she managed to finish the cake. "*Bargain Hunt*! It's a TV programme. It has Tim Wonnacott on it. People buy antiques and then sell them at auction and usually lose money – they're supposed to *make* extra money, of course. Pippy loves it as well. She always sits quietly on my knee while it's on, and watches it with me…"

I have *no idea* what she is talking about, thought Priscilla, feeling relieved that Elodea was at least not imagining that her dog understood shopping but disturbed that Elodea seemed to think Pippy watched television, let alone had any opinion on *which* television programmes to watch.

Elodea continued, "Anyway, when normal activities are in full spate we usually only watch *Bargain Hunt* on Thursdays because I am always doing something at that time of day on all the other days: Bible Study, WI, and so on. But at the minute everything else has stopped for August and I now find I have an absolute compulsion to watch it *every day*. So does Pippy!"

Priscilla had drifted away into her own thoughts near the start of this speech. The next remark that Elodea made, however, somehow managed to penetrate into her mind, and brought her back to full attention at once.

"And," continued Elodea, "you can *apply* to go on the TV show *yourself* but you have to be in a pair, so I applied for the *two* of us. I didn't think you'd mind!"

Priscilla choked on her coffee. This incident at least meant that she had to apply her serviette to her mouth, which gave her time to decide that she had better handle this carefully and not start by saying what she

42

really thought. "Do you think there is a *good* chance of us getting a place on the show?" she enquired, as calmly as she could.

"Oh no, very low chance unfortunately. It's very, very popular. Barnabus tells me that lots of students watch it but I fear that in my case I am one of the *other* sort of viewers. I'm turning into an old age pensioner far too early!"

Priscilla relaxed. She focussed on the positive, 'very popular'. There only seemed to be a very remote chance of having to refuse to appear on whatever this show might be! Priscilla filed this worry in the 'unlikely to ever happen' wastebasket section of her memory.

Then she realised that Elodea was looking quite sad and tearful at the thought of turning prematurely into an old age pensioner.

Amazingly, Priscilla actually thought of a truly comforting thing to say. "Nonsense! You aren't watching it because you are turning into an *old age pensioner*; you are watching it because you are a *perpetual student.* Which course are you studying at present?"

"That's one of the problems with my life: I'm not studying *anything* right now. I've just finished my seventh Master's degree and somehow I can't seem to raise enthusiasm for another. But I do miss studying!" replied Elodea.

Priscilla looked at her friend with wonder. Why hadn't she just taken *one* Masters degree and then read for a *doctorate* like a normal person? If Elodea had said she was addicted to *distance learning courses* with the Open University, Priscilla would have thoroughly agreed with her.

Elodea, who had cheered up at the thought that it was being a student that attracted her to the programme, had now wandered off, butterfly like, to another subject. "Anyway, I was just wondering…" she continued, while chewing with enthusiasm.

"Yes?" said Priscilla, wondering what Elodea did with all the calories she tucked in with such enthusiasm. They never appeared to settle anywhere on her figure.

She also reflected that Elodea must be in a strange state of mind today – she never usually committed such a breach of etiquette as speaking *while chewing*, and certainly not so in a restaurant.

"…Do you think that when Charles arrives he is going to notice the fact it's not *his* buddha?" Elodea asked.

"I should imagine he will notice fairly fast if he sees it at close range! I'll have to move it from the kitchen and put it on a high shelf at the back of the lounge! He is a chemist after all and I am sure his buddha must have been *real* silver; and this one is, er, white metal and not very well made. Charles only ever buys *very* good quality objets d'art! But he might not look at it closely. We'll have such a lot of other things to discuss. This will be the first time we have met in person since he sent it to me! All kinds of academic commitments – very limiting. If one of us was free the other wasn't, you know!" replied Priscilla.

Elodea forbore to comment on the length of time since Priscilla and Charles had met. She had long ago given up trying to fathom how Priscilla and Charles remained married when they only met so very occasionally.

"But," she persisted, "what are you going to say if he *does* notice?"

"I'm hoping that he might have forgotten that he gave it to me," Priscilla replied.

"And if he *hasn't* forgotten?" Elodea continued. She felt her friend should prepare for this eventuality before it occurred.

"I shall just have to tell him the *whole story*, I suppose. It will be tedious in the extreme to have to explain it all," replied Priscilla.

"All that glisters is not silver," mused Elodea, getting the quotation only partly correct.

"Gilded tombs do worms enfold," said Priscilla, completing the *correct* quotation and ignoring the fact that this no longer rhymed. "Very true, that speech. Talking of the buddha reminds me. How is *Paris* getting on?"

Priscilla was not really interested in Paris; she just wanted to change the subject. Nothing distracted Elodea faster than the subject of her own children! But Priscilla had made a bad choice of child and instantly wished she had not asked about Paris. Elodea looked almost as if she had been stabbed suddenly through the heart. Her whole body went rigid with distress for a few moments. Priscilla was still wondering what medical action she should take when Elodea recovered and replied, in a perfectly composed way, "He's in Afghanistan again. They were short of officers so he got posted almost straight back, attached to another regiment. Poor Belinda was quite, quite prostrate with worry and grief. She has gone back to her parents' house while he is away. And the baby is due in another two months."

"Baby?"

"Priscilla, you *must* remember! I *told* you! They have a honeymoon baby on the way! It's a girl. They know that from the scans. *Due in two months*. It is going to be a *very* lovely baby if it takes after *either* of its parents. I showed you the little dress I bought for

47

it. You *must* remember that. You do remember the *wedding*, I hope; you were there! But now Paris is likely to be on active service when the poor child arrives. How is Belinda supposed to cope? Of course she is mostly at her parents'. Her mother is really very, er…"

"Overpoweringly possessive," put in Priscilla, adding to herself, "I was surprised she didn't snatch Belinda back from the altar during the service. Which is odd because she looks very English, very unemotional – a very classically upper-class lady who is made entirely from ice like the Snow Queen. Evidently in her case it's very possessive ice. It is not surprising that she and Elodea don't seem to be bosom pals. Entirely different types!"

"She is *understandably supportive!*" corrected Elodea. "Very understandable, especially when you think about *Tom*." Elodea's face contracted again for a moment. Tom, Belinda's brother, Paris' army friend, who had died so young and so tragically!

"But Mrs de Woolf is so supportive that Belinda doesn't need any help from me at all," Elodea thought sadly to herself, "although I would love to help her if she needed me. No wonder her mother clings to her after losing Tom! If I lost any of my children I would never let the others out of my sight again!"

Elodea added out loud, "I would feel the same…"

Her voice trailed away. She *had* hoped to see more of Paris and Belinda now that they were married, but Paris and Belinda lived with the de Woolfes when Paris was on leave, and Belinda never visited Elodea without him.

Elodea shook herself metaphorically and corrected her expression into one of pleasure. "I am absolutely thrilled about having another grandchild, as you can imagine, because I *do love* babies!"

Priscilla felt she had better not remind her that she had said exactly the reverse a short time ago, and arranged her own face into a look that she hoped indicated a deep interest in Elodea's putative grandchild. "Silly me! Of course, of course, I remember. Expecting a baby, yes, lovely, super, wonderful. Let me know when it arrives!"

She moved rapidly on to an alternative subject.

"And you still have Barnabus and Angel's wedding to look forward to, when he finishes his D. Phil., that is!"

"Yes, I suppose they will probably wait till then. They did think they might get married next year *before* his final year. Angel earns a bit of money and they don't need much to live off," smiled Elodea.

Only because Angel lives with me, rent free, thought Priscilla, rather crossly.

"Angel's been very quiet around the house this week," she added, after a moment's reflection.

"That's because she has gone to France camping with Barnabus, in the Pyrenees. They are away for the whole month. They *must* have told you. I was thinking I might go to Japan with John but that was when I thought Barnabus would be around to look after Pippy and Mr Poggles. Of course they *need* a holiday. I don't mind that."

"Typical!" thought Priscilla. "I see why Elodea is so mumpish now. She spends her whole time running around after those two, and then just when she wants a couple of weeks in Japan with John and asks them to look after the dog, they hop off to go camping in France."

Priscilla drifted on with her musings. It was strange though, how ever had she managed not to notice that Angel, and indeed Barnabus, were missing. She tried to remember what Angel had said the *last* time she saw her, or even when that was! She *might* have said something about going on holiday. Priscilla had been thinking about her book a lot recently and had just replied "Yes" or, if that seemed inappropriate, changing it to "No". Had Angel left a note on the hall table last week? Yes, yes, now she came to think of it the last communication with Angel was a note which said "Gone to get some real French wine. See you when we get back." A little cryptic – clearly they *knew* she would think they were at the off-licence. She was prepared to bet that Barnabus was behind that note: he must have known she was not listening to them when they told her their holiday plans. He had a *wicked* sense of humour sometimes.

With a sudden cold feeling in her heart she did hope they had not also told her about their wedding plans and got her to agree to have them *both* move into her spare room following this big event. Surely not? She reviewed all the details that she could recall of any conversations they had held with her over the last month. When Priscilla returned to real life in Waterstone's, having carefully sifted all the small fragments she could dredge from her memory and, satisfactorily, recalling no evidence of any conversations about weddings or future accommodation, she realised that Elodea was still talking about something or other – probably something of no importance whatsoever.

What Elodea was actually saying at that moment was "And I *can't* leave her with Mrs Wigley although she offered, because of the wolfhounds and similarly the Vicar, although that's really the reverse problem because Pippy would be a nuisance. She does like chasing small birds…"

Priscilla returned to the words 'she does like chasing small birds'. She was baffled temporarily as to who the 'she' might be, being unaware of Pippy's predilection for bird chasing activities. Elodea did not have a *cat* now, did she? Was Elodea talking about the new baby? Couldn't be; it wasn't born yet. Maybe she was absent-mindedly referring to toddler Elodeus as 'she'. Yes, probably Elodeus: he was a very pretty baby so one could easily forget that he was a boy. Elodeus was a sturdy little child; he was clearly taking after Elizabeth and John. What was Elodea saying now?

"I wondered if you could possibly… I realise it's a terrible imposition!"

What was a terrible imposition? She didn't like to admit that she hadn't been listening, not after forgetting about Elodea's future grandchild's existence. On the other hand this was a *Smith* asking her for a *favour.* This had caused her quite enough disturbance in the recent past. But Elodea was looking expectantly at her, waiting for the answer.

Priscilla wavered. Surely it couldn't be anything too big or disastrous. Could it? Elodea was most unlikely to let Priscilla look after Elodeus, so it wasn't that. She did hope she *wasn't* agreeing to a holiday in Greece, but surely Elodea would describe that as a wonderful treat, not a *terrible imposition*. The words '*terrible imposition*' did have a rather sinister ring but she had to say *something*: Elodea was still sitting there waiting for her to reply. What should she do? What *had* they been talking about recently? Proofreading? It could be that. Priscilla clutched at this hopeful straw. Entirely forgetting that Elodea had just announced that she was not studying anything at present, Priscilla leapt to the conclusion that Elodea wanted her to proofread some of the work for her latest correspondence course. Could she be studying something classical? That *could* be it. Priscilla decided to take the plunge and rashly jumped down a metaphorical waterfall without finding out how high it was.

"Not an imposition at all; it would be a pleasure!" she heard her voice say.

"Are you *sure?* I don't want to burden you with too much!" asked Elodea, sounding anxious.

"Absolutely sure!" replied Priscilla. What other reply could she make now?

"How *wonderful* you are, Priscilla! You are a real *brick*, my *absolutely best friend ever!*" said Elodea with truly heartfelt gratitude. "Especially with Charles coming as well, but then she is *such* a sweetie, I'm sure she won't be *any* bother... provided you cover the kitchen with newspaper every night and shut her in there. And remember that she always bites people if they try getting into the house after ten o'clock at night. I have her and all her food and equipment in the car so you won't need to buy anything at all and I can get straight off to the airport as soon as we get back to your house. I've got my suitcase and the tickets and my passport so I'll just need to drive there."

Priscilla realised the dreadful gravity of her error. She had leapt into Niagara Falls unawares. She had evidently *agreed to dog sit Pippy*. How could she be this stupid and gullible? Elodea must have *known* she wasn't listening.

She looked at her friend's face. It appeared to be *totally* guileless and was glowing with heartfelt gratitude.

"I only booked the flight this morning, just before I came round to see you.   Last-minute booking. Very good bargain. That's how I knew there were cheap holidays to Greece available. I just booked it on an impulse. John doesn't know I'm coming yet because if you hadn't agreed to look after Pippy I wouldn't have been able to go. I phoned Cyril about Mr Poggles before I left because he wouldn't have minded if I had cancelled the arrangement again later because I hadn't gone! I *knew* you would help! It *is* a terrible imposition – I know that. You are *so good* to say it isn't! You really know when a girl is in desperate circumstances and needs help. I will never, never forget this, darling Priscilla!" she cried.

Before Priscilla could stop her Elodea had leapt out of her chair, flung her arms round Priscilla's neck, and given Priscilla a large and affectionate kiss on the cheek. Someone at the next table choked on their tea with the shock of such demonstrative behaviour. Everyone in the café seemed to be staring at them.

"What time is your flight?" said Priscilla, astonished by the serene sound of her own voice, as, in a vain effort to restore normality, she shoved Elodea back into her own seat. Priscilla had a horrible vision in her mind's eye of Pippy, mouth crammed full of precious proofs.

"Half past seven," Elodea answered.

"What would you have done if I had said *no*?" said Priscilla, with the word 'kennels' forming itself in her mind. Perhaps she could get the dog into kennels herself, once Elodea had gone?

"I couldn't have gone, not at all. She would never cope with kennels at her age, but I knew you would agree: you are such a super and obliging person!"

No I'm not, thought Priscilla. Just an inattentive and absent-minded fool. *Eheu! Cuiusvis hominis est errrare, nullius nisi insipientis in errore perseverare.*

Another thought occurred to her.

"And if I had agreed to go to the Greek Islands with you…?"

"I would have gone there *instead*. I really rather liked that idea myself! I'm not that fond of sitting on planes for hours and hours to get all the way to Japan. I would have just texted John and said, 'Gone on hols with Priscilla. Will let you know when I am back'. It would have served him right for leaving me here by myself *all the time*. We would have had to drive to Greece because I could hardly put poor Pippy into the luggage compartment on a plane, but the drive would have been *tremendous fun*!"

Was she telling the whole truth? *Apparently* she was.

Priscilla tried not to entertain a suspicion that she had been trapped by her friend's machinations. Elodea was, as she knew, entirely guileless. Elodea was a good friend! Pippy was very small and mostly very sweet and… Was there any chance that she could still retract her offer, explain that she hadn't been listening, explain that she was not a kind, good person but a horrible, unfeeling person who was habitually unhelpful? No, there was no way of getting round it. She had been Smith'ed again. No, not Smith'ed; classically vulcanized! Like rubber! Priscilla was not entirely sure what was done to rubber when it was vulcanized but it sounded appropriately painful. That was it! That was what the Smiths did, they vulcanized people! If it wasn't Elodea, it was Barnabus! What would she find she had agreed to do *next*?

She smiled to herself, very pleased with her new name for the effect the entire family had on her. But, just after this momentary pleasurable sensation, she realised that she was beginning to experience the dizzy feeling that being vulcanized usually induced. She experienced a vivid series of flashbacks about what had happened last time she agreed to dog sit for Elodea.

"Not in *your* house though! I am *only* having her in *my* house! No trips to Little Wychwell! No *house-sitting*!" she gabbled.

"No, no, not at all necessary," said Elodea soothingly. The last dog sitting episode in Little Wychwell had ended in Priscilla having an attack of strong hysterics, and Elodea did hope that Priscilla was not going to have a repeat attack right now in the café! She looked at her with anxiety. Priscilla did seem very agitated. She must calm her down and reassure her at once.

"No house-sitting! No Little Wychwell! Cyril is taking care of Mr Poggles. Coffee after church in our house is cancelled. I'm only away for *two weeks*. John didn't want me to join him for the whole month even when he first suggested that I might like to go as well. He said I could only come for *part* of the time because I am a *distraction*. But then I thought I couldn't go at all because of Barnabus being away so we gave up the whole idea. He is going to be *so* pleased with you because I can go now! He will be *so* delighted when I turn up! Oh! I forgot! It's not a conference or a meeting or a workshop this time, not for a whole *month*, of course. It's a…" She stopped for a moment to recall the right phrase. "…A *collaborative project!*" she finished with a flourish, feeling triumphant at getting the correct description.

Priscilla thought 'a distraction' was too polite a description of her friend by far! 'A disruption' would be more accurate. A mobile destruction machine, demolisher of peace and tranquillity, would be even better.

An hour later, Priscilla stood outside her house to wave her friend off while clutching a wriggling Yorkshire terrier under one arm. "Don't forget to ring John and tell him you are coming! Remember to send me a postcard!" she called, rather forlornly. Her words were probably lost in the noise of the car engine. She felt suddenly abandoned as the car disappeared down the road.

Priscilla struggled back into the house with her yapping burden and half dropped the dog on to the hall carpet. Pippy glared at her.

"Yes, yes. I feel *exactly* the same. Landed with each other again!"

Priscilla wandered into her kitchen and put the kettle on. When it had boiled she turned to fill the percolator and tripped over Pippy, who was wandering around looking lost. The little dog yelped with fright, looked hurt and sad, and ran away into the lounge.

Priscilla filled the percolator. She was just about to sit down in the kitchen when she realised the danger of having *that dog* in the same room as her proofs. She sprinted off to remove Pippy from the lounge and close the door. It was too late. Pippy had already had an accident on proof page one hundred and twenty-six.

Priscilla stood in her own hallway and screamed abusive words to no one in particular for a few minutes. Pippy, sensing her sadness and distress, came over and pawed at her skirt. Priscilla looked down at the dog in complete fury. But she had forgotten how impossible it was to be angry with the little wretch. Pippy's huge glowing eyes stared up at Priscilla adoringly, telling her that she, Pippy, was abandoned in a cruel world and that *only Priscilla* could rescue her. Priscilla's heart melted. She picked the tiny furry object up, and Pippy gave her a big wet kiss on the nose and wagged her tail.

"All right, precious, it's not your fault, is it, diddums? Nasty Mummy leaving you in a strange place. Never mind. Come and get a nice biscuit in the lovely kitchen!"

What would her students think if they saw her talking to a dog like this? Lucky no one else was around.

She gave Pippy half a digestive biscuit and then put her firmly outside in the tiny back garden; seized disinfectant, rubbish bags and carpet cleaner; and spent a furious half-hour in the lounge scrubbing the carpet.

She went out to dispose of the disgusting debris in her dustbin. Pippy, having tired of chasing blackbirds, slipped triumphantly past her the second the door opened a crack, and bounced back into the lounge again. Priscilla gave up and decided to deal with her own coffee requirements before trying to eject the dog again.

She walked through the kitchen to the percolator. A bicycle bell rang in the street – the one she had heard when Elodea was here. The same bell, most definitely, because there was something *odd* about it. The sound was wrong; she had thought that before. It didn't sound like a bicycle bell; it sounded more like a *temple* bell. Yes, that was it – a temple bell from the Far East. She looked at the buddha. He winked, very slowly, eye shut, eye open again.

This is it, thought Priscilla. Not only is Elodea mad but so am I. I already knew Elodea was quite insane, of course – years in Little Wychwell would make anyone lose their mind. But *me*? It has to be suggestive hysteria. Elodea has suggested the buddha winks, and now *I* am seeing it do so.

She poured a cup of coffee and walked back across the kitchen.

The owner of the bicycle with the temple bell rang it again. She looked at the buddha. Unbelievable! The 'silver' eyelid closed and opened as he winked again. Then all was still.

Could it be some kind of trick? Some kind of mechanical trick, like statues in medieval churches? What had she done to cause it? Ah ha! She had walked across in front of it! She waved her hand in front of the buddha's capacious stomach. She had previously assumed that the tiny hole in the centre was caused during the buddha's mass-produced process of manufacture. It must be a sensor of some sort!

Success! The bell rang; the buddha winked.

She picked the statuette up and looked carefully at it. She had always tried to ignore it as much as possible before. It had remained, almost untouched, on the work surface – a hideous reminder of the effects of biscuits on the stomach and why you should not lie about being distressed at losing a buddha statuette, but nothing more. She had dusted it, occasionally, but her kitchen was kept so clean and spotless that it was scarcely necessary. Elodea had been fiddling around with the thing earlier. Had anyone else ever picked it up and jiggled it around? Probably not – not since it had been removed from the brown cardboard box when Barnabus and Angel gave it to her.

Barnabus and Angel had been so delighted to be able to replace Charles' gift for her. She had *pretended* to be delighted at having the thing replaced by something that was not only equally hideous in her eyes, but cheap and poor quality as well. She had set it down by the biscuit barrel as fast as she could. Angel had suggested the lounge might be a better position but Priscilla had made some excuse about the buddha watching over the kitchen for her.

Could Elodea have flicked a switch on somehow?

Priscilla looked underneath – nothing. Down the back – nothing. Ah, there it was, just under his arm: a little tiny silvered switch. 'On' and 'off'. Elodea must have moved it by accident. It was not *just* a cheaply made buddha, it was *worse*. It was one of these sensor ornaments that you put in your garden to tell you when people were walking past it. Usually a crowing cock or a croaking frog.

While she was delighted to solve the mystery she was horrified to discover that she had been harbouring an object that could certainly be regarded as sacrilegious and was on the level of bad taste that she ascribed to garden gnomes. In fact a level below that which she ascribed to non-mechanical garden gnomes!

The combination of feeling disgusted and her depression at dog sitting again seemed to have only one possible cure. She opened a cupboard, got down a large bottle, and poured a generous tot of Tia Maria into her coffee. That might improve her outlook on life!

While she was drinking her *third* cup of Tia Maria laced coffee she decided the buddha might be *fun*! She would switch it off for now but perhaps she could use it to surprise Charles next week! Or to tell her where Pippy was straying about while she was in the house? No – the dog was probably too short to activate the sensor. There must be *some* amusement to be had with a toy like this! She could certainly surprise Angel and Barnabus with it!

Pleased with the idea of her own new secret knowledge and power she was, nevertheless, heavy hearted as she plodded off to the lounge to double check the page number of the page that Pippy had destroyed. Then she could go upstairs to her computer and reprint it. Her printer was as strangely erratic as all computer printers, and she envisaged that the apparently simple act of reprinting one page would take at least half an hour in reality. After that she thought she would take Pippy for a walk and calm herself down with some fresh air.

To her horror she discovered that she now needed to reprint the *whole* chapter, for when she entered the lounge she found Pippy lying in the middle of a pile of chewed paper, having made the rest of the proofs into a comfortable bed. The little dog leapt up, enchanted to see her; carefully selected one of the tattered fragments for a present; and trotted over to Priscilla to give it to her, with a happy doggy smile and a wagging tail.

Fortunately Priscilla was now so full of alcohol that she found this funny.

"Smippy Pith! No, let me try that again! Pippy Smith! You are just as bad as all your owners! But, and don't tell anyone else this, I do have an awfully soft spot for all of you!"

She picked up the whole tattered pile of destroyed proofs so she could drop them into the recycling bin.

Then she thought that she might as well leave them all for a nest for the dog to sit on, and lumped the heap of torn paper back down in the middle of the room. It was a mess but *so what*?

She decided to sit down on the sofa for a while herself before attempting any reprinting, but the moment she sat down the doorbell rang. Should she answer it? Or not? It was bound to be some kind of *botheration* but surely nothing else *too* awful could happen today? She no longer felt that she was even approaching the right mood to reprint the proofs and start reading them again from scratch. In which case she supposed she might as well answer the door.

She took a moment to focus on her visitor before realising that it was Barnabus' great friend Walls. Hadn't he finished his D. Phil. by now and gone home to the USA?

"*Walls*? What are you doing here? Barnabus and Angel are both away! Did they forget to tell you as well?"

Chapter 3

"Good afternoon, Professor, er, Professor, er…"
began Walls, nervously.

He had only just realised that he had no idea what the
woman's surname might be. How very awkward!
Buffy always called her Aunty Pris or Priscilla. Angel
just called her Priscilla. He knew she wasn't a real
relative so Smith would not be a good candidate as a
possible surname, except for the number of Smiths in
the UK? Maybe she was Smith as well. Perhaps that
was why no one ever used her surname? No, it was
too risky to try that. He decided to exercise one of his
devastating smiles on her instead and avoid her
surname altogether.

"Doctor, not Professor!" corrected Priscilla, but she
was pleased all the same, with both the smile and the

promotion to professor. "Since you are a friend of Barnabus, please just call me Priscilla!"

"Good afternoon, er, Priscilla!" he replied. He found using her first name very difficult. He hardly knew her, and 'Priscilla' seemed horribly disrespectful for someone of her age. He plunged on.

"I hope you are well on this fine day!" he began again.

Due to his nervousness some Americanisms were breaking into his usual impeccably English English. He had been attending the University of Oxford for seven years now, and when he was in Oxford he usually managed to speak faultlessly in the correct local language. English, however, was like any other foreign language, he thought sadly to himself. One attained correct fluency over years of practice but lost it all instantly when one was stressed.

"I know for certain sure that they are both away," he added, to make the motive for his visit entirely clear. "I have called to visit *you*, Ma'am!" he then added, with another hopeful and equally conquering smile.

"What has happened to my English?" he said to himself, despairingly. "Although Buffy will be most impressed when he hears that Priscilla has noticed their absence already! He had a bet with me that she would not have noticed they were away yet! I win!"

Priscilla just stood there, in the doorway, wondering why on earth Walls would possibly come to see her, but also feeling slightly dazzled by the smile and pleased with the 'Ma'am'. She felt, for a moment, like the Queen.

Walls made a desperate attempt to gain control of his linguistic skills, and succeeded. "Be assured, I have not come to see them. I have, indeed, come to see you. May I come in?"

He felt he should put a name somewhere in this speech but he still felt 'Priscilla' was too forward. If only he knew her surname, he thought with a touch of desperation. Buffy was a nuisance: he should have told him what it was!

Priscilla thought how fortunate it was that she had not yet reprinted her proofs, as Walls was too large to converse with in her hall. She stood back and ushered him through the hall into the paper-strewn lounge.

"I'm so sorry," she apologised. "Proofreading. My book. I need to put in a lot of work on it today so I can't give you very much time."

"Charmed to be allowed to visit at all!" said Walls graciously, wondering what strange method of proofreading she was adopting. He supposed she was too old to proofread on a computer screen. But why tear the pages up like that after reading them? Perhaps she was upset? Perhaps she had decided that everything she had written was rubbish? Walls did not yet know Priscilla well enough to realise that she believed any work produced by herself was, per se, excellent!

"What is your book about?" he asked politely.

"Agamemnon – a feminist perspective – revisited," she said, rather grandly.

"I should imagine," said Walls, after pausing to ponder swiftly over all the information he could recall about this gentleman and his family: murder of all sorts including infanticide, incest, affairs, rape, etc, "there must be quite a wealth of material there."

"Yes, indeed," said Priscilla. "The main difficulty is to reduce down to 250,000 words. You will be acquainted, no doubt, with the first edition. This is the first edition revisited. I have updated my earlier definitive work with respect to the current cultural perspective. You have read the first edition, I assume?"

"Ah, yes, your book. Splendid!" said Walls cryptically, hoping that this word was suitably non-committal and yet sounded enthusiastic enough to end the topic of conversation. He had just completed a D. Phil. in History but he had always chosen to study *modern* history and had only a very superficial knowledge of anything classical. He had never heard of Priscilla's apparently celebrated book, and nor did he at all wish to read it. On the other hand he did not want to admit to *not* having read it in case he was handed a copy to read, after which he would have to read it in case she asked him about the contents.

Priscilla knew that he studied modern history from Barnabus' prattle about his friend, but she had hardly had time to ask Walls himself about his academic interests when they last met, late at night in Coromandel Punt House. She felt quite sure that he had never read or even heard of her books, and wondered for a moment if she could amuse herself by seeing what he did when she handed him a copy of the *previous* edition of her book to *borrow*. She toyed with that idea for a few milliseconds and then decided not to tease him like that. It would only extend his visit. She wanted to find out why he was here, get rid of him, and then, unfortunately, she would now have to take Pippy for a walk. But, after the walk, she could finish her day pleasantly by taking just a few more alcoholic coffees and then lying on the sofa with some Beethoven playing loudly. She would abandon any plans to eat dinner – it was too much bother to go out and find some! Later, of course, she would have to feed the wretched dog and take it out again before she could retire to bed!

She looked at Walls hopefully, trusting she might find out the reason for the visit as quickly as possible and then be free of her uninvited guest.

But he had decided that he should be correctly English and be socially polite before he told her why he was there.

"A charming little house you have here. So convenient!" he said.

Priscilla sighed, audibly. Clearly this was going to be an extended visit! This was hopeless – she must now follow the correct social etiquette herself.

"Yes, indeed, I think so myself. Would you like to take some tea or coffee?" she replied, moving the time at which she might be free again forward by half an hour.

"I thank you. Coffee, if you would be so kind, Professor, Doctor, er, Ma'am!"

The word 'Priscilla' simply would *not* trip off his lips. As he looked at her he saw someone he considered to be a very fearsome senior don, who must be addressed suitably for her station, despite their combined rescue attempt when Elodea was kidnapped by Fran and the fact he was now rising to more senior academic levels himself.

Priscilla sighed again, louder, and went out to make a whole pot of coffee and then arrange it together with a plate of biscuits, two cups, two saucers, two teaspoons, cream jug, sugar tongs and sugar bowl on a tray. It seemed slightly harder to make coffee than it had been before she took her own last alcohol-enhanced cup! Another loud and doleful sigh came from her lips. She poured a large mug of coffee for herself while she was still in the kitchen, chucked another dollop of Tia Maria into it and knocked the whole thing back. She put the used but empty mug down on the tray. Then she set off for the lounge, bearing the tray with exaggerated care.

Must be careful not to pip over Trippy! she thought to herself. Something sounded wrong with that sentence, even while it was inside her own head. Never mind!

She need not have worried about falling over Pippy as the little dog had already discovered Walls and had scaled his knee. She was now bouncing around on his lap, chewing the end of his Givenchy tie. He was sitting there helpless and transfixed, watching the set of clothes that he thought of as 'English gentleman' attire, suitable for visits to elderly English ladies, being demolished by the dog's antics. Pippy seemed to think that the dangling tie was some kind of wild animal that was attacking Walls, and was rescuing him with great enthusiasm. Clearly Walls could have removed such a small tyrant very easily but he knew that dog owners were usually deeply attached to such creatures, and he needed to ingratiate himself with Priscilla, not infuriate her!

"Trippy!" said Priscilla, in her sternest voice.

Pippy turned and glared at Priscilla, stopped bouncing, and curled herself into Walls' lap, snuggling up to him affectionately for protection from Priscilla. In this position she could now devote her full efforts to continuing to chew the dangling end of the tie. Walls, choking slightly as Pippy yanked on the wrong end of his tie, managed to untie it, pull it free from his collar and hand the other end to Pippy as well, with a small and polite inclination of his head.

"You can keep it *all*!" he said to Pippy, exercising his usual big heartedness with respect to his personal property. "I have many more! It will not be missed."

Pippy, pleased at the apparent defeat of her tie adversary, got down from Walls' lap and went off into a corner, trailing her dead prey behind her. She lay down facing the wall and began to methodically bite it into very small strips.

"Is she a puppy?" Walls asked Priscilla.

"No, no. Quite old, I think. Not *my* dog! *Elodea's*!" Priscilla explained.

"Ah!" said Walls, "a Smith dog! I thought their dog was called Pippy. Have they got a new one?"

"Quite!" said Priscilla, thinking this was a sufficient explanation. "Charming little dog! Bound to be sweet, belonging to the Smiths."

That was a charitable and untruthful statement from Priscilla, who really thought that Pippy was a very spoilt and overindulged dog who was used to living in a house so chaotic that no one usually noticed the odd chewed-up possession. Priscilla watched the tie being shredded on the other side of her ex-proofs and did hope Pippy was not going to eat too many more things while she was staying here. Priscilla would have to move *everything* to a height that was over two feet from the floor. It was fortunate that Pippy had such poor jumping ability!

Meanwhile Walls had leapt up courteously, taken the tray from Priscilla and then lowered it carefully to the coffee table. He must remember to get all the English behavioural etiquette right! He looked at the two cups and one mug. Odd! Perhaps the mug was for him?

"Do you take cream or sugar?" enquired Priscilla, who had been grateful not to have to attempt balancing the tray while bending towards the coffee table in her current unfocussed state. She seated herself successfully and safely beside the coffee table.

"No, no, black, I thank you, Ma'am! No, no sugar!"

He usually took *several* teaspoons of sugar but he had seen the sugar pot with the tiny sugar tongs in it and felt safer not trying to juggle them in his huge fingers, calloused by years of rowing.

She poured coffee into each of the tiny bone china cups and handed him one, balanced on a very dainty saucer. She then filled the mug with black coffee, picked it up, drained it, felt a little better, poured more black coffee into her own minute cup with saucer, and took a small polite sip.

Walls watched her, feeling rather boggled. He wondered if he dare attempt to eat a biscuit but decided that would be unwise in case it caused a crumb situation on the furniture or carpet.

"I suppose, Ma'am, that you might be wondering about the reason for my visit."

"Indeed, you suppose correctly!" replied Priscilla.

She could do without such formality just now. This was like having to get through one of the introductory

81

meetings for new students at the start of Michaelmas term. Not the sort of activity that she had been planning for her evening at all.

"I wondered, Ma'am..." He coughed to clear his throat. He could suddenly see the enormity of the question he was about to pose. "...if you could possibly see your way to allowing me to sublet Angel's room for my own use for the next few weeks?"

"Clearly," thought Priscilla, "I must have taken more Tia Maria than I thought! I must have misheard what the boy just said!"

"I beg your pardon," she said. "I didn't quite catch that last sentence. Could you restate it for me?"

"I wondered, Ma'am, if you could see your way to allowing me a sublet of Angel's room for the next few weeks?" he repeated, feeling more and more annoyed with himself for the amount of American that was creeping into his English.

Priscilla was now rather more preoccupied with wondering how much Tia Maria she had been pouring without realising, than with any particular needs that Walls might have.

"I'm so sorry. I seem to be having a temporary hearing problem. I thought for a moment that you said that you wanted to sublet Angel's room for the next few weeks!"

He nodded encouragingly, to reassure her that old age had not yet affected her ears too badly. Poor old lady! She must be worrying about losing her hearing!

"Yes, Ma'am," he replied, soothingly, "that is *precisely* what I said! Your hearing is *perfect*!"

Priscilla's eyebrows shot up to her forehead. She lowered them again. He was not a Smith but he was one of their close associates. It was, as she knew only too well, not easy to refuse them once they had an idea in their heads. She decided to take the track of very firm and instant refusal to see if this worked before she was vulcanized yet again.

"I am afraid that is *simply impossible!*" she said, firmly.

"Impossible?" he gasped, shocked by the vehemence of her reply.

He looked completely downcast. She felt guilty and decided she must expand her reply further even though she had a terrible feeling that by doing so she was walking into some kind of vulcanizing trap!

"It can't be *sublet* by Angel it because it isn't *let.*" Priscilla explained, more kindly, "She just lives here, you know, for free. We were going to make a more formal arrangement but somehow we never did!"

It was all too difficult and she earns so little that I didn't have the heart, Priscilla added silently to herself. Angel kept telling Priscilla that one day she would give her a large lump sum towards the rent, and Priscilla kept agreeing that that would be fine. Angel's budgeting abilities were unsuited to her tiny wages. Indeed Priscilla had also frequently 'lent' her extra small sums of money with no expectation of the money ever being repaid. One couldn't be cross with the girl: she was so unsuited to coping with the difficulties of normal life, like budgeting! Priscilla had now simply accepted her as another pseudo-member of her 'family'. She already had three pseudo-nephews and a pseudo-niece in the shape of Elodea's children, and she had now added Barnabus' fiancée as an extra pseudo-niece. In fact, since Angel now lived with her, rent free, she almost regarded her as a pseudo-daughter. Although, she added to herself, her *own* daughter would most definitely not have got a rowing Third in Engineering – she had better have achieved a high First in Classics!

But Priscilla didn't want *another* pseudo-nephew.

"And," she ploughed on, hastily, "I would really prefer to leave the room empty while Angel is on her vacation with Barnabus. I don't need the rental, you see, and I quite like to have…"

She heard her voice trail off. She had made the mistake of looking directly at Walls, and his dark eyes were pleading with her.

"Please!" he said. "My situation is *very desperate*, otherwise, I assure you, I would never have been moved to call upon you and make such an outrageous and incommodious request!"

At last, he thought, English!

He smiled at her, using his 'devastating with a touch of pleading helplessness' smile. This had never yet failed him with a female!

What a good-looking young man he is! Priscilla thought. And clearly in great need of her help! But the word vulcanized had shot into her brain again. It was bobbing about in front of her eyes in large red letters. But she did now feel sympathetic enough to find out the reason for his request before she refused to grant it to him. She knew he was very well endowed with money, so why did he want to stay with her?

"So what *is* this urgent and pressing reason that requires you to stay here for a few weeks?" she asked.

Priscilla had imbibed a large quantity of Tia Maria but her logic was still operating, and at just this moment she had a sudden thought. However, due to the Tia Maria she also voiced the thought, very loudly, before Walls could even begin to reply.

"Barnabus! Elodea! Or Barnabus! Or Elodea! Or both of them! One of them thinks, no, both of them think, that I am not going to be able to manage by myself with Angel away. They think I need company!" she wailed.

"Ma'am!" said Walls, attempting to feign surprise.

She fixed him with a stare that was usually reserved for inattentive students in lecture rooms. He crumpled.

"Ma'am, I admit it. You were not far off there. I will admit that Buffy may have mentioned that he hoped you were not lonely while Angel was away," he said.

It was Barnabus who, following this dreadful thought, had then produced the brilliant suggestion that perhaps Walls could use Angel's room while they were away. This would be the perfect solution for Walls' current dilemma and he would also be able to keep an eye on the 'old girl'. Walls had been unconvinced by Barnabus' idea that Priscilla would be so delighted with a substitute lodger for her spare room but his own situation was sufficiently problematical for him to attempt the manoeuvre. He did not think getting the request granted would be difficult. After all, Priscilla was female, and females were usually putty in his hands. He had forgotten, from his earlier acquaintance with her, that Priscilla was a fierce and independent lady who neither wanted nor needed any looking after and was, furthermore, a senior academic, used to crushing precocious geniuses and making them feel small, unintelligent and totally untalented.

But until this afternoon he had decided that the suggestion was not the best option for himself. He did not want to share an elderly Fellow's house. He had decided instead that if his expected emergency occurred he would go straight to Heathrow and take the first flight on which he could find a first-class seat to anywhere that was not in the British Isles. Then, this afternoon, Elodea had sent him a muddled text message asking him to check up on Elodea's little angel as Priscilla might forget to feed her when

Charles visited next week. The text had continued with the information that Elodea was about to get on a plane to Tokyo. The whole text had made almost no sense to Walls and although the reference to 'little angel' had now been explained, Walls still had no idea who Charles might be, or why Elodea was going to Tokyo. It seemed an unlikely thing for her to do, especially as he did not think that Japan was particularly renowned for its cakes. But his emergency moment had come and this second suggestion that he visit Priscilla had made him decide, after all, to see if Priscilla could rescue him from his own tight spot. He returned to his quest.

"However, Ma'am, requirement for company aside, and I can understand that you are fine alone, I have my own pressing reasons which lead me to beg you to accommodate me for the next two weeks."

"You do?"

"Yes, Ma'am! I am in a situation akin to that of the man standing on the burning deck! Flic is visiting Oxford!" said Walls, in a voice that suggested that a pack of wolves was in full pursuit of him.

"Flic?" asked Priscilla, totally baffled.

"My *fiancée*, Ma'am!"

"Your *fiancée*!" exclaimed Priscilla. She had heard about Walls' serial conquests of numerous Oxford females from both Barnabus and Angel but she had never heard that he had a fiancée. This strange dialogue was beginning to make her feel as if she was in an Oscar Wilde play.

"Not a *real* fiancée!" he groaned. "At least, she is a *real* fiancée because I *will* have to marry her some day. She does have some good points. She is stunningly beautiful and she *looks* really cute and utterly sweet – *looks*, not *is*. Our affianced relationship can be ascribed to the desire for a business merger between our fathers. We have to agree. Allowances, you see. They can cut us both off."

Priscilla was struck by the strangely medieval behaviour of the over-endowed parent.

"That's outrageous, Walls! They can't make you keep to that! This is the twenty-first century!"

"Ma'am, I will not conceal from you that I was originally fully compliant with the scheme. Flic and I thought, when younger, that marriage together would also suit us. We then both changed our minds but, fearing the loss of our allowances due to parental displeasure, we have remained, officially, as affianced as ever."

"So why are you so worried about her visiting Oxford?" asked Priscilla.

"Because, Ma'am, I have realised that she is no longer in a position of having changed her mind about the actual nuptials being a consequence of the engagement. Or, rather, she has changed it back to our original joint attitude. She is now reaching a 'certain age' and thus she considers being a bride-to-be a goal that needs to be attained before she gets any older. The ceremony, you know, the clothes, the flowers, the photographs, being the centre of attention! I don't know, whatever else it is that makes girls so silly about the whole thing. Being the opposite sex, the desirability of the whole concept baffles me, entirely!"

He stopped his monologue for a pause to consider the matter, and then continued, "Although, naturally, *I* would *also* look remarkably good when attending the ceremony wearing a full formal dress suit!"

Priscilla was about to make a derisory snort, in support of her own gender, when she pictured how he would look in such attire herself and, being forced to agree, decided to keep quiet.

She leant back into a more comfortable position. This looked like a long visit. In fact she was quite clearly about to be vulcanized again. Perhaps it would be easier not to struggle against it. She sighed yet again, but almost inaudibly this time. She would usually have ceased to listen to what Walls was saying at all so she could think about something else much more interesting. Listening to others bored her very rapidly, especially when they were talking such twaddle. However, in this instance, she was wondering if she could get out her interview recording device and switch it on, without interrupting his flow.

Alternatively, would he notice if she reached for some paper and a pen and recorded his words longhand? She dismissed both these possibilities but felt it was a shame as what he was saying seemed to be such splendid evidence for her new research paper: 'A Comparison of Chauvinism in the Ancient and Modern Worlds'.

Walls continued to talk; he seemed to be quite unstoppable. Priscilla had become an unnecessary component of the conversation: he appeared to be explaining the situation to himself.

"Since she has been engaged to me for quite a few years she feels it is unnecessary to look for an alternative prospective bridegroom. There I am, already captive. To state it in a nutshell, she is now expecting me to *close the deal*. I really thought we both shared the same opinions on the ultimate clinching of the whole arrangement but, as I said, *she's* changed her mind."

He paused for a few moments.

"She's decided to marry you without love?" interposed Priscilla.

"Is love essential for marriage? It never appears to be so! Furthermore, no one could say that I'm not a desirable catch! Handsome, intelligent, well educated and rich – the last one, I am sure, being the most important on *her* scale of values."

"And modest!" cut in Priscilla.

Walls ignored her and continued. "To be fair to her she is beautiful, well dressed, a key figure in high society and, of course, *also* rich..."

"So why not marry the poor girl then? You have wasted seven years of her marriageable life by not breaking the engagement earlier!" expostulated Priscilla.

She felt she should stand up for her own gender. This Flic girl seemed to have been sadly misled, in Priscilla's opinion. Walls might have thought of the engagement as 'for convenience and allowances' only, but even if Flic had agreed to agree with him

Priscilla thought, looking at things from the female perspective, that Flic was more likely to be thinking that Walls would *one* day grow up and come round to taking the idea seriously. Poor deluded child!

"*Why not?*" Walls replied. "There are thousands of reasons why not! Number one, because I don't love her! Not in the way Buffy loves Angel. Buffy loves Angel *with* her faults; I don't even love Flic *without* her faults! Number two, I want to stay as Peter Pan for a bit longer, you know. I want to always be a little boy and have fun! Well, maybe not a *little* boy – I like to have *grown-up* fun!"

"So I have been told!" said Priscilla with a slight 'tut' noise.

"More seriously though, Ma'am – and I know you will appreciate *this* problem – number three, I have just been offered a research fellowship here. Flic won't see how important that offer is and she certainly won't want to live in academia. If I marry her I also have to go home and re-embrace the lifestyle of the rich, famous and idle. If I throw this fellowship away that will be the *end* of my academic career!"

Priscilla could finally see his point of view. Giving up a research fellowship was clearly completely untenable. She became an instant turncoat.

"I can *entirely* see the problem! You *can't* give a research fellowship up. Quite *unthinkable!*" she exclaimed.

"You may well say so! Flic, however, will see that as *completely unimportant.* She is coming here in two days to pin me down with a date for the grand event of the season – that's our nuptials, you understand. I have been forewarned about this visit by several mutual friends. *She* thinks *I* don't know she is on her way. I need to leave my room looking as though I have gone away. And find a hiding place which she will never suspect. I feel this would be an ideal refuge, here, in this house. If you will consent to accommodate me, Ma'am?"

Priscilla was now in full agreement with Walls. He must not throw this academic opportunity away.

96

Giving him a room was the least she could do, but she could see a few problems with the plan.

"Won't Flic ask someone where you have gone, or text you, or email you, or something? Or ask one of your *mutual friends* herself? They don't appear to have any sense of honour! How are you going to get round that one?"

"I agree, Ma'am," said Walls, "there are many possible hazards, very true, but I am going to text to her that I am en route to join Buffy and Angel, camping and trekking in the Pyrenees. I will send this message *just before* I know she is due to arrive here. I will add that there is no phone signal in the area of the Pyrenees where we will be staying. Mobile phones are wonderful for concealment! However did you all manage deception in your young days when there were only landlines?"

Priscilla ignored this question. She had a question of her own to ask!

"Won't she *follow* you?"

"Flic? Go camping? Definitely *not*! Trekking? Even *more* definitely not!"

"Won't she try contacting Barnabus and Angel?" demanded Priscilla.

"No, no. She doesn't know any of my Oxford friends very well. Heavens, Ma'am, she scarcely knows *me* these days!"

"Why not just tell her you have changed your mind? Tell the truth?" asked Priscilla.

"That, Ma'am, would be a gross incivility, so gross that I fear that I would not just have my allowance sliced by my enraged father, but I would be in danger of being permanently disinherited on top. You have also omitted to remember that the USA has a lawsuit culture. Flic could sue me for disappointment, deception, time wasting, damage to her nerves... Hundreds of things!"

"Then you could be free and poor but happy!" cried Priscilla.

"Me, *poor*? Manage a life of *poverty*? I doubt I could stand the shock of the whole thing! *Happy* would be entirely the *wrong* adjective! I might have to wear *socks* of the sort that *Buffy* wears! And that would be the thin end of the wedge!"

"I don't think Barnabus counts as *poor*!" corrected Priscilla.

"There you are then: *even worse*, I might be *poorer than Buffy*! I might have to purchase clothes from *Primark*!"

He winced and looked faint.

Was he joking? Priscilla considered him carefully. She totted up the approximate value of his clothes and jewellery in a quick piece of mental arithmetic. The total was so high she had to repeat the calculation. Still the same. No, probably he was not joking!

Walls watched the expressions crossing her face. He laughed. "Only *joking*, Ma'am!"

Well, that was a relief! But she could see that someone so extremely rich might find the change to research-fellow-without-additional-income a little hard to sustain in the long term. It was all very well to throw away a fortune for love, but he would be throwing away a fortune for not-love, which was entirely different.

"So, you see, the only thing to do is to get *her* to refuse to marry *me*!" he summed up.

"Brilliant!" cried Priscilla. "How do you aim to do that?"

"I wish I knew!" he sighed. "She is pretty determined to have the designer white dress, the veil, the shoes! I expect she is already considering options! And you know what a draw the whole wedding pageant is for women! No, for now, the only solution is to *hide*! Because if I meet her I will have no chance. I will be as putty in her pretty little entirely determined hands. She will have the date fixed and me in tow before you can say 'next flight to America'."

"Why not just move into a hotel?" asked Priscilla. "How about hiding yourself in the Randolph?"

"I can't move into the *Randolph*! *Flic* will be staying there, of course! Hotels are too *public*. She might check them all to see if I am there! I won't have to live here for *long*, only till she goes away again. She won't stay once she is sure that I am not here: insufficient expensive stores in Oxford! She'll be off to London, or Paris, or home! My acquaintances will keep an eye on the situation and let me know. All *very* cloak and dagger!"

"And how are you going to eat? Come to that, what are you going to *do*? Stay indoors all day?" asked Priscilla.

"Precisely. I shall stay in Angel's room with my laptop. The eating is not a problem! *You* are going to feed me, naturally!" Walls assured her.

"*I* am going to feed *you*?????" demanded Priscilla, open mouthed.

Priscilla was in the habit of eating as many of her meals as possible in college and using her own kitchen as little as possible.

He bowed to her. "I beg your pardon, Ma'am. If you prefer, *I* will be both chef and general factotum, but you will have to go to the stores for me because I can't leave your place in case of being seen."

Priscilla heard her own voice saying, to her horror, "Well, everything seems decided then! I'm sure it will all go wonderfully well!"

What was she saying? Far too many Tia Marias, she feared! But the loss of a research fellowship? Not to be considered! Also he was astonishingly handsome and his eyes... She exhaled happily. It would be quite good fun to have a handsome young man around the house, especially as Barnabus was away for several weeks so it was bound to be quiet. Walls might liven things up a little. Then she pulled herself up. She had momentarily entirely forgotten! *Charles* was coming here shortly. What would he think of her having a young, male lodger? She considered the situation and smiled rather wickedly to herself. You never knew –

maybe it would make Charles think that he should not have such very prolonged absences from his wife's life? Perhaps he would try to transfer his academic career back to Oxford or stop climbing so many mountains, or both?

But if Charles did either of these things it would be rather a nuisance. Having him there all the time would be a horrible disturbance to her work and a loud male disruption in her house. Even so, perhaps a bit of jealousy might not hurt?

Walls had watched anxiously as she frowned, smiled, frowned again and finally smiled, in a rather triumphant way. He wondered what she was about to say.

"So!" she said. "Are you moving in right away?"

"I'll just take a wander to my place and collect my gear. You will not regret this, Ma'am! I can guarantee that I will be a *faultless* guest. I offer you my deepest heartfelt gratitude for your charming offer of hospitality."

…Although I am beginning to wonder if this is the best solution, Walls thought to himself, since this lady is clearly quite eccentric, if not actually insane. If only I had more time I might be able to think of something more sensible. But one must run for any port in a storm!

"Won't Flic ask for you at Kings' Lodge?" suggested Priscilla, breaking into his thoughts.

"She may do. But it will be of little value to her as I have already specially asked the porters not to tell anyone where I am. Come to that, they won't be able to tell her where I am, because they don't know!"

"I won't offer to drive you round and help you move. Coromandel and Kings, you know!" Priscilla excused herself.

"Quite!" said Walls, although he also thought that the strong whiff of alcohol drifting towards him every time she spoke might also be a problem when it came to driving anywhere.

Priscilla picked up the tray and wandered towards the kitchen with it. Walls headed for the front door. She nearly fell over Pippy again. A bright and hopeful idea struck her.

"Could you walk the dog for me while you are staying here?" she asked.

"I regret, Ma'am, I would not want to risk discovery by Flic while roaming the local streets."

"Bother!" said Priscilla.

She had just made some airy plans for unloading the care of Pippy entirely onto Walls, thus compensating for having him in the house. Walls had no intention of figuring in any such scheme. He had been much entertained in the past by Buffy recounting the difficulties of taking Pippy on walks, and consequently he had no intention of risking the experience himself.

"I apologise most deeply for this!" said Walls, adding another polite bow, while achieving startling levels of correct 'upper-class Oxford English'. He continued,

"Many, many thanks for your very kind hospitality! I will see you shortly, er, Professor, er, no, Doctor, er, Ms, um…"

His attempts to address her correctly faded out as, still wondering what on earth Priscilla's surname might be, he held out his right hand formally. Priscilla balanced the tea tray carefully on the hall table, and Walls very solemnly shook her hand. He had considered blowing her a kiss, or even kissing her cheek, but decided this might be seen as disrespectful.

"One moment!" commanded Priscilla.

She reached up to the key rack by the door.

"Angel's door key. She has left it here while in France in case of losing it."

She handed the key to him with a small bow herself. She had only just noticed that that Angel's key was hanging on the rack but felt it sounded better if she pretended that she knew it was there.

Walls put the key carefully in an inside pocket, bowed very low and then left, closing the front door carefully and quietly behind him.

He was a charmingly polite young man, mused Priscilla, registering the very quiet click of the door. So much more peaceful than the sort of crash Barnabus usually produced when leaving a house. Walls was also clearly very strong academically, although that had to be balanced against his being a male chauvinist of the worst variety!

She was, as always, regretting being steamrollered into a ridiculous scheme. Why had she agreed to sacrifice the wonderful peace that she fancied resulted from Angel's absence, even if she had not actually noticed that Angel wasn't there, to accommodate a male person whom she barely knew? She had, she realised, been vulcanized yet again. She did wish the collective Smiths and their friends would understand that she *liked* living in a household that was composed of *one person*. Just one! That way she always knew exactly what everyone in the house was doing. She had every room available for her own personal use. No explosions. No chaos. No one else would be found using the bathroom or the kitchen. There was cleanliness and tidiness everywhere. Two *was* a crowd! She added a quick addenda to that thought: obviously it was not a crowd if the second person was Charles. But three was *definitely* a crowd, and here was Walls to make that magic number up when Charles arrived!

Something seemed to have gone terribly wrong with her whole day, ever since she had answered the door to Elodea this morning. Next time she was reading proofs she would bar the door against all entrants and refuse to take any notice of the doorbell, no matter how often it rang.

She washed the coffee cups. So much for Walls *offering to wash up*! Her irritation increased. She crossed the room to put the percolator back on. A temple bell rang gently. She looked at the buddha. It winked very slowly at her. Had she not switched the thing off? Had the switch broken already? Oh well, she would leave it on now – it might give Walls a surprise. Serve him right for invading her little sanctuary! She put the kettle on and ate most of the biscuits from the tray in an absent-minded way while the kettle was burbling up to a full head of steam. She must relax, calm herself. What she needed was to drink a couple more coffees, with just a nip of Tia Maria in each, before Walls returned. Then things might look brighter again! *Si bene commemini, causae sunt quinque bibendi; hospitis adventus, praesens sitis, atque future, aut vini bonitas, aut quaelibet altera causa...*

Chapter 4

Priscilla awoke the next morning in some confusion.
She had her own pillow under her head and was lying
under her own duvet. However, she was,
inexplicably, also lying on the settee in her lounge and
had a small dog curled on top of the duvet. There was
a strong smell of frying bacon wafting across the
room from the kitchen.

How very odd.

Priscilla tried sitting up, experimentally. The small
dog shot up in delight, bounced on her chest, flattened
her back into the pillow and washed her face all over
with a very drooly tongue.

Insanity! It was the only possible explanation! She
must be hallucinating the whole scenario. Was there

any insanity in her family that might provide a genetic explanation? Great Uncle Hubert had gone a little odd in old age – he had taken to chasing people down the street in his wheelchair – but he was over ninety at the time. Anyone else? No, no indications of likely inherited disorders of that nature.

She would assume she was still asleep but the dog was clearly real enough: her face was soaking wet from the prolonged attack of saliva. Also the smell of frying bacon? But why was she in bed on the settee?

Priscilla groaned. Her head ached. She struggled to remember yesterday. She focussed on the dog's face; it was very familiar. Of course! Pippy! Elodea! Was Elodea here, frying bacon? Perhaps Priscilla had been taken ill and Elodea had been nursing her? That was certainly possible.

The thought of Elodea was connecting brain molecules in her memory banks. Yesterday, yes, Elodea had called yesterday, and… Surely she, Priscilla, had not really agreed to dog sit for Elodea for a whole fortnight?

More memory stirred. Elodea was in Japan. So she could not be in the kitchen frying bacon at the same time. In which case, who was?

Priscilla shoved the protesting Pippy off her chest and rose to her feet. She was interested to discover that she was fully dressed under the duvet although she did seem to have taken her shoes off.

Could the empty bottle of Tia Maria next to an empty coffee cup and a half-empty lidless coffee pot on the coffee table explain the whole episode? It seemed horribly likely! That was it! Feeling depressed from being vulcanized by Elodea, she had added just a smidgen of comforting alcohol to her coffee. It must have sent her into a very deep sleep! She had probably decided to have a nap on the sofa, it was cold, she had brought her own duvet and pillow downstairs and instead of a nap had slept all night, worn out after all her work on her book! That was possible, although she never usually brought the bedding downstairs. And yet she felt there was something else. Something else had happened after Elodea left. Whatever could it have been?

She heard the faint sound of a temple bell accompanied by the crashing sounds of kitchen implements being used in an unrestrained and noisy way by someone without a hangover. Who on earth *was* it in the kitchen?

She brushed her hair back, with her hands, into a semblance of order, and attempted to trip lightly and casually towards the kitchen. Every footstep sounded like a cannon firing inside her head.

"*Bonum vinum laetificat cor hominis*, but not on the following morning!" she sighed to herself.

She paused outside the kitchen, hesitating to enter because it was most certainly inhabited by an unknown person or persons. Who could it be? Then an answer leapt into her mind. *Charles*! He had arrived early! Just like him! He had probably got the dates confused!

How embarrassing that she had been asleep on the settee when he arrived! What must he be thinking? Charles always loved English *bacon* for breakfast! It was definitely *Charles*!

Without considering further how Charles might have gained entrance to the house when all the doors were locked, she bounced into the kitchen as joyfully as someone of middle years, rather too short for her weight and suffering from a hangover, could trip. Charles, she thought. My *husband*. Such a long time since she had seen him!

She stopped abruptly as soon as she had passed through the doorway, and screamed very loudly. The sound of her own voice hit her ears like a fire siren going off next door to her.

The noise also very much startled the very tall, red-haired man who was in the kitchen. He was standing with his back to her and busily ladling bacon from *her* frying pan onto slices of fried bread on one of *her* big plates. His very long, very red hair streamed down his back but the word 'Coromandel' was clearly visible in between the strands of scarlet flowing down the back of his tracksuit top. Somebody from the college where she was a fellow then, but who and why and what was he doing here?

114

The man had jumped a foot in the air with surprise as her scream hit his ears. The bacon-loaded spatula had jumped with him, but the bacon had missed its footing, had completely failed to regain it, and had hit the floor with a greasy thud.

Pippy gratefully retrieved the whole rasher of bacon from the floor and dragged it into the hall to eat in peace, leaving a greasy trail across both the kitchen floor and the hall carpet.

The man turned round and smiled at Priscilla with the exuberant smile of a young, healthy, early riser who has already exercised and who, furthermore, has not imbibed excess alcohol the night before.

"Did you trip up over Pippy?" he asked. "I hope you are OK now! A very fine morning to you! Bacon sandwich?"

Priscilla's memory made a rapid and spectacular effort, joined a floating collection of random dots up into a beautiful pattern, and reminded her of the complete programme of events on the previous day.

"Walls!" she cried, pleased at her sudden recollection of both his name and the reasons for his presence in her house. "Salve, Walls! No, no, no bacon, thank you. Have you by any chance made any *coffee?*"

He looked at her sympathetically. He did not drink alcohol himself, because of the athletic requirements that kept his body fit for rowing, but he was used to dealing with alcoholically indulgent friends. He helped her tenderly onto a kitchen stool and dispensed a large mug of black coffee without speaking further.

He was, however, no longer in awe of her seniority or her academic status. One could hardly remain in awe of someone with a hangover like that, especially after one had had to find their duvet and pillow, remove their shoes and tuck them up comfortably on their own sofa on the previous evening. She remained in the far distant heights of the Oxford academic hierarchy compared to himself, but he now felt her equal while inside this house.

Walls had been at Kings and Oxford for seven years now. He thought of it as his home far more than his family home. He was attached to his family but like many students, especially those progressing to postgraduate study, his college had changed from being his second home to being his first home,

Kings was aptly named. The name was not 'King's' but 'Kings' due to its foundation being ascribed to multiple monarchs. The first College founder was Henry VI, who also had the misfortune to be the first monarch during the period which is now called the War of the Roses – a long struggle between Yorkists and Lancastrians, who all thought they had the right to the throne. Henry VI had decided to support the academic community at Oxford and had signed a charter to found an Oxford college and provide money for its maintenance by donating the revenue from some of his royal estates. Scarcely had the foundation stones been safely laid and most of the outside walls built, when Henry VI was deposed by Edward IV.

Far from seeing this event as a disaster, the cunning dons, all full members of religious orders at that time, rushed to petition Edward IV for further revenues to complete their building work, explaining that they would much prefer to have been founded by *him*. Nothing loath, Edward provided a new founding charter and additional revenues from some of his royal estates. The college replaced the head on the founder's statue with Edward's, and put Henry VI's stone head up as a gargoyle.

Nine years later they had to reverse the position of the stone heads, for Henry VI returned to the throne. They had only just fastened Henry VI's head back onto the statue when Edward IV regained his throne, and the process had to be reversed again. Edward V disappeared in mysterious circumstances. His disappearance was far too rapid for him to have time to rewrite the charter, so he is missing from the College sequence. However, Richard III's head soon replaced Edward IV's, and, using the same ruse, the dons were granted another new founding charter and more revenues. Following the defeat of Richard III by Henry VII the college gained another gargoyle, another head for the statue, another founding charter and even more revenue. Kings' dons must have been some of the few people in England who were disappointed at the resulting national stability and peace as the Tudor dynasty held the throne securely.

Kings now had an appropriate name, enormous revenues, a whole pile of charters in a strong box in its library, and a short row of royal gargoyles.

Kings' dons had a 'Vicar of Bray' attitude to their sovereigns. Since Henry VII was the last in the long chain of founders the result was that Richard III and his followers, like Thomas Coromandel, the founder of Coromandel College, were now permanently *persona non grata* as far as Kings were concerned. This fact has been putatively suggested as the original cause for the rivalry between the students of Coromandel and Kings, but there is also a strong belief that it originates in the events following a Michaelmas feast in the 1700s. On this occasion a minor argument between two students, one from each college, is supposed to have resulted in a brawling riot that spread throughout the quadrangles and buildings of both colleges. This event resulted in considerable damage from arson, and three deaths. However, Augustus Storian Illium, the noted Kings historian, suggests that the tales of this event may be purely apocryphal since, if it happened at all, the authorities from both colleges evidently managed to 'hush it up', for there is no trace of its occurence in any official records.

Walls, research fellow in History at Kings, who cared nothing for the rivalry between the colleges, or, indeed, medieval tales, now spoke soothingly and quietly to Priscilla, senior don of Coromandel, who also thought the long-running feud was entirely silly.

"I think you may have had a *little* too much *coffee* last night. You looked so comfortable asleep on the sofa I decided not to try to put you into bed. I do trust you slept well?" he said.

Priscilla was grasping the mug like a drowning woman clutching a lifebelt, and sipping the coffee with her eyes shut. Her head contained a complete drum kit, which was being played by a very wild drummer. The light in the kitchen was far too bright. She groaned.

"I am *very well*, thank you," she finally responded, weakly, "though, as you said, a *little* too much coffee."

After she had drained the mug she opened one eye a crack and considered Walls more carefully.

"What have you done to your head?" she asked.

"Disguise! Excellent, don't you think?" asked Walls.

"Not entirely successful. I can still see who you are quite well," responded Priscilla.

"Ah," he countered, "but *not from the back. You* didn't recognise me *from the back!*"

Priscilla decided not to inform him that she could hardly have recognised him as she had entirely forgotten his existence at that moment, whether viewed from the back or the front. Instead she said, in tones as soothing as his own, "I don't think you need worry about wearing disguise *in the house.*" He was clearly more paranoid about this Flic than she had been aware. "I don't think Flic is going to enter my kitchen unexpectedly!"

"Ah no, it wasn't intended for wearing in the kitchen. I had completely forgotten that I was wearing it!" replied Walls.

He removed the eye catching confection as he spoke, and threw it across the room to land neatly on the other stool. "I got it from the Party Shop. It's only a cheap party wig, but it's good, isn't it? Lucky I have such short hair underneath!"

"Surprisingly effective!" said Priscilla, closing both eyes again as the bright flash of red shot across her gaze. In truth she thought it was probably only effective if viewed from the back, especially as the position on his head had become maladjusted while Walls was wearing it.

"You see, wearing this wig and Angel's tracksuit top I can bike down to rowing practice with *no danger of recognition.* No one would ever think a *Kings* man would be wearing a *Coromandel* tracksuit top! Perfectly disguised! Went to rowing training this morning with no worries!"

A weak point in this concept had occurred to Priscilla. "Does Flic know about the college rivalry? Or care?"

"No, but it's not *her* I'm worried about seeing me when I go to rowing. Between five and seven in the morning her presence in the streets of Oxford is *most* unlikely. The thing is that I don't want *anyone* to know I am still in Oxford except for my very *best* buddies – that's you, Buffy, Angel and the rest of the crew. You see, she might start snooping around asking questions, and there are a few people, mostly women, who might actually *rat* on me!"

Priscilla was touched by her elevation to being one of his best buddies, and decided to spare him a rebuke for the end of his speech. She said to herself that these poor women who might betray him were probably some of Walls' many conquests, who found his glib promises of eternal devotion were slightly flawed when they discovered that he already had a fiancée, as well as several other girlfriends! What a complicated life the boy must lead!

"You weren't on the river in a *Kings* boat wearing a *Coromandel* sweatshirt and a long red-haired wig, surely? In any case, isn't the possibility of being seen on the *river* a minor flaw in your plan? If I was Flic it would be the first place I go to look for you! She must know how keen you are on rowing. And surely some of the other people who know you are likely to have seen you in the boat! The Coromandel crew, say?"

"It could have been a problem if I had gone out in an eight, yes, but I stayed in the boathouse and used an ergo. The eights aren't going out so much anyway because it's out of term. I am just keeping up my fitness levels, you see. Of course I won't be in the First's boat next year in any case, because I have completed my D. Phil."

He sighed at the thought of his great age and status.

Priscilla was wondering if he would notice if she staggered over to the sink, turned the cold tap on full and put her head under it, when he handed her a plate with a gigantic bacon sandwich on it.

"There you go!" he said, cheerfully. "*Breakfast!*"

She looked at the greasy, tomato sauce laden, monumental creation glistening on the plate. Her stomach heaved but, on the other hand, her nose was worshipping the delicious smell. She boldly picked up the sandwich and took a massive bite. As she chewed the delectable confection the drummer in her head packed up his kit and went to find another venue. She progressed through the entire sandwich. The light in the room seemed less bright. She no longer felt nauseous. She was well again!

"Wow!" she cried with enthusiasm. "You *can* cook! I must admit doubting your abilities when you offered to do so yesterday!"

Walls bowed.

"While that sandwich hardly counts as culinary genius I have, many times, discovered that a large bacon sandwich is most effective for friends suffering from an overdose of, er, *coffee!*"

She remembered something else, and smiled. "So, you can take Pippy for *walks* now. You can wear the wig to do that as well!"

"I already *did*," he said, with a heavy sigh. "Last night *and* this morning, while you were under the influence of too much coffee. But I won't be able to take her out once Flic is actually in Oxford," he continued, craftily. "She adores small dogs, and if she saw us and rushed over, she would be absolutely bound to recognise me!"

"Not at five in the morning! Flic won't be out at five in the morning!" reminded Priscilla.

She looked at his downcast face as he tried to find another plausible excuse, and took pity.

"OK, OK. I know what Pippy's like! I don't want to take her for walks either! Did she, by any chance, lie on her back on the pavement and make you pick her up? Crawl under a hedge to see what was happening on the other side? Make you sprint down the street in stiletto heels, looking *totally* ridiculous?" asked Priscilla.

Walls nodded, although he modified the statement. "I can sprint quite well in my stiletto heels but she *did*

126

cause my wig to fall off once! *So* undignified! As were the other two behavioural habits you have mentioned."

He was disappointed not to get a smile out of Priscilla, who did not seem to even notice what he said about stilettos, unless she was being deliberately obtuse. Walls' true objection to walking Pippy, even in the small hours, was that he felt walking a miniature and very cute dog made him lose all his masculine street credibility. Also Pippy was so *very* short, and he was so very tall, that he had to lean at an angle while walking as, otherwise, he would have kept sweeping the little dog up into mid-air, dangling on the end of her lead.

"I give in!" said Priscilla, seeing a possible plea bargain. "I'll take the little menace for walks; you can do all the cooking!"

"*Deal!*" said Walls, quickly, before she changed her mind.

"Where did you get that Coromandel tracksuit top *from*, did you say?" Priscilla asked.

"I found it hanging on the coat rack in the hall. I know Angel won't mind my borrowing it, especially under the current desperate circumstances!"

"Walls!" exclaimed Priscilla, "it isn't *Angel's*!"

"No? I did think it was about ten sizes too big for her! She does wear quite baggy things though. Whose can it be? It can hardly belong to Buffy – he would never be seen in anything labelled 'Coromandel'!" said Walls, who was not thinking very carefully about what he was saying about the size of the top. The identity of its true owner had never crossed his mind.

"Yes, well, Angel may be a *little* thinner than me! But not that much thinner! It's *mine*!" exclaimed Priscilla, sounding ruffled and cross.

"*Yours*! I know you are a Coromandel don but I didn't think it could be yours. I mean, I wasn't aware that…"

"I *did any sport*?" she finished for him. "I would have thought you would remember the fact that I am…" – she puffed up her chest a little – "…the best female punter in the Senior Common Room at Coromandel. I thought you would remember *that* from our previous meeting on the Cherwell!"

How could he have forgotten that? He slapped his forehead in mock apology and contrition.

"I *had* forgotten. I am *so* sorry! I didn't know College tracksuits were the required wear for fellows' punting races? I had," he added, ingratiatingly, and without a grain of truth, "always imagined you punting in a stunning floor-length white dress, so *elegantly!*"

Priscilla softened slightly, even while telling herself that she really must steal herself against this onslaught of flirtatious charm!

"Last year they decided to make the Coromandel and Kings punting race teams wear appropriate sportswear. Health and Safety stepped in or something! But I never wore a white dress before that! We wore subfusc and gowns – tremendous fun!" explained Priscilla.

Walls had a momentary and boggling vision of a set of dons in full robes racing up the Cherwell in two punts. He did hope they only wore black gowns and not their full-colour D. Phil. robes! He managed to keep his face straight and not giggle when he next spoke.

"I see!" he said, meekly. "I do hope *you* don't mind my borrowing it? I knew Angel wouldn't have minded and it never occurred to me that it might be yours. I feel I have overstepped the bounds of a polite guest!"

He bowed to her and, picking up her hand, placed a contrite kiss on the back of it.

Priscilla found she was blushing and then heard herself babbling in a rather pleased voice, "Oh no, not at all. No bother at all! It looks much better on you than me! Do use it if it's of any use! No trouble at all! It's a pleasure for me to help you out!"

How ridiculous! What was she saying! How was the wretched boy having this effect on her? She was well aware that this was how he affected every other female in Oxford but she also knew how *totally* insincere he was! *Amat ut invenit*! As bad as Ustin! No, not Ustin; Ustin was far more *intense* when he was talking to you. Ustin was even *believable*. Walls always made it quite clear that he was playing an uncommitted game and yet women still fell over their feet to get his attention. Ridiculous! She felt embarrassed for her own gender!

"I thank you!" said Walls, perfectly sincerely this time, and he kissed her hand again. She blushed again.

The temple bell dinged as Walls moved across the kitchen. It was set to ring on a particularly piercing note and the noise resounded through Priscilla's head in a most unpleasant way. She glared at the little buddha. He winked.

Walls had already prepared a washing-up bowl of steaming hot water and detergent ready to take the greasy crockery. What a domestic god he seemed to be! Maybe she could permanently swop him with Angel, who wasn't at all domesticated despite working as a waitress.

He recrossed the kitchen. The bell dinged again.

Enough! Priscilla bounced off her stool, picked the little statue up and immersed it in the hot water. That should do the trick! It would never ding at her again!

A few huge bubbles rose from the bottom of the bowl. Its last little breaths as the air struggled out of its little cavities! She had killed it! She felt a deep sense of peace and triumph spreading through her whole body. Nothing like murdering a small ornament to set you up for rest of the day! Was this how psychopaths felt?

"Is that part of your morning ritual?" asked Walls, watching her with his jaw dropping open. "Is it a religious devotional ceremony?"

"No, actually I have never drowned an ornament before!" said Priscilla, very cheerfully.

"*Drowned* it? I thought you were washing it. Some kind of ritual cleansing ceremony! I thought you must be a Buddhist when I saw it there in the kitchen!" he countered.

"While I fully respect the tenets of most religions I don't think that particular sacrilegious garden gnome counted as a religious icon!" retorted Priscilla.

"Was it meant to go in the garden? Oh, I see – a sort of intruder alert? Was that why it had a bell? Kind of neat idea!" said Walls. "I thought to start with that it had the little bell and the wink as a call to prayer, on some sort of timer, you understand. Then I realised it had a movement censor so I thought maybe it rang when you moved, as a reminder to be *frequently* devoted! The little chap and I were getting on quite well earlier. Ding! Good morning! Ding! Wink! Good morning!"

He saw her face and subsided.

"I didn't know myself that it made any movement or sound until yesterday after Elodea somehow managed to switch it on. Now I am hoping it will never transgress again!" she said, magisterially.

Walls fished in the water and lifted the statue out of the washing-up bowl. He dried it carefully on the tea towel. The silver coloured coating came straight off the ornament as he dried it, and stuck itself onto the towel in small fragments. A large dull green plastic patch appeared amongst the silver.

"I am truly contrite, Ma'am! I wasn't expecting that to happen! Should I have left it to drain instead of wiping up? I have *destroyed* it! My deepest apologies!" he said, sounding very guilty.

"I *prefer* it like that!" murmured Priscilla. "I can put it in the bin now!"

But she said it so faintly that Walls did not catch her words.

He continued, anxiously, "What to do for the best? I reckon that I might as well rub the *rest* of the silver off! It would look better *all* green now. You could have it re-silvered later? Agreed?"

"Yes," said Priscilla, wondering if he was actually serious. "Fine! Agreed!"

Walls found a damp cloth and finished removing all the silver coloured finish neatly and completely.

"*All* green now! It even looks as if it was *meant* to be that colour!" he said cheerfully as he placed it tenderly back on the work surface.

But as he put it down the temple bell rang. The buddha winked again. Clearly the mechanism was waterproof.

Priscilla picked it up, lurched somewhat unsteadily through the back door and deposited it firmly in her black rubbish bin. The bell dinged defiantly again as she firmly slammed the lid down.

"I say, it wasn't *that* far gone!" said Walls. "Terribly sorry! Will buy you another asap! You must think I am a complete clown! I can afford another one, easily. Don't consider the expense! What a dreadful house guest I am!"

"Not at all," responded Priscilla. "Never been more glad to see the back of anything!"

There was no point in keeping it as now that it was green and not silver, as there was not the slightest

chance of fooling Charles into thinking it was the one
he had bought, even if he only got the opportunity to
glance at it because she put it on a really high,
inaccessible shelf. So, *good riddance* to it! No more
'switch stuck in the ON position', no more temple
bells, no more winking!

But she would have to go and buy a brand-new silver
buddha now. It would be terrible if Charles was
disappointed not to see it when he called! The 'garden
gnome' would never have fooled Charles anyway, she
told herself. She had not wanted to upset Barnabus
and Angel by throwing it out before: they had been so
pleased with finding a replacement statue. But now
she *had* to get hold of a new one, and quickly!

Fortunately she knew a man who could help her out
with her little quest. She would go and see Tony,
Elodea's eldest son, who had converted to Buddhism
and now managed an alternative medicine shop in the
Cowley Road. She could go there today. He would
know where to get such an item. He probably even
had them in the shop. She just hoped that that sort of
statuette in real silver was not as overpriced as she
feared it might be.

She had already cancelled all plans to spend the day proofreading as this would be impossible in her current condition: the words would be jumping all over the page. It would have to wait till tomorrow even if she overran the 'final' deadline and her publishers were annoyed. She would have to tell them she had been *indisposed*, which would be true enough.

If she got a breath of fresh air by cycling down to the Cowley Road and back she might even manage to recover sufficiently to get some proofs read this afternoon. Two birds with one stone, as it were: health regained, and buddha replaced.

"How very gracious you are about the buddha!" said Walls. "My mother would have fits if I wrecked her ornaments like that, even accidentally!"

His mother's ornaments were worth a lot more money, and certainly less easily replaced, but, proportional to their income Priscilla's might have been the equivalent price. Strange thing for Priscilla to own in the first place and even stranger to possess an ornament that you seemed to dislike, but then *women* were hard to fathom at times! Especially elderly ladies like Priscilla! He had a vague memory, stirring deep in his mind, that this buddha was in some way connected with their rescue of Elodea last year, but he couldn't remember why! He had done a lot of academic study subsequent to that event and it had filled his memory banks with many other things.

But it was essential to keep his involuntary hostess in a good mood. So he kissed her hand once more, *very* apologetically.

Following the kiss Priscilla found herself humming as she wandered out of the kitchen to go to shower and change her crumpled clothes. Oh dear, Victor Hugo was quite correct: "God created the flirt as soon as he made the fool", but Walls was *undeniably attractive*!

Priscilla's warm happy feeling was shortlived. She skidded on Pippy's bacon fat trail and had to grab the doorframe to regain her balance. How embarrassing! How hilarious that must have looked! But, far from laughing, Walls rose politely from his breakfast and aided her through the door with tenderness suitable for a lady who might chance to be made of porcelain rather than flesh and blood. He smiled down at her. She felt slightly dizzy! Having him to stay could be *very* pleasant!

Pippy was lying in an enchanted bacon filled haze on the bottom tread of the stairs. Priscilla saw her only just in time and was forced to take the first two steps in one huge stride. As soon as she attempted this feat Pippy stood up and rushed away, dashing between Priscilla's legs. Priscilla span round, ending by sitting down heavily on the second step. Thank goodness that Walls did not seem to have observed this latest mishap, otherwise he might think that she was permanently drunk!

She rose from the stair with all the dignity she could muster, and caught sight of herself in the hall mirror. Dishevelled! Crumpled! Hideous! Frightful! She was even more impressed with Walls' gallantry under these appalling circumstances! She hastened off up the stairs to do something about her shocking appearance but still found that she was humming 'Greensleeves', and felt a lift in her step that had not been there for several years.

Chapter 5

An hour later Priscilla was spinning merrily off on her bicycle, out of Jericho, through St Giles and down to Broad Street. A quick ride past the Sheldonian, the Bodleian and Blackwells, and she was pedalling along Holywell Street, past the Holywell Music Room, straight out round the barrier and, dodging a few annoyed cars, on down Longwall Street. Just for once a street whose original name was still quite apt! She scooted along the inside of the queuing cars, waited for the traffic lights, and then cycled out through the last parts of the 'Gown' section of Oxford, over the elegance of Magdalen Bridge, and into the sudden and startling contrast of the 'Town' area of The Plain and Cowley Road.

Trying to see what was displayed in the window of the 'Ballroom' this week as she turned up Cowley Road caused a momentary dangerous wobble, to the annoyance of the driver behind her. It was ages since Priscilla had ventured so far south of the University. Many of the shops had changed hands and names and goods sold since her last excursion here, and she became uncertain as to how far up the road she had yet cycled. Could she have already passed Tony's shop without noticing it? No! There it was – the shop that Tony managed!

Priscilla swerved across the traffic, nearly being annihilated by a bus and, ignoring a chorus of angry horn blasts, she bounced up the kerb onto the pavement, clattered to a halt and flung herself off the bicycle with practised ease. She patted its handlebars as if it was a horse, and then chained it firmly to a handy loop of iron jutting out at the end of the shop window, right under the notice saying that bicycles must not be left there. Tony would not mind hers, she was sure of that!

She still had the key in the padlock when Tony advanced out of the shop door.

"Aunty Pris," he said politely and calmly. His voice had no modulation; he spoke entirely on one subdued note.

"I beg you," he continued, "do not leave your bicycle in that position. It is interfering with the calm vibrations of the shop front. It is also in danger of being illegally appropriated by a less-than-honest passer-by. Even if padlocked. Please, permit me to wheel it through the shop and leave it in the back storeroom. It will be perfectly safe there until you leave."

"Oh," said Priscilla, "but I wasn't going to stay very long. I just wanted to see you to …"

But he had already un-padlocked her bicycle and was carrying it through the door and past the raised flap of the counter to place it gently in the back room.

Priscilla had a degree of admiration for Elodea's eldest son. She thought about his recent lifestyle – at least the facts that she knew about it from Elodea's prattle. He was impossible to turn or divert from his chosen belief systems, he was a Buddhist, a fervent campaigner on Global Warming, he ran an alternative therapies shop in the Cowley Road. He was never hypocritical and adhered most strictly to the course of behaviour recommended by himself. He now refused to travel except by foot or bicycle, he ate only two bowls of rice a day, and only drank tap water. He was troubled by the distance that rice travelled to reach the UK and would have changed to only eating bread made with locally grown and ground flour, but he had decided that support of impoverished rice farmers was equally important.

Priscilla had quite recently *half*-listened to a very long lament from Elodea about Tony. When Priscilla untangled the fragments to which she had paid any attention, it seemed to be about how much Elodea admired his strong views and his faithfulness in following them himself but that Elodea was very concerned about how extreme Tony's behaviour was becoming and worried about whether such a diet was really healthy. Priscilla felt he could probably survive on it for a while – after all, many other people in the world managed to do so. However, Priscilla was aware that Elodea felt that any diet that did not include cake, preferably home baked by Elodea herself, was entirely deficient.

Priscilla looked at Tony, giving his appearance her full consideration. He *had* changed! She had not seen him at close quarters for quite some time. She had seen him quite recently, if briefly and at a distance, at Paris' wedding. He had, determinedly, cycled overnight to this event rather than travelling in a car with the rest of his family. He had then attended the wedding wearing his usual clothes, which he had also worn for cycling. Tony firmly believed that owning excess clothing wasted the world's resources.

Paris' new parents-in-law, being impeccably behaved members of the upper middle class, had ignored the situation and behaved exactly as if he was dressed in the tail suits or military uniforms of the other male guests. His own family was merely grateful that he had chosen to turn up. They were also relieved to find that he ate the same meal as everyone else, rather than bringing his own cold boiled rice. Fortunately he had decided that to bring his own food would mean a shocking waste of the food already prepared for him at the reception.

When he was younger Tony had looked very similar to both Barnabus and Elizabeth. Paris was so much more beautiful than any of his siblings that Priscilla omitted him from her comparison. However, due to his restricted diet, Priscilla thought that Tony was now looking far too thin and very pale. This effect was not helped by his head, shaven so closely as to be bald, and the fact that he was wearing a loose robe that was roughly woven from hessian. One might, in fact, call it a sack without much fear of contradiction.

"How delightful it is to see you again, Tony!" she said in the specially bracing voice that she usually reserved for either invalids or for undergraduates who were being, in her opinion, very stupid in tutorials.

"Antholian, not Tony. I feel I must re-embrace my original destiny. It is the name that I was given and it is the name I should use," he replied in his flat monotone.

"Ah!" said Priscilla in a way that might mean almost anything, and, before she could stop herself, added, "But then it should really be Antolianus."

"My given name," he said, leaning very slightly on the word 'given', in a way that was quite surprising among the other single-tone words, "is Antholian."

"Quite!" said Priscilla, again using this word in a way that might mean almost anything and she added, rather naughtily, "*Nomen ist omen!*"

He made no reply. She trotted around the shop, studying the content of the shelves for a few minutes.

"Interesting place you have here. I'd love to look around it. Quite fascinating!"

"Were you wishing to purchase something, or is this a visit of a social nature?" asked the expressionless voice.

"Oh, social, no, purchasing, no, both!" Priscilla had not anticipated how difficult it was going to be to explain her requirements to Antholian. He was so entirely serious and moral. It was not going to be easy to have to explain that one was trying to deceive one's husband by pretending one had not had his

146

present blown up by mistake. The whole affair suddenly seemed quite shocking. Priscilla felt sure that Elodea, and probably Barnabus too, must have told Tony about the exploding buddha incident at the time when it occurred. However, Antholian, like Priscilla herself, often did not listen to stories which appeared devoid of interest, and consequently he may not actually know about it. Priscilla did not want to have to explain the whole thing from scratch to this austere philosopher.

Priscilla finally thought of a neutral way to explain her case.

"I used to own a little silver laughing buddha, which Paris and Barnabus most unfortunately damaged irrevocably between them. I wondered if you could help me by suggesting where I could purchase another such statuette?"

This little speech seemed to strike a chord with Antholian. He reverted to speaking normally and looked much more animated.

"Typical of those two!" he sighed. "They were *always* breaking my things when they were little, pair of *perishers!*" .

"Yes, yes, so I just wondered if you had anything of that sort for sale in this shop," Priscilla persisted.

"No," he said, returning to his flat tone.

"No?"

"We only stock alternative therapies, not religious items. So you will find therapeutic items of all varieties: bracelets for rheumatism; cures and therapies using crystallography, aromatherapy etc. But you will not find items that are purely religious."

"Ah!" said Priscilla.

"Apart from this, even if we did stock religious items, my personal feelings would be particularly against stocking the item that you mentioned. As you know, I embrace the original pure form of Buddhism and do not agree with idolatrous statuettes. However, that is purely a *personal* viewpoint. I embrace the rights of others to celebrate or follow their religion in any way that they wish, or to not have religion. I was not aware that you yourself had now embraced the more traditional form of Buddhism."

"I haven't!" said Priscilla, simply, feeling it was better to stop there and not to embark on an explanation of the real reason for her temporary buddha ownership.

She continued, "I suppose you can't help me with the name of anyone else who might stock them."

"No."

He stood there impassive, apparently having no further interest in the conversation.

Priscilla wondered whether to attempt further social mores in an effort to extend the visit to a polite length. She looked at him. He looked back at her with no apparent interest whatsoever. She gestured past him to her bicycle and he lifted the counter so she could get through into the back room and retrieve it.

But as she reversed the bicycle she caught the pedal on a large cardboard box marked 'essential oil of lavender'. The pedal went straight through the soft side of the box and became wedged inside the hole of its own making. Priscilla had to drop to ground level to untangle it, balancing the bicycle awkwardly as she did so. She looked upwards to see how it had become so hooked inside the box, and above the bicycle saddle she saw black painted shelves, one above the other, right up to the ceiling.

The 'back room' was more of a corridor than a room. The stairs were on one side and, opposite the stairs, the wall rose right up to the attic level. She paused from considering her bicycle to look at the contents of the shelves. It reminded her of the sheep's shop in *Alice in Wonderland*. Open boxes of stock stood on the floor and also on the lowest shelves. The middle shelves were loaded with hoarded things that might one day be useful: carefully wound balls of string, smoothed out folded pieces of brown paper, plastic packing material rolled up and fastened into neat bundles. The top shelves, being the most inaccessible, were mainly empty.

However, right up on the highest shelf, Priscilla caught sight of a silver gleam. There was a solitary object up there! She stood up again and removed the pedal from the cardboard box by heaving it out with main force. Then she straightened up and reconsidered the mystery object. If she leant back far enough and tipped her head right back between her shoulders she could just see it. The bicycle, not appreciating her neglect, slid out of her hands and fell sideways, pinning her to the wall and embedding its pedals and handlebars into several more cardboard boxes with a loud crash. There was the faint sound of tinkling glass, and an extremely strong, sweet smell arose into the air.

Antholian hastened out to rescue her. He remained as calm as if he was in a state of meditation, rather than being a harassed shop manager whose pseudo-aunt had just demolished several boxes of very expensive aromatherapy oils with her bicycle. He lifted the bicycle off Priscilla and took it back into the main shop, where he balanced it carefully and safely against the front counter.

"It is indeed fortunate that this is not a busy period in the shop," he said, without a flicker of emotion in his voice.

Priscilla helped him to rescue as many the bottles as they could from the smashed boxes. Regrettably many of the lavender, chamomile and bergamot bottles had become fragrant heaps of broken glass and oil.

By the time they had tidied the area both Priscilla and Antholian were coated with large patches of essential oil and consequently had also both acquired a strong aroma – a heady combination of the three oils.

When Priscilla had finally finished apologising and when Antholian had assured her for the fifth time that the shop was fully insured for breakages and that everything that happened in life added to its meaning, Priscilla, who was nothing if not persistent, returned to her original quest. Unlike more tactful people Priscilla jumped straight in,   never even stopping to consider why something might be concealed on a high shelf in a back room.

"I was wondering about the little buddha on that top shelf," she said, gesturing towards it. "It's just what I need. I suppose it's old stock, from before your boycott of religious goods, and you had probably forgotten about it? Could I possibly buy it?"

"It is not for sale," he said, in a voice as flat as oil-coated water.

"Not for sale? What is it doing in the stockroom then?" queried Priscilla, very querulously as she saw her opportunity receding before her.

"It's not for sale because it doesn't belong to the shop. It doesn't belong to me either," replied Tony, not at all ruffled.

"Well, what is it doing on that shelf then?" demanded Priscilla.

"I am looking after it for someone," said Tony.

"Looking *after* it?" asked Priscilla, dumbfounded. A dog needed looking after, yes, or a cat or whatever sort of pet you might keep, but surely a buddha statue could look after itself?

"I know," he said. "I realise that sounds very strange."

He looked at her face and visibly relaxed. He laughed and his voice once more suddenly reverted to its natural modulation. "Look, Aunty Pris, the whole thing is a *bit odd*. I tell you what; it's just on closing time for my lunch break so I'll shut the shop and put your bike *back* in here, only next time you leave please don't try and get it out; I'll get it out for you! Then we can both go upstairs and I'll tell you all about it."

So he *was* a member of his family after all! In her experience there was nothing they all liked better than talking *at* her, preferably over a meal. Did she really *want* to know why he kept a silver buddha on a top shelf in his stockroom? She was not sure that she did. It was bound to turn out to be boring, and it was wasting valuable buddha shopping time. If he was not able to sell her this buddha then she needed to rifle through some more shops to see if she could find another one. Yet this could be a great opportunity! If they renewed their past acquaintance he might change his mind and she might still get an opportunity to buy *this* one. On the other hand, if his lunch was going to be boiled rice and tap water she did not want to partake of it. But actually, with her stomach in its current fermenting condition, she did not want *any* lunch. A reviving cup of tea though, that would be lovely! But did he drink tea? Did he only drink water?

"*Only* if you have *tea to drink*!" she said firmly.

"Green tea, properly made in a Chinese china pot?" he offered.

"Done!" replied Priscilla.

She watched him turn the shop sign from 'Open' to 'Closed' and lock the door. She had, when a child, planned to one day own a sweet shop, and she had particularly looked forward to the power she would be able to wield with her own Open and Closed sign. Her mind wandered off into a dream filled with huge glass jars of sugarcanes, peppermints, lemon delights...

"Do you think you could just move back to the base of the stairs so I can put the bicycle back out here without jamming you on the wrong side of it?" broke in Tony's voice.

Priscilla retreated to the very back of the dark stockroom. She was about to achieve another childhood treat: being allowed into the enticing looking back room of shops and up the back stairs to the flat above. When *very* small she had a friend whose mother owned a millinery shop. Her own mother did not really approve of the connection but Priscilla remembered the joy of being allowed to walk through the front of the shop and right into the forbidden paradise at the back, behind the counter. The milliner's shop was attached to a large house with a big back garden but the most thrilling part of visiting it was getting into that part of the house which was right above the shop. If you lay down on the floor in that room and put your ear to the floorboards you could hear the conversations in the shop. No one ever said anything of the slightest interest but that was hardly the point!

The stairs up to Antholian's flat were scrupulously clean. His flat was scrupulously clean. There was almost no furniture. The next room was a bedroom. The door was ajar and this room clearly had just a futon on the floor. The room she was in contained two floor cushions with a very small table between them. The only other furniture was a small narrow refectory table with one bench attached to it. She could see a small kitchenette with a microwave and a kettle. Another open door revealed a cold and unwelcoming bathroom with a solitary, small, pile-free towel on the towel rail.

It was nothing like the chaotic Old Vicarage, which had been his childhood home, except for the walls which were completely covered with shelves and the shelves being completely covered with books. Yet he diverted from his other relatives' habits because his books were, apart from a single volume which was sitting, shut and neatly bookmarked, on the refectory table, neatly and precisely arranged on the shelves. If the rest of the Smith family had lived here many of the books would have been flowing gently in tottering piles around the whole flat. The other Smiths seemed to regard this state as unavoidable and impossible to correct, apparently believing that the books wandered around by themselves, under their own volition, and that their readers were thus freed from any responsibility for the books' final resting places.

Priscilla was amazed and impressed by the tidiness and order. Her own books were also always filed correctly on her shelves so that she could find them quickly and easily, in exactly the place that she expected. At least this *had* been the case before Angel, and consequently also Barnabus, began to inhabit her house. Now Priscilla was forced to spend excessive amounts of time in retrieving her books from the kitchen, the bathroom, the hall, the bedrooms and even the stairs. She carefully flattened any turned-over corners, smoothed the pages, dusted them gently and replaced them on the correct shelf with a loud and enraged 'tut', which noise and actions Angel and Barnabus never seemed to notice.

"Your *books*!" She stepped over to admire the shelves. "Filed *according to the Dewey Decimal System!*" she added, admiringly.

"Indeed!" said Antholian, but expansively this time. His face broke into a wide and beaming smile. "So few people *notice* that!"

"How *wonderful!*" sighed Priscilla.

Here was a member of the Smith family who would never make the mistake of sitting down on her proofs. Ever. Tony had not pursued academia in the way that Barnabus did but he *was* a philosopher and, even more amazing, a *neat* philosopher! Any eccentricities from which she had previously thought he might suffer had paled and faded. Here was a man who valued books, not only for their contents but as *entities in themselves*, to be treasured and cared for.

She and Antholian stood for a moment, in full accord, and looked around the beautiful, although not expensive, library. The covers were neat and unruffled; the backs were straight and aligned; the volumes were dust free! Priscilla could instinctively tell that none of the books had *ever* had the corner of a page turned over, let alone a page bent or torn slightly. They had *never* been sullied by comments inked onto the margins. Priscilla had never realised that Tony was a kindred spirit, or known how much he must have suffered when he lived in the chaos of 'Chez Smith' itself, where the rest of the family so enthusiastically embraced the doctrine of Erasmus with respect to book lovers.

Elodea and John were not so impressed with the tidiness of their eldest son. 'Chez Smith' he still had a room that was almost thigh high with the debris of his life to date. He could not, clearly, have such objects cluttering up his own flat and yet he was equally opposed to their destruction lest he should be forced to increase global warming by buying new possessions should he ever require any of them again. Elodea increasingly felt that renting a gigantic skip together with a bottomless bucket rubble chute might prove a helpful ally in rediscovering the floor in her upstairs rooms, once the sanctuaries for her very dear but long-departed and grown-up children.

Tony had stopped admiring his own books and was carefully preparing a pot of green tea in a Chinese pot with a wicker handle and tiny cups. He looked relaxed. Priscilla felt calm and relaxed herself.

"Since this is an important social occasion I will join you in drinking tea rather than water," he announced.

Priscilla bowed, very formally. She felt honoured by his dietary change.

He gestured at the floor cushions. Priscilla looked at hers, doubtfully. She had been quite a floor cushion aficionado in her student days, and even when a *young* postgraduate, but it had been quite a few years since she attempted to find comfort on such an object. She kicked off her high heels and left them by the cushion, hoping Tony would not be offended by stockinged feet. Then she paused to consider how to continue. Fortunately Tony was still fully occupied in the mystical process of tea preparation, also a ceremony that she felt was most important, and thus would not be likely to notice exactly how she achieved a resting place on the cushion. She decided to throw herself sideways and made a, not entirely successful, crash landing. A considerable effort of rocking and she managed to get her feet forwards and sit on top of the cushion rather than being prone across it. She felt rather like a pixie on a super-large toadstool. She did trust she looked rather more like a pixie than the beached whale that she feared she might actually resemble.

A few moments later Antholian carried a small tray carefully over, placed it symmetrically in the centre of the table, and then knelt neatly down on the front edge of his own cushion. Priscilla wished she had thought of that approach. Could that be how she used to get onto them? She wished she would remember. She did hope she could get *up* from her cushion when the time came *without* requiring Tony's assistance, for she feared extensive 'pins and needles' if she stayed there for any length of time.

He poured the tea out, very formally, into the handle-less cups. Priscilla gave up trying to reach her cup from her pixie position. She managed to shuffle herself off the centre of the cushion, and finally achieved a kneeling posture similar to that of Tony. She raised the cup carefully and sipped slowly at the scalding hot tea. It was, indeed, delicious. She finished the cup in a state akin to ecstatic meditation except for her feet, which were making loud protests about being underneath the rest of her weight.

Antholian bowed, in so much as one can while kneeling on a floor cushion, and poured her another. She abandoned her feet to their crushed and mortified fate beneath her, and sipped the second cup very slowly, too.

It all seemed so relaxing and she was so tired after her night on the settee and then after having cycled *all* the way out to the Cowley Road. Like many academics Priscilla regarded areas of Oxford beyond the central university area as being in the 'here be dragons' section of the map.

After a third cup, enjoyed in mutual and happy silence, Priscilla tried to remember what the purpose of the tea, or 'lunch tea' as it might be called, had been. The tea had coursed around her entire body. She was feeling mentally cleansed and calm. For once she did not seem to be thinking of anything at all. She did hope that Tony had only put standard green tea in the cups and not something stronger from an alternative, or possibly illegal, branch of herbalism. She was not sure that illegal substances, unlike normal foodstuffs, were included in the items that Tony forbade himself to imbibe. No, surely he was too ethical to encourage the illegal drugs trade when it caused so much havoc among the poor of the world? Perhaps she was just very relaxed because both he and his flat were so entirely serene.

But she had to remember the *reason* for her visit. What could it have been? She filtered gently in reverse through her retained memories of the morning. She could hardly be paying a visit just to admire his orderly bookshelves and drink tea. Something *glittery*, she felt. Her memory seemed to be sadly awry. She sniffed, as surreptitiously as possible, at the contents of her cup to see if it was scented with anything except tea. A huge blast of lavender struck her nostrils but it was not coming from the cup, it was rising from her own sleeve! Ah ha! The aromatic oils! Perhaps it was the overdose of aromatherapy that was making her feel so strange. Lavender, bergamot and chamomile all mixed together! Was it a dangerous combination? she wondered vaguely, but she felt so entirely relaxed that she didn't really care either way.

Antholian seemed to be in a similar state. He was smiling at her. She had a feeling that they were there because he was going to tell her something, or else that she was going to tell him something.

"What was it you were going to tell me?" she asked, deciding to take a stab at it being him telling her something.

"I was going to tell you all about Flipper!" he said, after struggling with his own memory for a few moments.

"The dolphin?" asked Priscilla.

"What?" asked Antholian.

"I forgot; you are probably too young to know about Flipper the dolphin. He was on the television many years ago!"

"That could explain his rowing tag! Flipper is his *tag*. He's not a dolphin; he is one of Barnabus' friends, you know, one of the ones with whom he went to Nepal!"

"Ah, *yes*!" Barnabus had taken a gap year in Nepal after his degree. That made sense! What a good grasp of grammar Tony had! Why had she not become closely acquainted with him before now? Was he skilled in the Classics? It only required that for him to be entirely perfect!

"Flipper was one of the rowers in the First Eight with Barnabus, as well as going to Nepal with him, so they have been friends for ages. Anyway Flipper runs a sort of ethnic shop now, very ideologically sound, just down the road from here. Not like my shop, though: furniture and things, not therapies. He and Finn – he's another of Barnabus' friends – stayed behind in Nepal to source local stuff that they could sell in England after the rest of them came home. I think Flipper and Finn moved on to Tibet to look for stuff as well. Or did they all go to Tibet from Nepal in the first place? Anyway, whatever they all did, Finn didn't stay with Flipper for long. He went off; took a job in a bank in the USA or something. He had got tired of being altruistic or needed the money, or something, so Flipper said. Maybe they had a bit of a row. So Flipper stayed on and stuck to his task alone and got all the local sources set up and then, once the supply lines were set up properly, he came back to run the commercial end of the business *here*. Most of the profits back go straight back to the suppliers. So it's all fair trade, very *ethical*."

"*Splendid!*" said Priscilla, who had already drifted off into a consideration of a tricky section in the revised version of her book and had no idea what he was saying any more. It was a disappointment to find that when it came to making long, tortuous and uninteresting speeches Tony was so very similar to all the other Smiths.

"Anyway, Flipper's making a lot of money for the craftspeople there and making quite a name for himself here too, supplying stuff for interior designers and people like that. So it's all worked out pretty well."

"Good!" said Priscilla since he had paused with an upbeat sort of note at the end of the sentence. She looked at his face. 'Good' seemed to be a satisfactory and sufficient answer. She retreated back to the editing problems in her own mind.

"Anyway, this morning, Flipper appears in my shop. He isn't really a friend of mine – I only know him through Barnabus – so I was a bit surprised. Then he said he had a favour to ask me. He said he would have asked Barnabus if he hadn't been hopping around mountains with Gabriel."

"Angel!" corrected Priscilla, automatically. She had returned to the conversation when her subconscious registered the word 'Barnabus'.

"Angel! I knew it was something like that! Well what he asked me to do seemed a bit odd but I suppose it makes sense, really. He said he had a whole boxful of these little buddhas and he wanted to keep one back for himself. He thought if he left it in the shop the woman who works with him – he's actually doing well enough to employ someone to help him, you know – she might *sell* it absent-mindedly. He lives above the shop, like I do here, so she might go and sell it even if he left it in his flat because he lets her use his flat for her coffee breaks. If they ran out of buddhas, you see, and a customer wanted one, she might nip upstairs and get his, to be helpful and make another sale."

"Hmmm!" said Priscilla. Since there was again a pause, again this seemed a sufficient answer.

If she had been listening she might perhaps have registered the fact that there was a whole boxful of laughing buddhas available for sale at the shop just up the road. If Antholian had not been so ideologically fervent that he was parsimoniously sparing of unnecessary purchases, then he might have thought to suggest that Priscilla paid a visit to Flipper's shop and *bought* one. "For all sad words of tongue and pen the saddest are these: It might have been" is a concept expressed so well by John Greenleaf Whittier. It was also a phrase that would arise in Flipper's head later that day when he found out about Priscilla's visit and, due to the combined efforts of Priscilla, Tony and Barnabus, had to reframe his entire evening's plan. Flipper actually remembered the quote as "For all sad words of *mice and men* the saddest are these: It might have been", but under the circumstances the misquotation was understandable.

That was later. For now Antholian continued with the tale of Flipper's loan of the buddha.

169

"Well, Flipper said, could I keep it for him because he doesn't just want it for himself; it's more important than that because he wants to give it to his mother for her birthday and he'll come back and get it on the day. I said I didn't mind, but where on earth was I going to put it? I didn't want it in the shop or my own flat. So he came out to the back room himself and found the big ladder and put the buddha right on the top shelf, all by itself. He said no one would see it up there and, it's true, unless you are bent double near the floor it doesn't really catch your eye at all. He seemed very worried about it. I did say why couldn't he just put it in a box or in a drawer or keep it at home under his mattress or something. He said it was better here. I offered to get him something to cover it up with to keep it clean – a box or something – but he said it would be fine as it was and that he couldn't be bothered going back up the ladder because he was in a great hurry to get back to his shop because he was working on his own today and had had to close the shop while he was here as it was. So I said I would cover it *for* him but he just said it was fine like that and rushed out."

"How odd!" said Priscilla, realising there was a pause, and feeling that a story this long *must* contain *some* odd features. She had often found 'odd' a useful comment to make in the middle of other people's long monologues. She was now halfway through rewriting a paragraph in her book. She had never felt this paragraph was phrased entirely correctly in the original edition but, until now, she had never quite seen what she could do to amend this. The page of proofs was floating in her mind's eye and she suddenly realised that with a transposition of sentences, and a few other minor changes, her points would become much clearer to the reader.

"So there you are!" continued Antholian. "Flipper's being quite successful as an entrepreneur but it's *good* entrepreneurship, you know. His heart is in the right place, all very sound, trying to benefit the right people, as well as himself of course, so I didn't mind obliging him. Not at all! He's a great guy!"

There was total silence from Priscilla this time as she was fully occupied with her knotty paragraph. Tony carried on, almost to himself.

"I don't know many successful business people. Most of my university friends haven't done anything very much. The only successful entrepreneur who is an alumni friend of mine is called, funnily enough, Walter *Friend*. He wrote the S.T.I.N.K.S. system of classroom control and the F.R.A.U.D. business model."

"What?" asked Priscilla, feeling she should try an interjectionary question in *this* pause. She had sorted out her problematic paragraph and decided to experiment with a return to the room for a few moments.

"I suppose you don't have to apply S.T.I.N.K.S., being a lecturer rather than a teacher. The thing was, you see, he took a PGCE after he graduated and he got so tired of these nonsense theories that he was expected to take seriously and apply, or at least *pretend* to apply, because otherwise he got marked down. You know, he had to write lesson plans based on S.M.A.R.T. and that sort of thing. So he sent this entirely facetious spoof paper to an educational journal giving details of his new S.T.I.N.K.S. system for classroom control based on the 'anachronym': S, start calm; T, take control; I, illustrate your points; N, no shouting; K, keep calm; S, success! He thought they would be bound to notice that the word he was using implied less than serious intentions. In fact I seem to remember I helped him to make up the meanings – we did it in about thirty seconds. It was all a joke!"

"Don't you mean acronym not anachronym?" said Priscilla.

"No," said Antholian. "It's the word Walter used to describe this nonsense himself but they didn't even notice that. 'Anachronym' is beginning to be used seriously as well! Of course you know the rest. S.T.I.N.K.S. took off, implemented in all state schools. He gave lectures, wrote books, received royalties – money rolling in everywhere. I thought he was starting to believe in it all himself. In fact I wrote to him and asked him if he had no *integrity* left! Anyway, he wrote back and said he did but everything was too far out of his control for him to *do* anything. He assured me that he had written another audaciously fake system and this time he was sure that people would notice the ridiculous nature of all such systems and reject them for ever. He wanted to create a showdown like the one at the end of 'The Emperor's New Clothes'."

"Mmmm!" said Priscilla in an encouraging tone, but she had wandered off into her own thoughts again.

"So this time he wrote a fake time management system for business. Really it should have been impossible to not realise this was a spoof. But no one important did. It became, naturally, even more successful and has also now been extended into the educational goals sector in a totally irrelevant way. His new anachronym was F.R.A.U.D., as follows: F, find time; R, relax and stay calm; A, appropriate actions; U, understand the intention; D, achieve your destination. Teachers have to use both that *and* S.T.I.N.K.S. when writing lesson plans now. You would have thought that when he specially chose the acronym F.R.A.U.D., people could not have failed to notice…"

A huge lorry thundered past in the road and broke Priscilla's train of thought. She started listening to the conversation again. Antholian continued.

"But instead of seeing the meaningless stupidity of such systems, which was his entire original intention, everyone still went for it! He's a *multi-millionaire* now. He says he still suffers *occasional* scruples but when he considered the whole picture, he concluded that his systems were no worse than any of the others that people get made to apply. In fact he decided that they might even be more effective and less bother."

"Humph! *In regione caecorum rex est luscus!*" said Priscilla.

"Precisely!" agreed Antholian. " But however cynical one might feel about this sort of activity he made a *mint* of money with it. Terribly *ideologically unsound*, of course, but, you know, if I cared at all about money I *might* feel quite *envious!*"

Just for a moment Priscilla thought she heard a minute sigh from Tony.

"But what else could you need in life that you do not already have?" she asked. "Books, green tea, ideological satisfaction, living in Oxford!

Disiderantem quod sati est neque tumultuosum sollicitat mare ... non verberatae grandine vineae fundusque mendax."

"Absolutely!" said Antholian, and he beamed at her again. He had not realised how much Aunty Pris understood him. In fact he had always thought that she, like most other relatives and friends of the family, tended to prefer his bouncier and slightly less eccentric siblings. Clearly she *did* understand his lifestyle choices. He breathed in deeply and the overpowering scent of lavender flowed into his system again. Then he caught sight of the large clock on the wall.

"Goodness, look at the time! I must reopen the shop! I tell you what, though. Something has occurred to me. I can't sell it to you but I could *lend* you Flipper's buddha. He was obviously worried about it leaving it in my *shop* in case I accidentally sold it which would be no better than it getting accidentally sold from his own shop. That must be why he put it so high up. If you had it in your house there is no danger of it being accidentally sold, and he could just as easily pop up to Jericho to collect it for his mother's

176

birthday as get it from here! You are also much less likely to have a break-in than I am here. People will try to get hold of some of the alternative medicine because there are always rumours about it containing illegal drugs. Someone tried to break in last week but Boris Spassky stopped them."

"Boris Spassky?" asked Priscilla. She was paying full attention since he had made the suggestion that she might get hold of the buddha after all, and for *free* as well!

"I borrow one of the next-door-neighbour's Great Danes at night since the last break- in here. The neighbour keeps five in the flat over his shop, so he can spare one for me to use as a night-watchdog. He's called Boris Spassky – the Great Dane, that is, not the next-door-neighbour! Nothing is going to get in past him. But I don't see any harm in you *borrowing* the buddha. I'll go and get it down and you can take it back with you."

He sprang nimbly up from his cushion, took the tray into the kitchen, carefully washed, dried and put away all the utensils, and then dashed down the stairs to

177

reopen the shop. Shortly afterwards Priscilla could hear him returning her bicycle to the shop and getting the ladder out to reach the top shelf.

She was having some problems in her attempts to follow him. She had carefully waited till he left the room before attempting to rise from the cushion but she had now found that both feet were indeed soundly 'asleep', and when she managed to persuade one out of its coma it rewarded her with agonisingly painful pins and needles. She managed to stretch her legs out straight and wiggle her toes while trying not to scream. The second foot awoke in the same state as the first. After a few minutes of excruciating toe wiggling she managed to get off the cushion onto all fours and then propel herself back into a vertical position, one more usual for the motion of the current day *homo sapiens*. She had great difficulty in jamming her shoes back on and by the time she had descended the steep stairs, Antholian was back behind the counter and the buddha was safely wrapped up in brown paper and secured tightly in her bicycle basket by the means of some twine threaded through the wicker sides of the basket.

178

"Just in case you go over a pothole!" said Antholian, feeling pleased with his forward planning.

"I am truly grateful!" said Priscilla. "And thank you for the tea as well!"

"Do come again!" said Antholian, entirely sincerely.

He had broken off with his girlfriend last year as they had disagreed disastrously about whether having children was ideologically sound in an already overcrowded world. Now his social life seemed to consist almost entirely of solo philosophising, often for weeks at a time, unless you counted conversations with customers. Most customer conversations were unsatisfactory although some could be very stimulating. So a social hour with Priscilla had been very pleasant for him.

"I will look forward to it!" said Priscilla, also with perfect truth.

The whole visit had, she felt, been very enjoyable. She felt positively refreshed and cheerful as – trailing scents of lavender, chamomile and bergamot in her wake – she wandered out of the shop with her bicycle.

When she arrived home Walls courteously opened the door for her and then reeled backwards. Pippy took one sniff and fled upstairs.

"New perfume?" suggested Walls, as gallantly as he could.

"Aromatherapy!" replied Priscilla, who was, by now, feeling extremely peculiar. She had found pedalling her bicycle uphill unusually difficult: the bicycle had seemed strangely heavy and hard to steer. She had been glad to get off and lean it against the wall outside her house.

"Can you retrieve the brown paper package from my bicycle basket and put my bicycle round in the back garden?" she asked.

Walls watched, surprised, as she reeled up the stairs and vanished into her room.

Pippy shot down the stairs, escaping from what she considered to be the truly rank smell of the sweetly perfumed oils.

Surely she's not been drinking again *already*? thought Walls. She must be using that weird scent to cover up the smell of alcohol!

Slamming on the red wig, just in case of onlookers, he trotted out to the street to find Priscilla's bicycle leaning against the front wall. He took it carefully through the house to the back garden. He began by attempting to untangle the twine festooning both the parcel and the bicycle basket, and then, being of a practical and non-recycling mind, went back to the kitchen to get some scissors to slice through the tangle. The parcel was *much* heavier than he expected. No wonder the old lady had looked a bit tired after pedalling along with *that* in her basket. He put the parcel down on the hall table and hung his wig neatly on a coat hook by the front door.

It was a good job he had decided to move into Angel's room while she was away, he thought. Someone ought to keep an eye on the old lady if she was drinking this much! Presumably Angel usually looked after her! These aging academics were not safe to be left by themselves! He hastened back into the lounge to get on with the little assembly project that he was completing in there. He did hope Priscilla liked the 'Changing Rooms' transformation that he was achieving in her lounge! He was a *little* dubious about her reaction but trusted in his own personal charm to get through whatever happened when she found out.

Priscilla sat groggily down on her dressing table stool and caught sight of herself in the huge dressing table mirror. She realised to her horror that she had two large stains of oily liquid across the front of her blouse. She looked down. There was another on her skirt. What could have caused it? She sniffed at one of them suspiciously. The scent was easy to identify. Of course, the aromatherapy oils! No wonder she was feeling so strange; she had been breathing in the heady scents for far too long. She didn't need a *rest*; she needed a *wash*!

She leapt up, threw off her scented outfit, put it into the laundry basket on the landing, closing the lid firmly, and then vanished into the shower for half an hour of blissful hot water and shower gel. Even after that there still seemed to be a suggestion of lavender about her person but it was very faint.

Priscilla chose her new outfit carefully. Despite her professed feminist standpoint, she felt it was more important to dress well with a *male* in the house.

When she left her bedroom, twenty minutes later, make-up redone, hair tidily arranged, elegant clothes pristine and fresh, carefully selected shoes with very high heels, she breathed in another delightful aroma, wafting up from downstairs. Her stomach reminded her that the only sustenance she had taken for lunch was half a pot of green china tea, and then propelled her as rapidly down the stairs as one could achieve in the killer heels she was wearing. She hastened into the kitchen.

Walls was there, wearing a natty 'designer label' exercise outfit of shorts and singlet, with a towel hung round his neck. He was frying the latest in a huge pile of buckwheat pancakes. The already-cooked ones were stacked high on a plate, and as he finished

183

cooking each he added it to the pile and popped a large knob of butter on top. The butter melted and ran across its surface.

Priscilla found herself actually drooling.

"Help yourself!" said Walls generously, making an expansive wave with the spatula which encompassed the pancakes, a huge jug of maple syrup and the coffee pot full of steaming black coffee.

Priscilla did. It crossed her mind briefly that Walls as chef might not improve her figure but *his* looked perfectly trim, so maybe she should not worry too much.

After her tenth pancake Priscilla felt replete.

"What I need now," she said, with no actual intention of taking anything of the sort, "is some exercise."

"If you step into the lounge," said Walls, feeling pleased that she had made this suggestion as he had wondered how to introduce the subject of his lounge transformation, "you will find I have provided the very means to take some!"

Presumably he was *joking*; he must mean that she would benefit from a digestive rest in a comfortable chair! She laughed, politely rather than sincerely, and wandered off into the lounge to study a good book for a while.

At the lounge door she came to a dead halt.

"Walls!"

"Yes!" he replied, innocently.

"Walls! My lounge! *My lounge*!"

This morning Priscilla had left behind a lounge containing the usual accoutrements of an English 'withdrawing room': tasteful carpet, two-seater sofa, two armchairs, a coffee table and so on.

The view that met her eyes now was staggering. Black exercise mats covered the carpet, and there was an exercise bicycle and three other large items of torture equipment which Priscilla could not even name. There was a set of hefty weights in the corner.

Priscilla could not even totter in and sit down to recover from the shock as her furniture was no longer visible.

"Ah, yes, *splendid*, isn't it! Now we can exercise as much as we like without having to leave the house! Freddy brought it all round for me this morning. He's lending it all to me. His Dad bought a house for him to live in while he was doing his D. Phil. and he had a gym set up in one of the rooms but Freddy never used any of the equipment; he is such a lazy slob! He's finished his D. Phil. now and he's selling the house so he doesn't want it and he said I could have *all* of it for the next few weeks because I can't get to the gym. Thought I could pop it all Angel's room but I'd kinda forgotten that these little old English houses have such small bedrooms. When they brought it here there was no way I could fit it into Angel's room and also, even if I cut the amount of equipment back, I was worried about stressing your upstairs floorboards with the weight of it all. I didn't want to shoot through the ceiling onto your head, so the lounge was *the only possible option*."

Freddy was the Honourable Frederick, not only titled but also very well endowed with money, and also a postgraduate friend of Walls. He was shaped as nearly like a sphere as was possible for a human. His hopeful family had installed the gym in his Oxford house with the idea of improving Freddy's health but he had remained totally uninterested in any form of exercise save walking the very short distance to college.

Priscilla held the doorpost for support. *Stressing* the upstairs floorboards? Lounge the *only possible option*? She was beginning to understand why Walls and Barnabus got on together so well. They were so *very alike*.

"*Mens sana in corpore sano!*" added Walls, after a rapid crafty glance at his palm. He felt that an apt classical quotation might help him out. He had persuaded Freddy and his father to teach him a collection of useful classical quotations this morning and also to fill him in on the life of Agamemnon as

described in the *Iliad* and in the relevant plays by
Aeschylus and Sophocles.

Since they had both been classically educated at an
excellent public school, they had no difficulty in
reeling off a whole set of information and quotations.
In fact they had entirely lost track of his original
request as they both out-quoted each other in, to
Walls, a completely incomprehensible way.
Eventually he had stopped them and got them instead
to write out, carefully and neatly, twenty useful
phrases, together with their English translations, on a
notepad. He had attempted to acquire some Ancient
Greek quotations too but the Greek alphabet had
proved too great a stumbling block and Walls had
decided to stick exclusively to Latin. The three of
them had been like naughty schoolboys, giggling
together over their plans.

Once the other two had left, Walls had filed the
notepad in Angel's room and transferred a selection
for use on that day onto the palm of his hand, using an
indelible pen. Unfortunately, as many tourists armed
only with a phrase book have found, it is one thing to
say a phrase correctly in an unknown tongue but it is

quite another to comprehend a reply in the same language. Priscilla's reply demonstrated this problem very effectively. She was not impressed with his quotation. In fact she prefixed her own statement with a loud 'tut'.

"Except, of course, that that is a common misquotation, caused by taking words out of their original context. What Juvenal actually wrote was *orandum est ut sit mens sana in corpore sano. fortem posce animum mortis terrore carentum, qui spatium uitae extremum intere munera ponat naturae, qui ferre queat quoscumque labores, nesciat irasci, cupiat nihil et potiores Herculis aerumnas credate saeuosque labores et uenere et cenis et pluma Sardanapalli.*"

"I stand humbly corrected!" said Walls, having no idea what she had just said and *still* feeling quite pleased with his new-found Latin ability since she had understood his pronunciation! She might not like the phrase but he must have got the pronunciation spot on or she would have mentioned it!

Priscilla was not listening to him. She was still transfixed by the new look of her room. She did not seem at all happy with her wonderful opportunity to exercise on top rate equipment.

"Walls!" she pronounced again. "*Where* is my furniture?"

"Still there!" he said, triumphantly. "It all fitted in together!"

"*Where?*" demanded Priscilla.

"The settee is behind the rowing machine. One chair is behind the bench press and the other is behind the exercise bike."

Priscilla refocussed on the scene more carefully. Ah, yes, those lumps covered with black dustsheets and pushed back against the walls *could* be her furniture.

"I forgot to take the dustsheets off! We put them on to keep your things safe and then I was so excited about being able to exercise! I'll whip them off in no time! We were careful to put them on so we didn't damage the furniture or get it dirty while we were moving everything about and assembling the equipment. Freddy's father *insisted* on using dustsheets. He went and found them all in the back of the horsebox. Did I tell you his father had come round as well to deliver the stuff? No, I don't think I did. They were in a bit of a hurry as they are trying to pack the rest of Freddy's stuff up today, so they just *left* us the dustsheets. They said you could keep them. Very generous people. Wonderful family!"

He began leaning over the equipment and whisking black dustsheets through the air rather like a magician revealing white rabbits. Her furniture reappeared, looking miffed and startled by its new role as background scenery for a gym.

Why had she allowed herself to be cajoled into sharing a house with an exercise freak of a rower? Spending time with Barnabus in his own house had been quite enough for her; she should have been warned by that. *Nemo liber est qui corpore servit.* Seneca was quite right so far but he forgot to mention that the effect spread through their friends and acquaintances!

191

It was no good *reasoning* with them: they would never understand that activities designed to improve rowing ability were not vital parts of life!   Her room was *ruined*, even if only temporarily, and what on earth would Charles think?

Then she realised that she *knew* what Charles would think. He would *love* it. After all he was an exercise freak of a mountaineer. Perhaps she could explain it as a special surprise she had planned for *his visit*? She would give up any idea of evicting all the equipment and leave it there to impress him. He might even think she had taken up exercise herself!

In the meantime the only thing to do was to behave as if it was not there.

She made a leisurely choice of a book from the shelf by the door, climbed over the exercise bicycle, half fell into an armchair and then, after readjusting her position, found the bicycle to be quite useful as a footrest. She opened *Odes* by Horace and left the room for better climes.

"I thought *you* might like to use it *as well*!" offered Walls, after a couple of minutes. He was troubled by her silence. Was she working up towards a sudden explosion of wrath?

"Sorry," said Priscilla, absently. "Did you say something?"

"Not really. Nothing. You're sure you are OK with all the equipment?" said Walls.

"Yes, I thought that was what you said. I was assuming that. Thank you. I'll enjoy it," replied Priscilla. She felt this reply covered whatever remark he might just have made as she hadn't been listening. She was no longer in the new gym; she and Horace were far away together. She continued, reading aloud absent-mindedly, "*Vitae summa brevis spem nos vetat incohare longam.*" Then, realising she was voicing her thoughts, she stopped speaking again.

"Absolutely, Ma'am!" said Walls, feeling nervous in case she might decide to interrogate him about the highest level he had ever achieved in Latin. His school had abandoned the Classics in favour of

Spanish, so that he had never studied these subjects. You never knew with dons; all such one-track minds. She might think no knowledge of Classics at all made him unfit to share her house.

He looked at her rapt face. She appeared to have drifted off again into her own world so he concluded that his reconstruction of the lounge *must* have been forgiven, and went back to pancake construction instead. She had, he felt, taken the whole thing *much better than he had expected.*

Priscilla was not quite as lost in Horace as Walls thought. She was continuing a second train of thought behind Horace's lyrical compositions and wondering if she could move in with *Tony* until Barnabus and his assorted associates had finished occupying her own house. No, not Tony: far too far out from the centre of Oxford, and the diet would be too *distressing* in the long term! She could move into *College rooms*? No: she liked to have life *outside* College. Coromandel, although it had been mixed for many years, was still, in its deepest soul, a *men's* college and she found this masculine atmosphere grew tedious after a very short while. Elodea's house? No: far too chaotic and ridiculously distant from Oxford.

She smelt more pancakes under construction in the kitchen. Even though replete she found herself salivating again. She scrapped her plans for moving out. Inconvenient, cavalier and annoying as he was, Walls certainly knew how to cook just the sort of food she liked.

She abandoned Horace, climbed out over the exercise bicycle, and tripped back into the kitchen.

"I think I could fit in just *one* more pancake!" she said to Walls.

Chapter 6

Antholian was shutting up his shop. He had had a satisfactory afternoon. Several ladies in search of eternal youth had invested in his cosmetic range. One of his favourite customers, a retired don, in her eighties, had called in to purchase and test yet another infallible cure for insomnia. They had agreed, as usual, that this 'cure' would be worth a try but that, in the event of it failing, one could have so many interesting thoughts in the darkest hours of the night. He suspected that she actually slept too much during the daytime and that this was why she could not sleep properly at night. However, she enjoyed calling in once a week for a chat and they still had many other 'infallible' remedies to work through. New alternative medicine insomnia remedies were created so frequently.

A charming young American lady had called in and had had to whisper in his ear the word 'constipation' as she was too embarrassed to say it out loud. He had sold her what he believed to be an effective cure, wrapping it carefully in brown paper so that no one could read the packet as she carried it home. He had also given her some excellent advice about eating more fruit, vegetables and fibre. She had blushed and thanked him.

Antholian had even had time between customers to complete sufficient study of *The History of Chinese Philosophy*, as edited by Bo Mou.

Yes, his afternoon had gone very well.

Together with the pleasure of Priscilla's lunchtime visit, he felt that he could say that the whole day had passed enjoyably.

He went upstairs and pulled a plain black hoodie and a pair of black tracksuit trousers out from under his futon. He opened one of the base units in the kitchen and removed some black trainers with a pair of designer sunglasses tucked into them. He changed his robe and sandals for this new outfit, pulling the hood carefully over his head and tying the cords tightly to stop any risk of the hood sliding off. Once he had the designer shades on he felt his transformation was complete. His aim was to prevent any of his customers from recognising him during the next part of his day's regular routine.

He ran swiftly down the stairs, hurried through the back door and walked the five steps along the shared back path that stretched between his own back door and that of his next-door-neighbour. He gave a good blow on the back door with his fist as Mr Fisher was rather deaf. Actually the volume of his knock hardly mattered because it was instantly greeted with the usual ear splitting chorus of howls and barks. He heard his next-door-neighbour fighting his way through the crowd of huge bodies to reach his own door.

"What is it?" came an unfriendly shout, as Mr Fisher opened the observation shutter in the door.

Mr Fisher then added, in a quite different tone but at the same volume in order to compete with the dogs,

"Oh, hi Tony, it's *you*! Come to get Boris, have you? He's raring to go."

He said exactly the same thing to Antholian every night. It was all part of the rhythm of their routine. Antholian heard all ten bolts being forced back behind the door and the huge key rasping round in the lock. Sometimes he thought Mr Fisher was just a little over the top with his security arrangements. Mr Fisher himself appeared, looking harassed and batting the rugby scrum of dog's noses back into the house with the aid of a leather bedroom slipper. He handed Antholian a leather loop at the end of a huge chain link lead.

"Come on then. Good boy!" said Antholian.

A huge lion-sized brindled dog fought its way out from the mass of its fellows and instantly set off at a speed that suggested it was about to attempt to score a try. Antholian had no choice but to follow. Antholian often thought that if he fell over it would make no difference to the speed with which he and Boris continued, except, of course, that he would be being dragged along on his face. They belted along the shared back path and through the dark passageway into the Cowley Road.

If it had not been for their unstoppable speed Antholian thought that he could have popped into Flipper's shop and explained about the buddha, although he did not want to reveal his identity even to Flipper when he was wearing this outfit; it was not his usual public image! They hurtled onwards as other pedestrians leapt out of the way and the occasional A-board shop sign folded itself up with a clunk and hit the pavement. They sped on and into Florence Park. Steering his massive charge around the flowerbeds, in order to avoid demolishing the floral displays, Antholian managed to turn Boris around by dint of making a slowly curving circuit around the entire park. Reaching the road again, they then both bolted back in the opposite direction. Someone had once told Antholian that Great Danes were quite placid and only walked slowly over comparatively short distances to those traversed by much smaller dogs. Clearly someone had forgotten to transmit this information to Boris.

Arriving back, breathless, at Antholian's own back door they bounced up the stairs to his flat. Boris drank a bucket of water and then lay down on the futon for a rest, peacefully free from the rest of his canine friends and relatives.

Antholian drew breath for a few moments, changed back into his normal robe, and then put a saucepan of water on to the hob ready to prepare his meal of rice. Perhaps he would add some thyme tonight? Or coriander? Coriander was always good with rice. He tuned into Radio 3 on his iPod and hummed happily along. People did not understand his diet – they thought it was restrictive and strange – but he felt they failed to understand the truly delicious nature of rice with a few herbs added. He was equally sure that if they joined him in the simpler life they would enjoy it and be healthier and damage the world far less. He was determined himself to lead by example, even if no one *ever* followed him.

He remembered that he had still not told Flipper about loaning Priscilla the little buddha. He would phone him now. He looked in his contact list but he did not have Flipper's number or his email and he did not have a connection with him on Facebook or Twitter either. He could have delayed his meal and gone to see him – he only lived just up the road – but the water was just coming up to the boil. Flipper's shop might be closed: it was late. Antholian felt that he did not really know Flipper well enough to make an informal house visit for no particularly urgent reason. Antholian also belonged to the mobile phone and internet communication generation, although, being older than Barnabus, he felt that using your mobile to have a conversation with someone in the same house, which was a thing he had seen Barnabus manage, was ridiculous. So, having concluded that all possible means of electronic communication were impossible, how *was* he to tell Flipper about the buddha? Then he had a bright thought. *Barnabus*, of course. Barnabus would have Flipper's number! He flung several handfuls of rice into the bubbling water and then rang his youngest brother.

Barnabus was reclining on a dry grassy slope high in the Pyrenees. The scent of mountain flowers floated above his nose. His girlfriend was lying peacefully at his side. The mountain herbs on which they were both draped, parched by the summer sun, were prickly but not in an uncomfortable way. He felt this was a perfect moment in his life, which he must remember for ever. He wished it would never stop. Then his mobile rang. Bother!

He sat up lazily to see which number was ringing and was surprised to see that it was Tony as they very rarely bothered to contact each other. Perhaps there was a family emergency? Barnabus pressed the 'answer' key hastily!

"Tony! Is everything OK? Mama? Dad?"

"Everything is fine," replied Antholian. "I just want you to either give me Flipper's number so I can text him, or otherwise maybe you could pass a message on to him?"

"Flipper?" asked Barnabus, surprised. He did not think Flipper and Tony knew each other, at least not well enough to text message each other.

"You do *have* his number? He didn't give it to me," Tony continued.

"Yes, yes, somewhere. Haven't rung him for ages but I am sure he's on my contact list, provided he hasn't changed his number recently. Yes, yes, I'm sure I have it. OK, what is it you wanted to tell him?"

Barnabus was sleepily peaceful with exercise and good food and mountain air. The reception on his phone was very poor and he had a job to make out all that Tony was saying. All the same he thought he had grasped the important points. Tony seemed to be saying that Priscilla had wanted to borrow a silver laughing buddha that wasn't Tony's but was Flipper's. At least it was Flipper's now but it was going to be for Flipper's mother's birthday, and that Tony thought that Flipper ought to know he had lent it to Priscilla. None of this made any sense at all. Priscilla already had a laughing buddha because he and Angel had given it to her. Why would she want another? Why on earth would Priscilla visit Tony? What was going on? However, despite the relaxation engendered by sun, fresh air and exercise, he did manage to keep in mind the fact that Flipper did not share his number with many people.

"I'd better not give you Flipper's number, Tony, old

man," he said. "Flipper's funny about giving his number to other people."

"*Antholian!*" corrected his brother. "You know I prefer my full name! I've told you often enough! I suppose I have to go round and see him myself then!"

"No, no," said Barnabus, feeling guilty. "*I've* got his number. *I'll* tell him."

"You won't get the message wrong?" asked Antholian, displaying the usual lack of faith that older siblings have in their younger siblings.

"No, of course not! How could I get something *that* simple wrong!" said Barnabus, with the knee-jerk reaction of a younger child whose older sibling does not trust them to achieve a perfectly easy task. "Cheerio then! Love to everyone!"

Barnabus rang off. He wasn't going to actually *ring* Flipper. It didn't seem all that important, even if strange, and if Flipper asked for details he would not be able to give him any as, in truth, he couldn't understand *any* of it. Phoning from here would cost a fortune and, on top of everything else, he wasn't sure how much charge he had left on his battery. So Barnabus composed a suitable text message instead, containing just the facts which he felt must have been definitely correct, if totally lacking grammar and punctuation.

"Tony wants to check OK to lend someone your mothers buddha which you lent to him best regards hope all well Buffy"

He did hope that made sense to Flipper.

"Who was that on the phone?" said Angel, not opening her eyes.

"Tony," replied Barnabus. "You know, my big bro'!"

"*Tony*? Your *brother* Tony? Is everything OK?" asked Angel.

"Everything is fine," said Barnabus, reviewing the text message he had just sent.

Why had Flipper lent a laughing buddha that was intended for his mother, to Tony? How very odd! Why had Priscilla called on Tony? No idea on that either. He could see that if Priscilla had seen the buddha in Tony's house or shop and decided to have it then Tony would have *had* to lend it on to her. Priscilla was a very determined person and Tony tended to vacillate and be easily persuadable when it came to handing over worldy material goods, since he saw them all as valueless. But why did Priscilla *want* it? She already had one. Had she started a whole collection of laughing buddhas? Why not buy another one instead of borrowing Flipper's from Tony? Could Tony be involved in the same line of business as Flipper these days? Was it code? No. To start with, Tony was totally unsuitable for that kind of work and, secondly, in that case he *would* have had a contact number for Flipper. All the same…

Angel smiled up at him. She was so beautiful! He kissed her and forgot all about borrowing buddhas.

"Come on," he said. "We had better start down the mountain or it will be dark. Don't want to be clambering about on these paths in the pitch dark."

Halfway down the mountain a terrible thought flashed across his mind. Flipper's mother was *dead*! She had died when riding with the first field of the hunt – fallen off jumping a bruiser and broken her neck. Too late to retrieve his message now! He did hope Flipper would *forgive* him! He must have *completely* misheard Tony, or else Tony, who was as bad at listening as Aunty Pris, had got the wrong end of the stick. What a *frightful* faux pas to refer to a mother as if she was alive when she was deceased! What could he do to correct things? Being male, he rapidly concluded that the best thing to do was forget about it and hope it had all blown over by the time he got back.

When he did get back he would take Flipper out for a drink and apologise profusely for the bad reception on the phone, his terrible forgetfulness and the resulting misunderstanding. Perhaps it was Flipper's *grandmother's* birthday present? He could have misheard grandmother as mother, *maybe*. He was, however, not perfectly sure that Flipper had a grandmother either; he had the feeling that one of them had pickled herself with alcohol and the other had gone too fast round a corner in her electric wheelchair. Yes, definitely one grandmother had died in an electric wheelchair crash because even Flipper used to think that was a humorous end. All very odd but…

Barnabus returned suddenly to the real world, for here was that tricky bit where they had to climb down the huge rock slide. He had better help Angel. He looked round for her. Angel, who was very well able to climb down all by herself, had already gone past him while he was lost in daydreams about the buddha. She was already halfway down the slide. Seeing him standing there, looking around for her in a confused way, she called up and waved to him.

"I'm down here, slowcoach!"

"Hey, wait for me!" replied Barnabus.

In the excitement of first negotiating the huge fallen rocks while trying to keep up with his annoyingly nimble girlfriend, and then having to solve the mystery of the correct path to follow below the rock fall since they had both failed to notice that there were several downward alternatives when they were travelling upwards, Barnabus entirely forgot about the whole phone call. His uppermost thought now was that Angel looked so lovely when she smiled up at you! They continued the descent hand in hand, planning what to eat for dinner on the way.

Back in the Cowley Road, conscience now quite clear of any worries about borrowed buddhas, Antholian *still* sighed. Despite the rumours rife among his family and friends, he did not *really* only drink tap water all the time. He tried to drink as much as possible but Oxford tap water was undeniably unpleasant. It lacked the crystal clarity of living water from leaping natural springs, and it tasted flat and far too full of calcium carbonate. But now he faced his usual evening's moral dilemma. If he made tea with the leftover water from boiling the rice, that would clearly save energy, and not waste the trace nutrition in the water, or waste water that had to be processed in the purification plant. But the taste of tea made with such water was so far from satisfactory, he would just have to ignore his scruples again and boil *more* water for the tea, thus wasting energy, water and trace nutrition. However, Boris could drink the rice water so that it would not be entirely wasted. That was most important – no waste.

He chose his tea carefully from the selection in the cupboard. Yes, a little Green Balance tea would be pleasant. He prepared this tea as formally as if he was his own guest. Eating frugally did not mean that one must lose all the ceremony of a meal, he told himself. He arranged his rice carefully in a classic blue and white rice bowl, rising in a beautiful pyramid shaped mound above the rim of the bowl. He took his chopsticks out of their case. He placed the tea and the rice on the low table.

Then he ate in splendid formality, kneeling on the cushion. He felt at perfect peace with the world. So did Boris, snoring sonorously on the futon.

Once Antholian had finished his meal and stood up again Boris sprang up, looking enthusiastic and drooling. Antholian got out a large china dog bowl and poured the cooled rice-boiling water into it. Boris strode over and drank it heroically. He did not like the flavour particularly either but he liked Antholian, the hero who rescued him from the rest of his family and took him for such lovely runs. Boris could stomach a lot of rice water if it made his friend happy. Boris ate pretty much anything if it was on the floor, even non-food items like bars of soap. He was well mannered enough not to help himself to items belonging to Tony that were not actually on the floor, although if he accidentally knocked them off shelves or the counter he considered them fairly won once they hit the floor itself.

Antholian felt that Boris's ability to deter unwanted intruders overnight made the passage of the occasional possession or item of stock into the dog's stomach worthwhile.

Antholian theoretically disapproved of non-working household pets as a waste of world resources but, as a Buddhist, he respected all life and anyway he reasoned that Boris was a *working* dog. He enjoyed Boris's company in the evenings. He did not expect you to hold long conversations or take part in meaningless activities, and yet he was another breathing being in the house.

Antholian picked up his book, lay down on the floor near the window, and let the room get dark naturally as he read onwards. When it became too dark to see the page he stood up, stretched and began to prepare to meditate.

Boris woke up, looked at him and stomped off down the stairs to start his night watch duty in the shop. Boris did not agree with meditation: he didn't like the smell of incense. Antholian shut the main door to the flat behind the dog. Boris would be quite happy downstairs for the rest of the night.

Antholian raised the sash window a few inches to let the evening air, unsullied by the day's petrol, flow gently into the room.

The streetlight outside his window flickered and went out with a slight pop. It seemed very dark outside. He looked to left and right. All the streetlights were out. There was still a street glow from lit shop windows and passing cars. Maybe a main fuse had gone on the street lighting circuit? It could not be a power cut as only the streetlights had gone out.

He took out some patchouli oil and poured it into a small lamp. He put several incense sticks into small holders: lemon grass, ylang ylang, orange. He had had quite enough of the scent of lavender when Priscilla was here!

Then he took off his robe. He preferred to meditate naked. In the dim room his pale skin glowed slightly and looked whiter than it was, and the tattoos of swirling lines that he had acquired in India during his gap year showed up as black against his skin.

He lit the oil and the incense sticks and composed himself in the lotus position just behind them. He breathed deeply twenty times. In, two, three, four. Out, two, three, four.

He was just about to start reciting his mantra when he saw the window, opposite him, begin to rise of its own accord. His eyes opened wide but he did not move. His meditation routine should not be disturbed by the random behaviour of a window. Perhaps it was a spirit?

214

The window continued to rise. Antholian watched it, unmoving but fascinated. The burning sweet scents of the oil were filling his head and making him vaguely dizzy. He felt strangely unmoved by the window's behaviour.

A few seconds later a man, dressed from head to foot in black, with a balaclava covering most of his face and with the only visible parts of his face darkened with charcoal or make-up, dropped lightly and soundlessly into the room through the now fully raised sash window. As he landed he reached behind to unhook a wire from his belt and leave the end trailing on the floor. He surveyed the room. He was holding a small handgun, ready to fire.

Antholian felt vaguely surprised but he stayed put, unmoving and silent. He was considering possible likely options. He wondered if perhaps he was having a hallucination induced by a combination of his restrictive diet, over-exercising with Boris, and the incense and patchouli oil. Or possibly he had already dropped into meditation and this was a vision? Perhaps he was, in fact, asleep on his futon in body and only here in spirit, dreaming this whole event? He

215

had a feeling that the scene before him resembled something he had seen in a classic film, or a classic TV programme. Dr Who? James Bond? No, not a film or a TV programme... A classic advertisement from the old days – that was it! He even knew what it was now.

The man with the gun was equally surprised. He had been roaming about on dark rooftops for a while so his eyes rapidly adapted to the gloom of the room. However, the presence of a lifesize glimmering white buddha statue did startle him. He looked more closely.

"Tony! You really gave me the creeps just then! I thought you were a statue!"

"Speak for yourself, Flipper! You rather startled me, entering in such a manner! I presume you have come to bring me Milk Tray?" said Antholian, who had recognised Flipper's voice.

Antholian was beginning to recover from his shock and was now feeling annoyed at not recognising Flipper in the first place. He reminded himself of an important rule: If you want a peaceful life you should always, always, always keep away from Barnabus, Paris and every single one of their friends. They had no idea how to behave themselves and all their friends were the same! *Younger brothers*! He should have had more sense than to even let Flipper come in through his shop door this morning! It just *encouraged* them!

"Is this some kind of joke?" Antholian continued. "Am I being videoed for YouTube or something? Or have you taken up armed robbery?"

At this point Boris, rather tardily as he had been distracted by hunting spiders in the stockroom, flung himself against the other side of the flat's door, broke the catch completely and crashed into the room with a low menacing growl.

"No, Boris!" cried Antholian, flinging himself in between Boris and Flipper. "Back! Down!"

Boris was growling low and ready to spring.

"No, Boris! *Friend*!" said Antholian, rather desperately this time.

Boris's slow mind processed this information. He looked disappointed. He stopped growling, sat down, scratched his left ear with his right leg, turned, and wandered sadly back downstairs.

"You are lucky I was here!" said Antholian. "He could have killed you, you know!"

"Or, indeed, *I* could have *shot* him!" said Flipper.

"You mean that thing's *real*?" said Antholian. "I have an interesting paper on the evils of weaponry. Perhaps you would like to peruse it."

Antholian turned towards the shelves.

"Never mind that just now!" interrupted Flipper. "The *buddha*. I have come to collect it!"

"Did you *forget* when your *mother's birthday* was? You could have used the usual door for *that* purpose, you know! Or did you try ringing the bell and I didn't hear you? So sorry; I don't always pay attention to external distractions when I am preparing to meditate. Did you think I was *out*?"

Antholian found he was babbling as he tried to make rational sense of Flipper's strange behaviour.

"The buddha, *quickly*! I need it right now! Let's just pop and get it!" said Flipper, hoping to get him to concentrate on the point in hand.

"It's not here. I thought Barnabus had told you! I lent it to my aunt, Aunty Pris, that's Priscilla really. She's a don and not really my aunt but it will be quite, quite safe. I thought it would be safer in her house than in my shop. You know, raids on the shop and things. But if you need it for *tomorrow* I'll walk up there with you and get it back tomorrow, or we can go right now if you really need to get it."

Antholian reflected that he had better not send Flipper to collect it by himself. If he usually entered houses like this then Aunty Pris might well have a heart attack.

"I got the text but Buffy only told me you *wanted* to lend it to someone, not who the someone *was*, or that you had *already* lent it! I hoped it was *still here*. I need it sooner than I expected. Things have moved faster than I thought. You have to come with me. After Buffy sent that text, it's not safe for you to stay here! *You* rang *him* first, I assume? And mentioned the buddha?"

Antholian nodded, mutely.

"We must go *at once!*" said Flipper.

Antholian was finding this hard to follow. Flipper's mother's birthday had moved faster than he thought? Surely not! Not safe to stay here? He wondered if Flipper was quite sane. Perhaps he wasn't: being very intelligent was not always accompanied by sanity. Could he be a paranoid schizophrenic? Or had he taken crystal meth during his gap year trip? That could cause lapses into paranoia at any time. He must try to humour Flipper and calm him down.

Flipper unhooked the wire from his belt and was just about to hand it to Antholian when he noticed something.

"I say, though, you can't come like that!" exclaimed Flipper. "Do you normally walk round outside in the nude?"

"Bother!" said Antholian. "I forgot. I was meditating, you see!"

He picked up his robe and sandals.

"Is that all you have to wear?" asked Flipper. "Because you are going to have a job to climb round roofs in that! For heaven's sake find something more practical! Come on, quick; we have hardly any time! You and Barnabus between you have wrecked everything!"

"*What?*" asked Antholian.

"No time to explain!"

"I have a *tracksuit*," said Antholian, rewinding the conversation to the issue of clothes, which had been the last logical thing that Flipper had said.

He had now concluded that the only rational explanation for these extraordinary events was that he, Antholian, was asleep and dreaming. It seemed an interesting dream, if rather peculiar. He wondered what would happen next!

"Put the tracksuit on and be quick! Meanwhile," Flipper said, as he swung his rucksack from his shoulders and fished in it, "I'll pop down and put this thing on that shelf."

'This thing' was another buddha, just like the first.

"You've got *another* one!" said Antholian, helpfully, and he then prattled onwards, "I suppose this is one of the ones you didn't want to give to your mother. Does the one you put here have a better expression or something? But you don't have to give *me* another one in exchange; the one I had was yours in the first place! They are very *heavy*. I noticed that with mine. Are they solid silver or some kind of lead or what?"

"Will that dog be all right with me if I go downstairs?" asked Flipper, ignoring Antholian's last speech completely.

"Yes, yes. Boris knows you are a friend now. He might lick you a bit but he'll be quite safe, but, hang on! I was just saying, you've *got* another one. Are you sure you need the first one back?" said Antholian, explaining more slowly and carefully this time.

"This one is not the same one as the other one! I am past explaining as I have entirely lost track of my original master plan, due to you, your aunt and Buffy. I am now implementing Plan F combined with elements of Plans A to E!" said Flipper cryptically, and, moving very quietly, he vanished down the stairs.

Antholian dressed himself in the tracksuit, trainers and designer shades again. Essential oils could cause vivid hallucinatory dreams. The ridiculous conversation he had just had with Flipper definitely proved he was dreaming. He must have finished meditating and gone to sleep on the futon and *then* started this dream.

"Gloves!" said Flipper, reappearing completely silently and making Antholian jump. Flipper handed Antholian a pair of soft black leather gloves that he had taken from his pocket. He put the original buddha into his knapsack and re-shouldered it.

"Now!" said Flipper. "Off we go! Through the window!"

"Why not?" thought Antholian as he was fastened to the hook and then told to shin up his own wall to the roof. Due to benefitting genetically from a tall and athletic build combined with years of climbing trees as a child and mountaineering in the Scottish Highlands as an undergraduate, he found this reasonably easy.

A ginger cat who was resting on the slates and had met him eye to eye as he scaled the guttering did not think much of the new addition to its roof. It spat and swore at him and then rushed over the rooftree to descend hastily into the dark back gardens and vanish.

Antholian turned to fling the hook back to Flipper but found Flipper was already scaling the guttering behind him without any mechanical help.

"Now, quickly. Try not to be seen, and go along the roofs as fast as you can!" ordered Flipper.

These instructions seemed contradictory but Antholian, having decided this was not real life, set off with confidence. Fortunately this misplaced confidence was exactly what he actually required in order not to fall. If he had realised the situation was real and then thought about the matter at all, he might have slipped off.

After successfully passing across the first three roofs they both heard the muffled sounds of a threatening bark from the direction of Antholian's house, followed by a sudden silence. Then Antholian's next-door-neighbour's dogs lifted their voices in a sudden cacophony. They could faintly hear Mr Fisher's voice rising above that of his dogs as he swore at them and told them to be quiet. The noise died down.

"F***!" whispered Flipper. "Only just in time! Good thing I kicked the window shut! They'll just think you are out!"

This made no sense to Antholian at all, but then dreams did not have to be coherent.

When they had worked along another three roofs there was an enormous flash in the sky behind them, followed by a deafening bang. The roof momentarily lost its solidity and rippled beneath them as if the Cowley Road was experiencing an earthquake. Fortuitously close to a chimney stack, they both grabbed it for support. The reverberating bang seemed to echo backwards and forwards several times but perhaps that was just a sound within their own ears. They turned and saw a dull red glow shining above the roofs on the opposite side of the road.

A Siamese cat who had been parading peacefully along the guttering shot past Antholian's head with a wild yowl. Roosting birds rose from trees and hedges, squawking in protest, and wheeled around the black sky – flocks of dark shapes twisting and turning, confused in the darkness.

Mr Fisher's dogs gave voice to a wild torrent of sound. They were joined by every dog in the whole gigantic triangle of Oxford that was formed between and around the Cowley and Iffley Roads. The barking relayed onwards through Headington and then gradually died away.

"Big mortar on that firework! Someone's wedding's going off with a bang!" said Antholian calmly as he turned back to the task in hand. In his new weird world the explosion seemed of no importance.

"It wasn't a firework," whispered Flipper, "it was my shop! Gas explosion!"

Flipper checked his watch.

"Right on time, too!" he added, with satisfaction.

Antholian wondered about the thoughts that his own imagination was creating. How very surreal this particular dream was becoming. Perhaps he should seek counselling himself?

"I'm *dead*, you see!" Flipper added cheerfully. "That should put them off the scent!"

Antholian wondered if he had vitamin deficiency. Perhaps he should add a little more variety to his diet. This was more a hallucination than just a nightmare. He was creating the *feeling* of everything as well: cold hard roof slates, the difficulty of maintaining a foothold, his fingers gripping in the cement on the chimney brickwork. He could even feel his nails snagging off. I suppose I will fall off the roof soon and then wake up just before I land or else start flying around the sky or something, he mused to himself. He hoped that he was not *sleepwalking* on a *real* roof. Surely he couldn't be, could he?

People were rushing out of the houses and shops and pubs and gathering in the road. The pedestrians who were already outside were running up the road and pointing and shouting. Somewhere in the distance an emergency vehicle's siren began to sound.

Further away in the city people opened their front doors or rushed to their windows to look out. People in the central streets turned towards the sound. They wondered if they had heard a huge clap of thunder or if the RAF were doing exercises with a low flying supersonic plane.

"Time to move on!" said Flipper. "Come on! Keep along the non-street side of the rooftrees as much as possible! Probably pretty safe. No one is looking this way anyway!"

"What?" said Antholian. Perhaps the patchouli oil *had* been polluted with something else. He did hope the owner of the shop had not been concealing her cannabis resin in a fake-labelled jar in his flat again. Something similar had happened once before. She liked to conceal her illegal substances in the cupboards in his flat in case her husband found them, apparently forgetting that the cupboards were for Antholian's exclusive use. He did wish she would remember to warn him when she did that sort of thing.

He followed Flipper onwards along the roofs. They pushed off from one chimney stack, dashed along the rooftree and grabbed the next one to restore their balance. Flipper was taking the roofs as casually as most people would progress along a flat pavement.

Antholian had a vague recollection that Barnabus and Flipper had both been 'free runners' when they were undergraduates at Oxford. Maybe that was why he was using this route. Perhaps he had forgotten about the normal way to progress along pavements! Barnabus and five of his friends, including Flipper, had spent a gap year in Nepal after they graduated, so whatever they were doing there he expected it included a spot of mountaineering too. What had they all been doing? Some kind of voluntary work, Mama had said at the time. Building a school or something, Antholian supposed.

In front of Antholian and Flipper loomed what appeared to be an insurmountable problem: a much higher block of buildings with a flat vertical wall facing them, no toe or finger holds! This could be the moment where Antholian's dream ended. He would 'land' in his futon with a gasp and a jolt from his heart. However, as in many dreams, a solution was also provided. A handy climber's wire cable had been left there, the end coiled on their roof, the wire lolling against the vertical wall up to the higher roof.

"You can abseil *up* this, can't you?" hissed Flipper from behind him. "Of course we don't have any abseiling harness, but you know what I mean – using your hands and feet?"

"Naturally!" replied Antholian, with confidence, and suiting the action to the word. He had spent so much of the time, when he should have been studying for his degree, in climbing up and down mountains and cliffs. A little less climbing and a little more philosophy study in a library would undoubtedly have improved the classification of his degree, but he had philosophically explained to his parents that true philosophers considered academic qualifications to be worthless sheets of paper. His parents had not really shared this view. Elodea had never recovered from what she considered to be the poor academic results of her eldest three children. Only Barnabus had encouraged her to believe that her ability to nurture geniuses was not entirely flawed. They were *all* so very *intelligent* but the first three suffered from lack of directed effort, or rather from lack of effort in the 'correct' direction. John was less troubled: he had simply ignored their academic progress once it was clear that none of them were going to study physics.

At last, Antholian thought happily, he would now be able to tell Mama that his viewpoint on the importance of physical exercise and climbing had been correct. If he had spent all that time in the university library he would now be *dead* due to crashing off a roof onto the street below.

The feeling of the wire between his hands, the cool night air, the clamber over the rooftops, the sheer length of time that this had been going on, had finally convinced him that this whole experience was not a dream but definitely real. He had no idea why he and Flipper were fleeing like this. Possibly Flipper *had* gone mad, or was under the influence of something illegal? He didn't think that Flipper indulged in that sort of thing. He thought he subscribed to the 'body being a temple' view of those who indulged in excessive and indulgent, in Tony's classification of activities as 'being of use to the world', physical exercise. In Flipper's case, as in that of Barnabus and Walls, this activity was rowing.

Whatever was *actually* happening was an adventure to equal anything that Barnabus and Paris had recently experienced. Antholian was becoming enthralled, absorbed into the beauty of the chase, the joy of the hunt! Were they chasing or were they being pursued? Were they the hunters or the prey? Did it matter? Primeval emotions were breaking through his acquired Buddhist calm.

Antholian now walked boldly up the vertical wall, hands slipping slightly on the wire with sweat. He was worried about how much they must both show up against the pale brickwork if anyone was looking upwards from the street below. He could sense Flipper, just below him, using the same wire. They must show up as a solid block of black. If they *were* being pursued they must travel quickly to the concealment afforded at the top of the wall. This was a hard physical struggle. Flipper had to reach up once and shove Antholian's foot back to position as Antholian slipped and began to swing outwards uncontrollably. Antholian, embarrassed by this fault, decided that he really must start climbing again and get back into condition, even if it meant taking a little ideologically unsound transport to reach the mountains. He had forgotten the exhilaration afforded by the physical challenge and the danger. As he swung up onto the next roof and carefully rose to the vertical position required to sprint to the next chimney pot he felt a fantastic rush of adrenaline, He was a caveman chasing a mammoth, a medieval huntsman after a white hart. No, he was the white hart. No, he was the mammoth. He was enjoying himself. He had not had nearly enough fun recently!

Flipper wound up the wire and stuffed it into his backpack before following Antholian. At the other side of the tall block another wire hung down. Antholian launched himself down it, feet on the wall, leaning outwards, sliding the wire gently through his hands. This direction was easy with gravity to help!

They continued and reached the muddled block of buildings that filled the narrow gap between the Cowley and Iffley roads as they converged at the Plain. Two more helpful wires assisted them across the buildings, and they finished with a single-storey jump down into the Iffley Road.

"Phew!" said Antholian as they landed. "You know, when we started off I really thought this was *all a dream.*"

"Definitely not! If *only* it was!" replied Flipper. "No time to explain. Streetlights all still on here. Quick, into that car!"

There were no pedestrians at that end of the Iffley Road; they had all rushed round into the Cowley Road to see what the bang might have been. Only a very drunk female tramp appeared around the corner from the Plain, waving a bottle of methylated spirit and singing incoherently. She reeled into a wall and descended to the pavement in a heap.

They ran up the pavement to the first of the parked cars. Flipper fished what Antholian assumed was the car key from his pocket and they flung themselves hastily into the ancient Volkswagen Beetle. Flipper persuaded the car to start. It gave a deep groan and then cranked itself into motion. They accelerated up the Iffley Road and, with a casual disregard for speed limits and even red traffic lights, made their way towards Donnington Bridge. Antholian found high speed car travel very frightening. It was several years since he had even been *inside* a car. He clenched his teeth and clung to the nearest door. Flipper did not seem inclined to talk either. His jaw was set and he looked tense. He parked the car by the bridge itself, and Antholian followed him as he sprinted down to the towpath.

"Is that parking *legal*?" asked Antholian in a whisper. He did not really like to question what Flipper was doing as he knew now that he was taking part in a greater plan which he did not understand. He had begun to feel unreasonably tired, despite the excitement of the moment. He was usually asleep by this time of night.

"No, but it's not *my car*," hissed Flipper in reply. "Hopefully someone will tow it away. Joyriders, eh? What can you do about them?"

They started along the towpath, travelling away from the city centre, at a speed that Antholian felt Usain Bolt might have considered normal but which he, personally, was finding rather stressful.

Flipper suddenly braked, turned and flung himself down behind a large bush. Antholian followed, relieved that Flipper had stopped before his own heart had.

He felt he should state some points of principle, one of which had been deeply troubling him since they had leapt into the car. "You know I don't usually enter vehicles powered by *fossil fuels*! And definitely not *stolen* ones! I'm not sure which aspect is worse!" he whispered.

"A first time for everything!" replied Flipper, cheerfully and without scruples. He was fishing in his rucksack. "Here. Put these on."

'These' were a Kings College rowing lycra and a wig of short blond curls

"*Disguise*!" added Flipper, in case Antholian should have any doubt about its purpose.

"Isn't it a bit late at night for rowing? And it's out of term!" objected Antholian. "We'll stick out like a sore thumb!"

"Late night training. Ergos and weights. We are postgraduates, so we are living here all summer. We are both jogging back to college down the towpath."

"We might fall in. It's rather dark!" Antholian demurred.

Antholian was regaining adult caution. He was several years older than Flipper and had developed the concept of consequence as well as action.

"Joggers' head torches!" said Flipper, happily, handing him something else. "Not so you see better – they are really pretty useless for that – but they stop anyone else being able to see your face clearly!"

"We couldn't possibly be doing rowing training at this time of night," objected Antholian, still fixated on this idea. "I know! We could be training for a marathon run as well, and we started our twenty-six mile run *after* doing an evening's rowing practice, so that is why we are still in our rowing lycra!"

"OK, whatever you like!" replied Flipper, whose rapidly redesigned plan had, admittedly, been a little woolly on the supposed motives of two rowers running along the towpath at night. Flipper had felt that this was a very minor and unimportant detail in his plan. "But remember, keep in the part! No conversation about anything else!"

Flipper transformed his own appearance by converting his very short dark hair into a long blond mane which any heavy metal lead singer might have envied. He tied the wig neatly back in a pony tail with a rubber band. They put the head torches on.

"Ready?" he asked Tony.

"Ready, but, *wait*. One more thing!"

"Quickly then! Speed is everything. We have spent far too long here!" answered Flipper.

Antholian had suddenly remembered the barking in his own house, the barking that had stopped so abruptly. In the effort of hurrying along rooftops he had not really thought what the barking meant except that the pursuers, whoever they might be, must have entered his house. His face contorted with distress and he gasped out the two words.

"Boris Spassky!"

"Who? The chess player?"

"No, the dog. The dog in my house. Is he…" Antholian was suddenly unable to say the dread word. He pictured Boris's noble frame lying still and silent for ever on his floor.

"No, no, no, not *dead*. Tranquillised, I would think," replied Flipper in soothing tones. He was afraid that Tony might be about to insist on going back to try to rescue the dog. "They won't want to leave any trace of their visit. They were only there to collect the buddha. They thought no one was in. They won't leave any signs at all that they have been there. Boris will just have a long nap!"

"Thank goodness, as a Buddhist, you see, mustn't be the cause of harm to any form of life…" Antholian trailed off with a slight gulp. I am very *fond* of Boris, he added secretly to himself. He knew that Flipper thought he was 'soft' and, while he was prepared to suffer for his principles, he didn't want to look completely pathetic by voicing attachment to a dog.

"If we don't go now it will be *us* you are harming!" said Flipper, more firmly.

"But, just a minute!" said Antholian, thinking of a fault in Flipper's soothing statements. "They already blew up your shop! And think they killed you! They won't care about adding a *dog* to the tally!"

"No, no, *they* didn't blow up my shop. *I* did!" responded Flipper. "Lovely controlled explosion, well planned. Shouldn't have damaged any other buildings!"

"Why on earth would you blow your own shop up?" Antholian was genuinely staggered.

"Destroy all the evidence, leave an exploded body, get them off my back. If it wasn't for you and Buffy all would now be well!" replied Flipper.

Antholian ignored the last line as it made no sense.

"Body? *Whose* body? Who exploded?" demanded Antholian.

"Mine. *My* body, of course!" said Flipper. "I told you! I'm *dead*!"

He had been keeping a body donated to a body farm for research in his freezer for some time in case of just such an emergency requirement. Forensics could now find out what happened when someone exploded like that so it was a bona fide use. Having to dress the thing in his own clothes and prop it up over his gas cooker so it got the full force of the faked gas explosion was something he preferred to forget. He certainly wasn't going to explain the situation to anyone else, especially someone who was this sensitive about a *dog*. If it hadn't been for that text message from Buffy to his phone, just when he had set up the explosion irreversibly, things would have been so much simpler. His phone had now blown up but it was all too late: the message would have been tracked before it reached the phone.

"If whoever it might be is so harmless and doesn't want to leave any trace of their passage through the world, then why are we running?" persisted Antholian.

"They are not *harmless*; they just won't want to leave a trace of their visit to your place. It's not the same thing at all. The *dog* can't *describe* them. It would have been quite different if *you* had seen them. There would still have been no sign that they had been there; you would have seemed to have gone out for a midnight jog. Very sad – slipped in from the towpath, found drowned. A tragedy!"

"I can *swim!*" protested Antholian. "And surely inquests can tell if you were tied up or drugged!"

"But you can't swim if you are held firmly but kindly, upside down by your ankles with your head under water!" retorted Flipper in an almost inaudible hiss. "Look, this is not the time or place for discussions! I assure you that if we don't move I am going to be *really* dead and *so are you*. Come on. Stop wasting valuable time. *Run!*"

And Flipper suited the action to the word.

Antholian was now completely baffled. He had
invented an explanatory scenario in which Flipper
was a drug dealer, smuggling heroin into the country
inside buddhas, and this had fitted in well with the
'unknown people' being rival illegal drug traffickers
who were having a 'drugs war' with Flipper. It didn't
seem at all likely that Flipper *would* have become a
criminal, given his background and education, but,
Antholian had mused to himself, the prospect of
unbelievably vast sums of money can corrupt *anyone*.
However, Flipper blowing *his own* shop up simply
didn't fit in with this theory!

He hastened after Flipper back on to the towpath. This
time Flipper had turned in the opposite direction and
taken a route back towards Oxford, travelling at a
reasonably easy jogging pace.

"Fine evening!" Flipper called to Tony. "Pleasant for
a training run, eh, Rob?"

"Yes, indeed, *James*," replied Antholian. If Flipper
was going to call him *Robert* he felt he could

rechristen Flipper as James. James was simply the first name that came into Antholian's head, but the line 'Bond, James Bond' rapidly followed it into his mind. He had now come to the definite conclusion that some kind of secret service work was the only explanation, and he felt like giggling hysterically. The whole episode still seemed entirely ridiculous and yet Flipper definitely thought there was real danger following them. Who could it be? Why? What? He was so glad Boris was *probably* all right, but was Flipper lying about whether Boris would be harmed? And whose body could Flipper have blown up? Clearly *not* his own! Had Flipper *killed* someone?

As they went under Donnington Bridge they saw a female tramp lying, apparently unconscious, by the side of the towpath. There was a strong smell of neat alcohol rising from her body. Her head was face downwards in the grass.

Flipper, most surprisingly, raised his voice and spoke very loudly and clearly.

"Funny, I could have *sworn* I saw that tramp somewhere else, Rob!" he announced.

"Hard to tell in the *dark*!" whispered Antholian back, helpfully. Really Flipper should be careful about speaking so loudly, even if the woman did appear dead drunk. "But she *does* look like the one near the Plain."

"Keep in character!" whispered Flipper back. "We *haven't come from the Plain*!"

Antholian felt annoyed. It was Flipper who had started shouting about the tramp, not him! Another mystery to add to the rest of them! Flipper drew slightly ahead and they carried on along the dark towpath in single file. If anything, the light from their head torches made navigating through the surrounding darkness worse than if they had no lights at all. They could only see clearly within the small cone of bright light; everything else seemed darker and more impenetrable. Flipper, so used to rowing, thought Antholian, probably knew his way along here with his eyes closed, even if he had usually travelled on the river and not on the towpath. He did hope so as they *must* stay on the path. If one of them fell into the fast flowing river it would be very difficult to get out, especially in this darkness.

Almost invisible strands of thin mist, carrying the smell of the night river water, cool and slightly rancid, rose towards them, stirring memories. Antholian thought how he had often wandered along this towpath on summer evenings with his girlfriend. A romantic walk in the dark and then both lying on their backs in the grass to watch the stars and planets whirl above them! Sometimes there were shooting stars...

"Not much further to go now. We must have done *at least* twenty-three miles, Rob!" said Flipper, conversationally.

"Yes, *easily* that far!" puffed Antholian, who was beginning to feel as if he had indeed run twenty-three miles.

Unseen by the two young men, two phantom rowing eights shot past, racing side by side, moving soundlessly on the dark and empty river. Coxes shouted, unheard by the living joggers. Another eight glided smoothly through the water, and another. One crew ended a joyful downstream sprint and began to turn across the river, ready to row back against the current. Their spectral cox waved towards the bank. Was he waving to the two joggers, or to spirit spectators lining the towpath?

For a millisecond Antholian thought he *saw* a turning eight. He could even see the plain, dark blue oars – a Christ Church crew! He blinked, and the vision was gone. Just the darkness of the flowing river, with bats and night insects flitting about above it.

An invisible rowing coach riding an invisible, old fashioned, bicycle rode straight between Antholian and Flipper, and they felt the breeze of his passing as a night chill.

Nearer the bank the spirits of two, very serious, Edwardian gentlemen in straw hats and blazers were rowing a wide-bottomed rowing boat, taking two giggling Edwardian lady spirits for an excursion on the river. Each lady carried a parasol. One held hers unfurled and twirled it merrily. The other one had hers furled and was using it to poke one of the gentlemen as she made fun of him. Antholian thought he heard the mocking laughter of a girl drifting from nowhere into his ears. It reminded him of many painful youthful experiences. He felt sad suddenly.

The memories evoked by his senses as he jogged up the towpath, marooned on the tedious dry land, were making Flipper feel sad too. He would never row in a college eight on this river again! He had not wanted to continue rowing after he graduated. He had not felt any angst at the time – giving it up was just a sign of progression from university to adulthood. However, just now, he felt the excitement. He remembered the agony of physical effort, the thrill of success. He could almost hear the splash of the oars, the swish of a passing boat, the swearing of a cox. He thought momentarily that if only he had planned better he could have concealed a skiff somewhere near Donnington Bridge earlier in the day and they could have rowed up the river instead of jogging.

Then Flipper shook his head to wake himself up. He must be getting sleepy! What nonsense his thoughts had become! He chided himself for being so silly. They could hardly have rowed in this darkness, especially in a coxless pair! Even if they could have plotted a safe course, they would have been most conspicuous, rowing all alone up the river. The additional possibility that Tony could not row did not even cross Flipper's mind. *Everyone* that *he* had known at Oxford *could row*!

Less of this sentimental twaddle, Flipper told himself! Remembering to keep exactly in character, he began to make light small talk about the nineteenth-century Corn Laws. He considered these a calming topic, entirely appropriate to the circumstances of it being necessary for him to keep Tony calm yet also functioning and awake enough to keep running at this speed. Flipper associated Corn Laws with calm because when he had studied them for A-level they had always sent him to sleep. He trusted they would not have quite this effect on Antholian. Antholian was confused by the choice of subject, one about which he knew almost nothing other than having heard the phrase 'Corn Law'. Then he realised that Flipper was assuming that he had read History because Barnabus had read History. As far as Antholian could remember Flipper had read PPE so, since he himself had read Philosophy, they could have discussed a philosophical topic more easily. But a change of subject was irrelevant really because Antholian's own replies were, by now, limited to "Yes", "No" and "Um" as his breathing was too fully engaged in getting his legs to move to achieve sentences.

Flipper suddenly stopped. Antholian only just avoided either crashing into him or swerving into the river.

"Sorry, Rob, old boy!" said Flipper, loudly and cheerfully. "Lace undone!"

He bent over his trainer.

"I thought I heard another runner coming up behind us," he added, equally loudly and cheerfully, "but I must have been wrong!"

Antholian looked back into the darkness as Flipper fiddled with his lace.

"I can't see or hear anyone!" he whispered.

"Off we go again then, Rob!" announced Flipper, continuing to use his jolly and very loud voice.

"Right ho, James!" said Antholian, nearly adding the sentence that his father had always used when they were all safely strapped in the car after prolonged visits to relatives: "Home, James, and don't mind the horses!" He had no idea where the phrase came from, other than the days of horse drawn carriages. He had asked Dad once and Dad had claimed it came from the words of a 'well known' song. He had not asked further as Dad's musical taste did not match his and he thought he might *play* the aforesaid song to him. Oops! He really must concentrate on the towpath and not let his mind wander; he had nearly veered into the river!

Behind them the female tramp seemed to have made a rapid recovery from her drunken stupor. She had been loping along a short distance behind the men until they stopped so abruptly. She now appeared to be playing at 'statues', stuck in a particularly difficult pose with one leg off the floor. As the runners began to move forward again she replaced her leading foot on the floor and, having waited a few moments to give them a start, continued behind them with rather more caution.

They reached Folly Bridge; they reached Carfax. Antholian was beginning to think that the danger had been entirely imaginary. Perhaps the whole episode *was* a

'wind-up' of some sort. Perhaps Flipper had only pretended that some mortar rocket fireworks going off were his own shop blowing up. Barnabus and his friends had always had very strange senses of humour. He did hope this wasn't some sick form of *You've Been Framed*, with himself as the patsy.

"Would you like to go in front now, Rob?" called Flipper as they began to pound up Cornmarket.

He screeched to a halt for a moment. When Antholian drew level with him Flipper spoke quickly in a low voice, "Going well so far. Provided Buffy hasn't been sending any more stupid texts to my mobile, things might yet work out! Now, I need *you* to lead the way! Go, *go, go!*"

"Where are we going?" gasped Antholian, who was very breathless and beginning to feel confused due to insufficient oxygen reaching his brain. His diet did not really give him enough energy for this much exercise. The night air was cold, and he had entirely lost his adrenaline rush.

How obtuse he is! thought Flipper, having entirely forgotten himself that Tony still had very little idea of what was going on.

"Your *aunt's*, of course!" whispered Flipper, as discreetly as someone can in the middle of a brightly lit Cornmarket. "*You* have to go in front because *I* don't know where she lives!"

"It's a good thing she doesn't live in the opposite direction to that in which we have been travelling then!" retorted Antholian.

"You said she was a *don*! Almost bound to live north or west!" replied Flipper. "Although I suppose she *could* have lived in Iffley," he added, as an afterthought. "Lucky she didn't! Now go!"

"Will I ever find out what is actually going on?" asked Antholian.

"Hopefully not! Just *go!*" replied Flipper.

They set off again, Antholian in front this time. He was running purely mechanically now because, apparently, he *had* to do so. He could barely remember the reason why he had started running in the first place. His breaths were coming in rasping pants. His heart felt as if it would explode. Blood sloshed between his ears. Sweat poured down his face, rapidly becoming cold and clammy in the night air, and ran into his open mouth in a salty stream.

Flipper, realising Antholian's level of exhaustion, pulled beside him again to encourage him by keeping in step with him and, continuing to exercise his theory about soothing conversations, he moved on to a discussion of Peel's sacrificial repeal acts. Antholian's brain appeared to be entirely concentrated on the mechanics of motion, when Flipper was suddenly interrupted by a surprising contribution from him.

"Twenty-sixth and final mile, Rob!" called Antholian, cheerfully and loudly, as they left the centre and headed north to Jericho.

Antholian had wanted to tell Flipper that they were getting close, since the poor man did not yet know where they were going. He hoped he had mustered enough strength to produce the correct 'fit marathon runner' tone of voice. He felt as if he had *actually* run at least *one hundred* miles by now, not well under five! I just hope I can *find* Priscilla's house in the dark! he said to himself. It's *years* since I have been there. What if they are all out? Or all gone to bed and refuse to answer the door? Flipper seems to be quite good at breaking and entering; he could get us into the house. But then *what if we get arrested for burglary*? Surely Aunty Pris would never press charges against us – not against me, anyhow?

They pounded onwards. The distance from the centre of Oxford to Priscilla's house seemed to be increasing exponentially in front of Antholian. Random images poured into his mind, distracting him from the ghastly noise of blood pumping around his skull and swishing and booming in his ears. He had a horrible vision of Boris Spassky with a gunshot wound in his chest, covered with blood, lying on his side, big paws still for ever! It was all very well for Flipper to say Boris was *fine*; Flipper seemed to have scant respect for human life, let alone that of dogs! Tears began to pour down his face, mingling with the sweat.

Antholian knew he must think of something else. He imagined Mama and Dad in Japan, enjoying themselves, not knowing he was in some kind of danger. No, that thought was just as bad! He thought of his shop, looked round its shelves in his imagination, all so satisfactorily neat and tidy. But this was no use either as, suddenly, some mystery invaders, masked and wearing black, burst in and started smashing everything, tossing everything aside to find the buddha.

Buddhism! His most important mainstay! His reason for being! The sort of activities that Flipper and Paris and their ilk got up to was *against every principle that Antholian held*. What was he doing taking part in this escapade? Barnabus and Paris and, yes, *definitely* Elizabeth and *even Dad* were all going to find this breaking of his pacifist principles utterly *hilarious*! How *humiliating*! But Mama would not do so. No, Mama would explain to him that principles were very important but could be dropped, in times of extreme need, emergency or catastrophe, without any fear that you had besmirched your soul by betraying your principles. Antholian remembered her saying that *very* phrase, quietly, in the corridor outside his grandparents' dining room, when he was a fervent eleven-year-old vegetarian and Grandma Smith had provided an entirely carnivorous version of Sunday lunch. Mama would *never* laugh at him, no matter what he did, no matter how much she disagreed with his ideas. Antholian suddenly felt about seven again. He would like to scream "Mama!" and have her appear, tell him it was only a game, put everything right. This was ridiculous: he was a capable adult. He had to think of something *calming*. He decided to recite soothing philosophical thoughts. Flipper could join in and stop going on about repeal acts. But all that ran through his mind was the first verse of 'Row, Row, Row your Boat'.

He began to sing the little ditty quietly as he ran. "Row, row, row your boat, gently down the stream; merrily, merrily, merrily, merrily, life is but a dream!"

Flipper joined in, inventing a verse of his own. He was using most of his brain to concentrate on a taxi, which seemed to be somewhat inexpertly trailing them. He did hope the occupant was the person he *expected* it to be. If it wasn't then they could both be about to *die*, which seemed a shame after all the bother he taken to get them this far. They might as well have stayed put in the first place and just had a shootout in the flat. But he now diverted a small area of his brain to compose amusing and encouraging verse for Antholian.

"Run, run, run, your feet, quickly down the road; merrily, merrily, merrily, merrily, life is such a toad!" sang Flipper, cheerily.

Antholian laughed and felt a little better and far less breathless. They took turns to produce increasingly ridiculous and scurrilous versions of the little song. Their relationship changed from younger leader with older, rather annoyed, follower to that of two young men who were simply having fun.

When she had reached Folly Bridge the female tramp had glanced hastily around, removed her coat and hat, and dumped them at the side of the towpath. The tramp had been transformed into a quite conventionally dressed student wearing a Coromandel scarf round her neck. She leant on the parapet of the bridge for a while, studying the screen on her iPhone. Then she turned and strolled towards the city centre.

Near Christchurch she had hailed a taxi. The taxi driver was a man around her own father's age.

"Can you give me a fare to…" – she looked closely at her iPhone – "…Jericho?"

She did hope that she had pronounced that word correctly. English pronunciations were so strange sometimes.

The taxi driver looked at her doubtfully. Bit late at night for respectable single females to be walking around alone. She smiled at him. Her voice had an American twang but she seemed a sweet little thing. Must be a student, he supposed, even though it was well out of term. She looked about his own daughter's age. Couldn't be up to anything of any harm.

"OK," he said. "Hop in!"

She got into the back.

"Where exactly in Jericho?" he asked.

"I'll tell you when we get a bit closer," she said.

"Fair enough!" said the taxi driver. Bit drunk, he supposed. Forgotten the address where she is staying! He trusted she would remember how to get to the house but if not, *she* would be paying for the extra length on the journey and not him.

"Funny business tonight," he said, conversationally. "Gas explosion in the Cowley Road. Whole 'ouse blown up. Rumour is there's someone dead in it, if not *several* someones. Blooming nuisance: the Plain onwards closed for the duration! Have to divert right round Headington."

"Oh look!" she said. "There are my two friends! The ones I'm staying with! No point in arriving before them! They've got the key to the front door! Just follow them a bit behind!"

This passenger was definitely on the odd end, thought the driver. He trailed behind Flipper and Antholian for a short way and then hit a problem.

"I can't go the wrong way down one-way streets, ducky, even if your friends do!" he said. "You can either get out here or else I can go round and get to the other end of this particular street by a different route but following the correct rules of the road."

"Whatever!" said his passenger, then, "Both!"

He looked round at her. She seemed confused. In fact she looked as if she was listening to someone else, rather than him. She stared at her iPhone. Perhaps she was making a phone call.

The taxi driver pulled into the kerb. He turned round so he could see her better.

"Are you going to get out here or am I getting to wherever we are going by a different route?" he asked.

"I'll get out!" she said, flinging the door open and putting a foot through it.

"Not quite so fast! I'll need paying before you nip off, ducky!" said the man.

"Freaking hell!" said his passenger, grabbing her purse, and she added, under her breath, "*Another* delay! *Freaking* hell!"

Meanwhile Antholian and Flipper had turned into Priscilla's road and Antholian was relieved to find he knew which house he wanted. He could remember its position perfectly. *There it was*! Even more marvellously, the lights were all on. Aunty Pris must still be up! He saw the house as a beacon of hope and safety, never considering what might happen *after* they entered. They skidded to a halt and rang the doorbell.

"Such a bother, *both* of us forgetting our *keys*, Rob!" said Flipper, keeping carefully to his role play, while they waited for the door to open.

"Absolutely, James!" responded Antholian, who, with his goal achieved, was now beginning to feel that the whole adventure was quite good fun. He spoke in an appropriate upper-class accent, likely for a Kings rower, "Frightful bore! How fortunate that our housemates seem to be in!"

There was an uncomfortably long delay, a noise of scrabbling, and what sounded like squeaks of protest from behind the door. Then Walls' voice called out cheerfully, "Just a minute. *Apologies*! The dog is refusing to move away from the door!"

"Odd thing to say. *Aunty Pris* wouldn't have a *dog*! She doesn't like them very much!" whispered Antholian to Flipper. Then he realised something else. "S***! Aunty Pris has a *male* visitor! Maybe Charles is here; he was supposed to be visiting her *soon*. That could be *awkward*!"

The door opened.

Chapter 7

After feeding her a further pancake Walls felt that Priscilla had probably forgiven him the lounge-to-gym conversion but he had thought of an extra idea that should improve her opinion of his continuing presence in her house.

"I had a good idea!" he said. "I thought I could help you proofread your book!"

"*Help* me?" said Priscilla. "*Proofread?*" This was said in a tone which would have warned most people, or at least those who were less optimistic, less determinedly friendly and less companionable than Walls, that this was *not* a welcome suggestion.

"Speed it up a bit, you know. Do some of the proofreading *for* you!" continued Walls, completely ignoring the tone and still feeling that he was really being generous in offering his time in this way.

He took an opportunity, while pretending to adjust the washing-up, to study the phrases written in indelible ink on the inside of his palm. He selected a phrase to use.

"I am quite practised at proofreading, having just completed my own D. Phil.," he assured her and then added, with a slight flourish, "*Non ignare mali miseris succerrere disco!*"

He particularly liked that phrase because it made him think of disco dancing. It had a lovely swing to it, as well as a very suitable meaning!

Priscilla was delighted to discover that he knew *some* Latin. Quoting *mens sana in corpore sano* did not indicate any knowledge at all – it was such a common quotation, as well as being in error – but this quote suggested that he had had some *solid* classical education after all. Perhaps she *would* let him help read her proofs? She did not like to let *anyone* else touch her precious pages and, of course, his proofreading would be of *no value whatsoever* – she would have to do those pages herself whether he read them or not! Here she preened herself inwardly. Unlike the rest of the world, she herself would *certainly* not miss *any* mistakes. Her own proof editing was perfection itself. But, and here she smiled to herself, she felt that reading her book would *do him good*! She would particularly enjoy watching him read a discourse that was written from the feminist standpoint – it could hardly be other than beneficial for anyone whose body was so very saturated with male chauvinism as that of Walls. She topped his Virgil quotation with another.

"Hic tibi ne qua morae fuerint dispendia tanti,
quamuis increpitent socii et ui cursus in altum
uela uocet, possisque sinus implere secundos,
quin adeas uatem precibusque oracular poscas
ipsa canat uocemque uolens atque ora resoluat
illa tibi Italiae populos uenturaque bella
et quo quemque modo fugiasque ferasque laborem
expediet, cursusque dabit uenerata secundos.
haec sunt quae nostra liceat te uoce moneri."

Walls had caught his oar on the 'phrase book' crab once again. He listened, fascinated, beginning to wonder if she would *ever* stop spouting incomprehensible Latin. At least he *thought* it was Latin, but could it be Greek this time? After listening carefully he decided it must be Latin as he recognised a few words, like et, bella and quo, but he did not feel certain enough to *commit* himself to this assumption! He wondered if she was going to conduct the rest of the day's conversations in Latin? That would be *very* awkward. If that should happen he was by no means certain that he had enough non-committal Latin phrases in his little lexicon to keep throwing one in and hope it was appropriate. Of more immediate concern was the question of what on earth she was saying now? He hoped it was not a set of instructions on how to proofread her book. Maybe it was a refusal to let him help?

Priscilla's speech finally ended. The pause at the end seemed to be becoming interminable. She was looking at him expectantly, waiting for his answer. A meaningless and therefore hopefully appropriate reply was Walls' only option.

"Quite so!" he said.

Fortune smiled upon him; this seemed to be a suitable response. Walls continued, "I'll finish the washing-up while you go and get the proofs, and then we can have a go at them together."

What an evening this was likely to be! thought Walls, splashing around in the washing-up bowl. Not quite what he had originally planned earlier in the week! He sighed! He had sent a text message to his date for the evening telling her he was unfortunately unavoidably ill and that he would contact her again when he recovered. He had also sent a huge bunch of red roses to make up for his absence. In his experience this was a gesture that never failed to mollify angry females! He did hope his date did not run into Flic by chance in the city centre. How terrible if they happened to collide in a coffee bar, spoke to each other, mentioned his name and then compared notes on where he was supposed to be. No, that probability was so low that it must be nearly zero. He was becoming jumpy and ridiculous. It was the strain of all this Latin!

Priscilla trotted off upstairs to bring down some proofs, giggling to herself. She had not been tutoring students for so many years without seeing right through Walls. Clearly his Latin phrases had been learnt by rote to impress her, but she had really enjoyed watching him squirm with gathering panic as she continued her quotation – a quotation which, in her eyes, was so well known and, in any case, *trivially* easy to translate. It was disappointing to discover that she could not, after all, enjoy sharing classical languages with her unwanted guest. However, she reflected, he had taken the bother to impress her by learning some quotations, and this activity would have been very good for him – it would have *marginally* improved his classical knowledge!

She paused before selecting which of her chapters to proofread this evening. It was, she decided, sweepingly, no use whatsoever to attempt to continue from the place she had previously reached! With the interruption to her thoughts caused by Elodea's visit and the disturbance of Walls she would have to spend too long resuming her previous level of immersion. The only thing to do was to start right again at the beginning, with Chapters One and Two. The

Introduction and Contents could only ever be proofread *last of all*, only when she was entirely sure that everything else was correct.

She returned down the stairs, bearing a huge pile of printed pages stacked in a pristine cuboid with perfectly straight sides. She carried the paper as carefully as if it had been a rare Ming vase. Swinging from her arm was a plastic carrier bag containing two notepads, in which to note the corrections, which must never, never be actually written upon the pristine pages; two identical black ballpoint pens; and two pairs of manuscript gloves.

As she descended she discovered, too late, that Pippy had, once again, decided to curl up on the bottom stair. Fortunately Walls was leaning on the wall waiting for her to return and leapt forward, catching the stack of paper with one hand and arm while nimbly restoring Priscilla's balance with his other hand and arm. Pippy gave a cross squawk and fled under the hall table, nearly tripping Walls up as she did so.

"Are the proofs OK?" asked Priscilla, in the desperate voice one might use if one had just accidentally fallen over while carrying a small baby and dropped the child.

"Perfectly OK!" Walls assured her. "Just a slight bend on some of the corners!"

Priscilla, by taking a very deep slow breath, managed to prevent herself from screaming that a slight bend was not *OK*, it was a *disaster*. She could not help comparing Walls to Tony. Tony would *never* have thought that slightly bent corners were OK!

"Let me straighten them out, *immediately*!" she cried. "It might not yet be too late…"

He held the pile while she gently corrected the damage, as far as it was possible to do this.

"Quite a pile!" said Walls, in what he hoped was a cheerful way. He was trying not to sound as daunted by the apparent size of the task as he now felt. He had not expected the feminist perspective on Agamemnon to take up *quite* so many pages of print.

"I *only* brought down chapters one and two!" said Priscilla, wrongly assuming that his reference to the size of the pile was sarcastic and that he meant it was very much *smaller* than he expected. "This should be quite sufficient to occupy us for the rest of the evening, if we do *precise* proofreading! If we *should* finish faster than expected I could always pop up and get the next two chapters!"

Walls groaned silently and followed her into the gym, aka the lounge. He held the pile while Priscilla tenderly and carefully spread pages out over the floor and all the gym equipment, except for the exercise bicycle, which would have bucked the paper off from its shiny slopes. Walls began to wonder if she was about to attempt balancing pages on parts of him as well. He could clearly cancel out any idea of *using* the exercise equipment this evening!

In a rash moment, while watching the paper distribution, he had the temerity to, very mildly, suggest that, just possibly, proofreading on her computer might be easier, and that then she could possibly just email a chapter to his own laptop, and then he could proofread it on there too.

He received the withering look that Priscilla usually reserved for the rare occasions in tutorials in which students appeared to have entirely forgotten to study the subject concerned before writing their essay.

Walls subsided, completely crushed.

Eventually she completed her arrangements and sighed with satisfaction.

"That is *the whole* of Chapter *One*. I shall leave Chapter Two to *you* to read for now. Before you begin, remember to *always* don these manuscript gloves! Turn the pages with great care and do not, *under any circumstances*, roll or fold the corners or the edges! Do not, *under any circumstances*, write on the pages themselves! Make any comments you might have upon this notepad, including a careful note of the page and line number. Remember to put a heading on each page that you use in the notepad which designates the number of the chapter that you are reading. You will find the chapter is in *reverse* order.

I always print all proofs in *reverse* order, so you will need to invert the pile and turn each page over as you read it. Chapter Two is, possibly, a challenging place to start but since each chapter can be read as an individual essay I feel you should still also be able to fully enjoy the contents of the prose as you proof edit. You will, of course, not be able to cross reference your reading with the Contents, References, Notes, Appendices or Introduction as yet. I always check the peripheries as my final check since they are so interlinked with everything else. You may use the hall. There is no space left for you in here as the room is now fully occupied with the proofs that *I* am about to read."

Walls, his heart sinking, meekly and obediently went into the hall and consigned himself to an uncomfortable position on a very small, very hard chair. He struggled mightily and succeeded in completing a *scan* read of the first ten pages. The book appeared to consist of deeply feminist rhetoric interspersed with, to him, totally incomprehensible quotations in Ancient Greek. Numbers by each quotation suggested that, possibly, a translation might exist in an appendix which he did not have, although this was more likely to be a numbered reference to the original text. Not that he felt that having a translation of the Greek would have made much difference to his comprehension of the main body of text. He had begun by feeling fairly confident of being able to follow the gist of the English text, especially with his new-found classical knowledge, courtesy of Freddy and father. However, most of the content seemed to be baffling, and the small remainder that he could understand was extremely annoying. After ten pages of Priscilla's feminist standpoint he was definitely coming down in favour of Agamemnon's culturally male chauvinist standpoint on women, violent and ideologically unsound as it admittedly was.

Pippy had leapt onto his knee as soon as he sat down on the chair. She now prevented him from moving to ease his cramped limbs by growling every time he disturbed her comfortable position. The sun fell gently onto him, flowing through the small window by the front door. After those ten pages and despite the discomfort of his perch, the weight of Pippy's small furry body and the cramping pains in both his legs, he found he had dozed off. He jerked awake ten minutes later, now slumped forward and having added an additional racking pain in his neck.

This was no good!

"I think I shall have to continue my reading in Angel's room!" he called to Priscilla, chucking Pippy unceremoniously off his lap and having her turn, growling, and sink her tiny teeth into his trainer in revenge.

"Oh, do stop being silly, dog!" he added, as he wiggled his toes to ease the violent pins and needles in his feet. The motions inside his trainers drove Pippy to a frenzy of yapping and more pretend attacks on his feet and yet, strangely, still there was no reply from Priscilla.

He glanced into the lounge-gym. Priscilla was lying on the floor, warmed by a beam of sunshine. She had her head resting lightly on the end of the bench press and was clearly blissfully asleep.

Walls patted his own pile of disordered papers, already in a state which would horrify their owner when she next saw them, put them gently down on the hall table, beside the mysterious brown parcel which Priscilla had brought back on her bicycle and, sweeping Pippy out with him, went out into the tiny back garden to sunbathe for a while. He lay on his back on the small patch of lawn. Pippy lay on her back on his stomach. The sun was warm, the ground was warm, but the birds were astonishingly noisy, and small insects crawling through the grass struggled over the new mountain range that had appeared before them. Walls could have sat up and swatted them but it was the sort of afternoon sun that renders one completely inert, even if being tickled by minute feet and, occasionally, bitten. Pippy got down from time to time to chase butterflies around the garden and then quickly returned to her perch and re-engaged her stomach in sun worship.

At the end of the afternoon there was a cooling in the air. It was not going to be a sultry hot August night, but damper and cooler. Walls and Pippy decided to return indoors, restored and very happy.

Walls went into the kitchen to consider the problem of the next meal. He fished around in the fridge, the freezer and the kitchen cupboards. It became clear that Priscilla must usually 'eat out' – there seemed to be a desperate shortage of ingredients. He had brought the bread, bacon, pancake ingredients and maple syrup with him but for this meal he would be forced to rely on Priscilla's stores, unless he disturbed her and asked her to go to the store for him. On the whole it would be easier to cook from what he could find here: she might be awake and proofreading and before he knew where he was he would be set back to work without dinner.

Pippy 'helped' him to hunt through the cupboards with wild enthusiasm. She had great confidence that he would find the mouse, for which he was clearly hunting, any second now. Eventually he found enough ingredients to concoct a gigantic lasagne, bursting with herbs, minced beef and tomatoes even if not with quite as much onion and garlic as he would have liked. Walls enjoyed cooking full blown, calorie loaded, gorging meals. He was always hungry because of all the exercise that he took. He had been pleased, so far, to find that Priscilla also had a robust approach to meals although the results of a hefty diet without exercise were quite evident in her case. He

279

did hope he could convert her to using the gym equipment for its original purpose rather than as a proof holder. He was evangelical about the benefits of exercise, and here was a woman requiring conversion to his belief if he had ever met one!

Priscilla came to as the lounge grew chillier. She had a feeling of déjà vu, as she again awoke to wonder where she was, but this time was momentarily horrified to find that she seemed to be in a mysterious black torture chamber. Then she recognised her own converted lounge. Surely it could not be tomorrow morning *again*? Walls would think she never used her bedroom if this carried on. She focussed on her watch with an effort. Hopefully the time was seven in the evening and not seven in the morning! A wonderful smell of cooking floated in from the kitchen. Walls cooking again! Goodness, she would never fit in any of her clothes if he stayed here much longer.

She stumbled into the kitchen and he poured her a black coffee from the percolator. What a gift the man was! No wonder Flic was so keen to close the deal on her wedding.

Her happiness in his skill was shortlived as he handed her a *very* long list.

"Can you step out to the nearest 7-11 and get this lot, please? I'm kinda short of ingredients. I fear I may have cleaned you out."

She did not look enthusiastic.

He used his most entrancing smile and added, "Pretty please with a cherry on top?"

She slumped over the list. Why did young men eat *this* much? Why had she ever let him into her house? This would take at least an hour of trudging round Sainsbury's or Tesco's. And she would have to take the car – no hope of getting this lot in her bicycle basket – which meant driving right out to the bypass superstores. Then she had to find everything on the list, put it all into the trolley, out of the trolley, into the trolley, out of the trolley, into the car, out of the car... Perhaps she could translate that last sentence into Greek and publish it as a modern piece of Greek verse?

"I can *pay*!" he offered, misinterpreting her reaction.

"No, no, the money is fine. I can *afford* it!" she replied.

She sighed. The lasagne, cooking gently in her kitchen, smelt really delicious!

"*Equo ne credite, Teucri, quidquid id est, timeo Danaos et dona ferentes*," she said, almost to herself.

Walls had a quick look at his palm. He thought he recognised that one! Ah ha!

"I am not," he said loftily, "even vaguely Greek, so that quotation does not apply."

She laughed.

"OK, OK, you win for knowing that one! I am off to the supermarket but dinner had better be *ready* when I get back!"

"Assuredly!" he replied.

Priscilla drove her car through the bypass traffic to the supermarket, pushed the trolley around with unnecessary violence, and had to restrain herself from physically attacking the harassed young mother in front of her because her momentarily unwatched toddler had emptied an entire kilogram of sugar over the till conveyor belt. Another day of proofreading entirely wasted!

By the time Priscilla returned to her own house with a car boot full of shopping she was ready to evict Walls and tell him to just go away, go home to the USA and marry Flic right now!

But Walls, with the lasagne bubbling and ready in the oven, was watching for her return. He was ready to open the front door for her courteously, rush out to the trunk of her car, collect all the bags of shopping in one go and whisk all the contents neatly away in less than five minutes. The whole house was permeated with the delicious smell of lasagne. Really, thought Priscilla, how lucky she was. The boy was quite a marvel to have around!

Walls, with consummate gallantry, had assisted her to climb onto one of the kitchen stools, and handed her a cup of coffee. Now he lit two candles, switched off the main light, and handed her a large glass of red wine. Even the fact that she had just been sent out to buy the wine herself did not prevent this charm offensive from working as he had hoped.

After a large plate of lasagne and two cups of coffee she found that it was hard to think of a more perfect lodger! She did hope Angel was not going to hurry back *too* soon. She had, in the very bottom of her mind, almost begun to think that it was rather a *nuisance* that *Charles* would be calling here just when *Walls* was staying!

Walls could see he had risen in her estimation. He had rather hoped she might abandon proofreading after dinner, but he had reckoned without proofreading being seen as a *treat* for the privileged. They decamped to the lounge-gym. This time Walls was absolutely determined not to be consigned to the hall. He ignored Priscilla's suggestion that he might like to continue to work in the hall as there would be more space, and assured her that he could easily fit into the lounge. He then climbed over the equipment to reach the settee and lay down on it with Chapter Two, gloves carefully donned, pages meticulously piled on his stomach. Priscilla, despite the weight of the lasagne in her stomach, proofread Chapter One by crawling around the floor, as she always did. Pippy, finding that page sixty-four had floated out of Walls' own pile as he scaled the exercise bicycle, carried this prize off and settled underneath the settee to chew it in peace. For the next two hours there was silence. Walls, admittedly, was reading with his eyes shut, his mouth slightly open, and his breathing slow and relaxed, and was thus entirely untroubled by the sad loss of page sixty-four. Priscilla was concentrating so hard on her own work that she failed to notice his lack of progress.

Finally Priscilla felt that the proofs for Chapter One had been thoroughly analysed, and all the necessary corrections noted carefully down.

"You know," she said, straightening up with some difficulty, "this is the first progress I have made with editing since Elodea bounced in on me! If we can just keep this pace up for the next three days I might get back to where I was when she called."

Walls, hastily opening his eyes, did not feel enthused about this predicted scenario. He had been lying there awake for some time, ever since there had been a loud bang in the distance. He had heard it half in his dream, half in reality, but had assumed that it was probably fireworks going off at someone's wedding reception. Priscilla was so engrossed in her own reading that she did not even seem to have heard it.

But he had decided to remain as he was, reclosing his eyes tightly in the hope that she *had* noticed that he was asleep and decided not to *bother* him. He also thought that he should remain quiet and still so that he did not disturb the 'genius at work'. This settee was quite comfortable and he had a lot of his considerations to work through.

He pondered his big dilemma. Did he really want to break up with Flic, irrevocably and finally? For ever and ever? It was a difficult question. Did he only *not* want to marry her because he was *supposed* to be marrying her? Would he find her more attractive if he *wasn't* doomed to marry her? Would he *want* to be engaged to her if he *wasn't*? Was she really a selfish, greedy shopaholic, or had he caricatured her in his own mind? He had got *used* to being engaged to her. It stopped him even having to consider commitment to anyone else. Had he always, underneath, actually *expected to one day marry her?*

The more deeply he thought about it the less and less he found he had any inclination whatsoever to actually marry her. But if he broke off with her the financial consequences would be disastrous. Could he live off a research fellowship? It would be hard! There was only one solution and that was to make *her* break the engagement. He had always thought that she would find someone else while he was away at Oxford. He had been over here, hardly ever seeing her, for such a very long time now! But although she amused herself with other men quite as often as he amused himself with other women, she appeared to still be determined that *he* was going to be her trophy husband.

Priscilla's speech roused him from his thoughts even though it induced a feeling of desperation and despair at the suggestion of days and days of proofreading looming before him.

"Time for a coffee break?" he said hopefully.

"Yes indeed!" replied Priscilla. "Then we can settle down and swop chapters so that we can check on each other's work."

Or, rather, so that *someone*, i.e. me, can proofread Chapter Two *at all*, she added to herself.

"Have you discovered many errors?" she asked, wickedly, as she had noticed his total immobility.

Walls had been planning to take a night jog in his red wig next and then retire to bed. Was that the time? It was much later than he had thought. If there was to be *another* chapter tonight he might have to join his late night jog up to his early morning run!

"No, no, *no corrections at all*," he said glibly. "All *entirely perfect* and *completely fascinating!*"

They went out into the hall. He spied a possible distraction.

"By the way," he asked, "what is inside your parcel?"

"My parcel?" queried Priscilla.

"The one you brought back this morning!" Walls reminded her.

"Goodness, I had entirely forgotten! It's *another buddha*!" she answered.

"*Another* buddha? The same as the one you put in the trash can?"

Walls felt entirely dumbfounded. What an odd woman she was! He had got the impression that she had positively disliked the previous ornament.

"No, no, not the *same* at all. At least, yes, much the same but made from genuine silver and hopefully without bells and winks this time! I borrowed it from Tony."

"Tony?" asked Walls.

"Barnabus' oldest brother, Tony. But it's not his; it belongs to Flipper."

"Flipper? The Flipper *I* know?"

"Yes, yes, the one with a shop in the Cowley Road!"

Walls was surprised that Priscilla was quite so closely connected with the *whole* of Buffy's life. In particular he was puzzled at the thought of a friendship between the volatile, if highly intelligent, action man who was Flipper, and Priscilla. Walls knew that Buffy regarded Priscilla as a *real* aunt, even though she was unrelated to him, and Walls was perfectly prepared to make use of her himself. He liked exercising his charm on ladies of any age, but he couldn't quite visualize her and *Flipper* being mates!

"You *know* Flipper?" he asked.

"No, but Tony does. He was telling me how well Flipper was doing with the shop. The buddha is for Flipper's mother's birthday but it's not yet so Tony was keeping it safe for him and he thought I could keep it safe here just as well. Till after Charles has visited me!"

Walls gave up trying to work out the whole sequence of buddha related events. What Priscilla had just said made no logical sense at all. Especially as Flipper's mother was, sadly but definitely, dead. Priscilla herself was just thinking that Tony's explanation for the buddha being in his house was rather illogical. It was only as she voiced the reasons herself that they sounded quite ridiculous. However, she did not mind why the buddha was in Tony's stockroom, provided she could borrow it while Charles was here and then get rid of it as soon as her husband had left again, without having any hassle or unnecessary expense!

Walls *loved* opening parcels. He had not lost his childish thrill of finding what was inside them.

"Can I open it *for* you?" he asked eagerly.

"Of course! I know what's inside it anyway!" she replied, able to feel indulgent by giving away a task which she did not want to do!

He picked up the strangely weighty parcel and carefully unwound the rest of the string. This was quite difficult as he was still wearing the thin manuscript gloves, because easing them on and off his large hands was so trying. He peeled back the brown paper to reveal the little silver statuette. It must be solid silver – it could hardly be that heavy otherwise – but in that case it would be worth a very large amount. Did Tony realise how valuable the statuette was when he lent it to Priscilla? Walls doubted it: he had heard all about Buffy's unworldly brother from Buffy. Barnabus despaired of his big brother's future, in the way that many anxious relatives worry about those who are truly happy just as they are.

"It looks *pretty well identical* to the one that Charles sent to me!" sighed Priscilla with great satisfaction.

The one Charles sent to her? Walls did wish he could remember what the story had been about the original buddha. Vague memories returned to him: something to do with *Paris*. Paris, Elodea's middle son, the one who was the bomb disposal expert. The bomb disposal expert! Of course! Paris had blown the original buddha up and it had all been Buffy's fault!

"It's an utter marvel!" he said absently, not meaning the buddha. He was really thinking that his recovery of memory was a marvel.

"Shall I put it back in the kitchen for you, where the other one was?" he added helpfully.

"Not the *kitchen*! Charles is coming to visit. I want him to think I *appreciated* his gift. You can put it on one of the shelves in the lounge. I don't think I can reach to put it onto them myself any more, not with all that stuff in there."

He was just heading off to do so when she remembered something.

"Just a minute! The one Charles gave to me had quite a loose head. I only got a few seconds to look at it, because Barnabus rushed in and then Paris blew it up straight afterwards, but I do remember that the *head* was *loose*. Does that one have a loose head? Be careful in case it does!"

Walls took the head in one of his muscular hands and gave it a little turn to see what happened. It was on a screw fitting. Despite Priscilla giving a squeak of alarm he carried on turning it. Like most men he could not resist completing a mechanical action just to see what happened.

The head came off completely. It was joined to the body by a very short screwtop connection around the putative neck. He looked inside.

"It's full of some kind of packaging. No wonder it's so heavy! I thought it must be solid silver! I suppose they put some kind of heavy packing in to keep it safe while it's being transported so the sides don't get dented. I'll shake it all out and it will make it much lighter for you to move around on the shelves!"

Priscilla made another squeak of protest but he had already turned the body upside down and was shaking the contents out with enthusiasm. Small square plastic bags fell out and hit the floor with loud thunks. Pippy was delighted. She seized one and began to tear it to pieces. Things that looked rather like rather roughly made beads spilled out and she ate several, swallowing them in a thoughtful and experimental way – an interesting new delicacy!

"What is it? Some new kind of plastic packing?" asked Priscilla.

Walls had picked up one of the bags in his white-gloved hand. He held it up. Beyond his matt, white-gloved fingers the contents of the transparent plastic bag shifted and   glittered and shone beneath the hall light like, well, there was only one thing in the world which glittered and shone like that!

"Unless I am much mistaken, these are uncut diamonds!" he gasped.

"Diamonds?" cried Priscilla. "There must be thousands of pounds worth in that pile!"

"Not just any *any* diamonds!" said Walls, who had been studying an article on this trade quite recently. "Judging by some pictures I saw in a recent article in *Time* magazine, these are *blood* diamonds!"

"*Blood diamonds!*" said Priscilla faintly. "I have a hall carpet covered with packets of *blood diamonds!* Oh hell!" she added. "And that confounded dog's *eaten* some of them!"

Walls sprang to try and retrieve the packet from Pippy, who growled ferociously and backed into the lounge, under the gym equipment and then beneath an armchair. She stuck her small head out from the base frill of the chair cover and growled even more fiercely.

"Her stomach contents must be *awfully expensive!*" sighed Priscilla. "I suppose they will work their way through!"

The whole event was too much to deal with. Priscilla was concentrating on the small, more homely details of Pippy's behaviour as a defence mechanism.

"How we can retrieve them from Pippy's stomach," said Walls, "is a matter about which I prefer not to think!"

They turned back to the pile on the floor.

"But these diamonds are not just expensive, they're *illegal*!" Walls continued. "*Blood* diamonds! *Blood* diamonds! The sweat of labour on starvation wages, suffering, injury, mutilation and death, have tainted them! Banned from legal jewellery sale in nearly every country in the world but still cut, concealed and sold! No wonder Flipper is doing well with his store! *He's a diamond smuggler*! I would never, *never* have believed it of him! Never! Surely Tony isn't in on it as well? Buffy says that Tony has very strong moral principles! Could his principles be *fake*? Could he just be covering for his *real* activities?"

While Walls continued his horrified burblings Priscilla was registering the degree of prosecution threatening her friends. What if Tony *was* involved? Even Flipper counted as a *friend* because he was the friend of Tony and Barnabus. What would Elodea say if Priscilla was *responsible* for reporting the matter and if any of them were caught and *put in prison*?

"We have to report this to the police, *immediately*!" said Priscilla. "But we *can't*! We *can't*! What if Tony and Barnabus are *both* involved? They both know

Flipper! Elodea would never forgive me! Even if it was *only* Flipper that I ran in! *You* can't be involved," she continued, with relief in her voice, "because you *didn't know*! Or did you? No, because if you had known you would have said the head didn't come off! Wouldn't you?"

After a pause she added, "I have to sit down!"

She sat down abruptly on the carpet, her head spinning, her eyes closed. Walls, who usually only ever consorted with young, fit people, felt helpless in the face of the necessity to give first aid for the elderly. What if she was having a heart attack? Exercising all the knowledge he had acquired from feature films, he decided the thing to do was to go and find a glass of water.

At this precise moment, before he could move towards the kitchen, the doorbell rang.

"*Don't answer it!*" hissed Priscilla, opening her eyes.

"I *have* to!" whispered Walls, although he had no idea why this was the case. He just felt a compulsion to do so.

They listened.

"Two men outside! Who can it be?" gasped Priscilla.

"Two *young dudes* with *posh English accents*!" Walls amplified Priscilla's description. His guilty conscience supplied an instant answer which was, as it happened, entirely correct. "Oh no! It *must* be *Tony and Flipper*! Flipper's obviously *understandably distracted* because Tony told him that you *have his buddha*. He's come to get it back. It *must* be them."

But Walls' adrenaline-active brain was now producing more soothing suggestions as well. He continued, "Or, if it isn't them, it must be some of *my* mates unless you know a lot of young, posh Englishmen! Which," he added, "you do! How stupid can I get? Just realised! Probably some of your postgraduate students or research fellows! Coming to seek elucidation of a tricky question, so urgent that they must ask you right away, even at this hour of the night? That's it! That's who it is!"

He felt more cheerful after voicing his second theory and even more cheerful after his third theory, and added, "See. No problem, for sure! We've both just got the jitters! You can decline a bit of Latin for them or whatever else they want from you, and then they'll walk! I'll *let them in*!"

"*No*! Not just yet! *Quick*! If it *is* Tony and Flipper they mustn't know we've found out!" babbled Priscilla. "Witnesses! Flipper would have to kill us! The diamonds! Hide them! Hide the diamonds! Shove those plastic bags under the hall table and cover them over with that brown paper! Get the head back on the damn thing. Then give it back to them and get rid of it! *Get rid of it*!"

Walls, realising that the delay in answering the door was becoming unacceptably long, called out in a loud, cheerful voice that scarcely trembled, "Just a minute! *Apologies*. The dog is refusing to move away from the door!"

"Won't they notice the diamonds are missing? The weight! It's too light!" he gabbled in a whisper to Priscilla as he shoved the diamonds under the hall table as rapidly as he could, according to her instructions.

"Just *hide* them, like I told you," hissed Priscilla, "then answer the door! We'll have to cover up somehow! We'll just pretend we thought they were worthless packs of packaging if Flipper notices they are missing!"

Walls felt more cheerful. He and Priscilla could easily have thought the diamonds were just glass packaging beads. Maybe they *were* just glass packaging beads! Maybe his own imagination had just been running away with him! It was the time of night and the effect of reading Priscilla's awful book! He wasn't thinking clearly! He had read that magazine article about blood diamonds and so he had projected the idea that the packaging beads were diamonds because the little square bags looked the same! He and Priscilla would have a good laugh about it when the others had left!

He finished shoving all the small packets under the hall table, placed the brown paper lightly over the top of them, and straightened himself up. Pippy had heard the noise as he pushed them across the floor, and dashed out to help him in his tidying efforts by grabbing another little package and hurrying back with it to 'her' chair. Walls was looking under the hall stand; Priscilla was looking at the door. Neither of them saw her. Both of them had entirely forgotten about Pippy's stolen treasure.

"Perhaps they *are* just glass beads for packaging! Maybe I was *mistaken!*" he muttered to Priscilla.

He sprang hastily to his feet, realising how long they had left the door closed, and then leapt towards the door and grasped the lock handle with a hand that was suddenly trembling.

"*Quidquid agas prudentur agas et respice finem,*" hissed Priscilla from behind him.

He opened the door.

Chapter 8

Walls boggled for a moment at the two blond lycra-clad young men who were waiting expectantly outside the door. Then he recognised Flipper's face beneath his golden locks. Flipper was mildly surprised to find Walls in residence at Priscilla's house but his well-trained face did not even flicker.

"I guess you are surprised at how very fast we ran that practice marathon!" he cried, heartily and confidently, advancing boldly into the house and towing Tony over the step behind him. Then Flipper summarily wrenched Walls away from the door so that he could shut it firmly behind them.

Antholian was too exhausted to even be surprised that Walls was there, although he did feel grateful that Aunty Pris's visitor was not a complete stranger. He had seen Walls with Barnabus often enough to recognise him as one of his younger brother's friends. Once he was released from Flipper's iron grip on his shoulder, he staggered across the hall. He narrowly missed Priscilla, who was standing motionless, clutching the buddha to her bosom, and collapsed into a surprisingly comfortable, nose down, prone position on the staircase.

Pippy flung herself angrily out of the lounge and sank her tiny teeth into Antholian's leg. He opened one eye, registered what was attacking him, and closed the eye again. The whole Smith family were accustomed to Pippy's theory that anyone, including family members, who entered a house after ten o clock at night was a burglar. They had all suffered attacks like this for years. Antholian knew that Pippy would realise who he was in a few moments. The small pain from the bite was nothing compared to the agonising muscle and chest pains that he was already experiencing.

Walls and Flipper, callously accustomed to the sight of exhausted rowers collapsing after long races, were left unmoved by Tony's condition and ignored him completely.

Priscilla turned towards Tony. She was short-sighted. It was very late. Her nerves were in tatters. She had totally failed to see through the disguise, especially as Tony was face down on the stairs, so she had no idea who these two blond young men were. They must be rowing friends of Walls'. It seemed a very odd thing to have been rowing in the middle of the night but you never knew with indefatigable rowers! She supposed they had decided to make a social call on their friend – that age group seemed to have no idea that some times of night were *inappropriate* for *social* visits! What a time to get chance visitors though, just when she had blood diamonds hidden under the hall table!

"Lovely to see you, whoever you are!" she squeaked. "Would you like a glass of wine, or even water?" She was relieved to discover the harmless nature of her visitors and very pleased with herself for remembering, even in this moment of stress, that, being rowers, they might not imbibe alcohol, but her voice seemed to have risen by at least an octave. She continued on the same high, nervous, shrill note, "Maybe a cup of coffee? I suppose you are both

305

friends of Walls'? Very welcome. Very, very welcome. I am Priscilla, Walls' temporary landlady!"

Please don't look under the hall table! she added to herself.

Priscilla was upset about the diamonds, Walls reasoned to himself, and that must be why she had lost her mind completely. Surely, even if upset, she could still remember who Tony was, even with a wig on? Under the circumstances Walls decided he had better not just identify Flipper but also remind her *who Flipper was*, so he spoke, carefully and clearly, in the tones usually used by native English speakers who are attempting to communicate with foreigners who have been so careless as not to learn how to speak fluent English. "Priscilla, no! Or rather, yes, one of these gentlemen is a friend of *mine* but *you* know one of them rather *better* than I do! That's your *nephew Tony* lying on the stairs! This one" – waving his hand – "is *Flipper*! He *owns the buddha*."

"Tony! But Tony doesn't row, he didn't go to Kings, he never dresses like that and he doesn't have blond curls!" protested Priscilla.

"It *is* me, Aunty Pris!" coughed Antholian, from his face-down attitude. He felt that attempting to return to a normal vertical position was not an option at present.

"Why are *you* both wearing *gloves*?" asked Flipper. "Are you practising a song-and-dance act?"

Walls gave him a mock cuff around the head.

"Don't make racist allusions!" he said. "We were just proofreading. *Keeping the proofs clean*, you know!"

Antholian had heard about Aunty Pris's proofreading habits from his mama. The story of the pregnancy disaster was an old chestnut in their family. Antholian was very careful with his own books but even he thought that wearing gloves for reading computer printed proofs was going too far. In his currently overwrought state such behaviour seemed extremely hilarious. Antholian descended into hysterical giggles, rolling around on the stairs and groaning "My stomach! My stomach!" as the laughter caught his strained muscles.

Pippy had, by now, recognised him, licked the blood from her own teeth marks apologetically, and climbed up to rest lovingly on his back. But she did not like her bed to shake with laughter. She jumped off in an offended way and ran back into the lounge to guard her little diamond-filled nest.

Flipper was completely puzzled by this explanation about the gloves. "You were reading *antique* proofs?"

"Don't ask any more!" sang Walls, à la Lloyd Webber.

Flipper decided to ignore this strange sidetrack entirely, and turned courteously to Priscilla.

"I do apologise for our irruption into your house at this late hour! I was just popping in to see if I could *retrieve* my *buddha*. I see you are holding it in your arms. How convenient! I had accidentally forgotten the correct date for my mother's birthday and have found it is a month earlier than I thought! Silly me! Very bad on dates, don't you know? Absent-minded academic of the year! Dr Spooner – nothing on me!

Without the spoonerisms! If you would not mind awfully, I really need it back right now!"

"Why didn't you tell *me* that story?" said Antholian, aggrieved. "I would have believed it, and then I could have popped straight out, cycled up here by myself, brought it back to you and saved all that running about!"

He was feeling tired and very fractious.

"Oh, do *shut up!*" said Flipper, who was feeling rather exhausted himself. He had already died this evening and, on top of killing himself, had then to rescue two other people from the consequences of their own idiocy. Tony could at least have the grace to keep his mouth closed! He rejected the idea of shooting Tony to save time, turned back to Priscilla, and prised the statuette gently from her arms.

"Thank you enormously for taking such good care of the little fellow for me," he said. "I may have to leave Tony with *you*; he seems a little *tired* from our run. I'm trying to get him fit for a Cowley Road traders charity run in October! I'm sure he can find his own way home tomorrow morning if you could just accommodate him for the rest of the night! I'll collect the buddha and pop right off! Got to dash! Need to get it wrapped up. Ribbons, fancy paper, *you* know!"

But, as he took the weight of the buddha, his face changed. He looked horrified and then suddenly, looking much younger and very much more vulnerable, his face crumpled up.

"Please, *no!*" he said. "After all this, after *all this!* Months of investigation, planning, danger, being dead, all gone! *Please don't tell me you two took its head off!*"

He sat down on the hall chair in an attitude of complete despair. Then, after discovering how uncomfortable the chair was, he got up, shoved Tony's prone figure over a little and lay down next to him on the stairs, but on his back, eyes closed, apparently inanimate.

Walls and Priscilla looked at the two motionless figures, then, nervously, at each other. Clearly Flipper was very distressed. Should they confess that they knew all and that they had hidden the diamonds? Or should they deny everything?

"We, er, we thought the head was a little loose," said Priscilla, who felt, as the eldest of the two guilty parties, that she should speak for them both, "so we gave it a turn and a lot of *packaging* fell out. It's all right though. The head went back on fine, nothing broken! I'm sure your mother won't even notice!"

"Where..." said Flipper, faintly and still with his eyes shut, "*where* is the *packaging*? Not that it matters now – it will be covered with both your fingerprints and your DNA. I might as well have *really* blown myself up!"

Walls and Priscilla exchanged looks.

Priscilla was feeling more and more nervous. She had not felt so guilty since her mother last caught her with a school uniform pullover tied around her waist by the sleeves in a manner which would stretch the knitted material out of shape. In her mother's eyes this had always been a crime nearly as heinous as murdering someone.

311

"The, the, the *packaging* is all under the hall table. We, er, we had only just got round to unwrapping the buddha from Tony's lovely brown paper parcel," she quavered.

"Just a minute!" said Flipper, suddenly gaining hope and sitting bolt upright. "The *gloves*! The *gloves*! Were you, by any chance, wearing the gloves at the time?" Then he added, "No! I'm just being silly! Of course you weren't!" and collapsed again.

"Yes, yes, we *were*. We were *wearing the gloves*. We were just about to proofread again, you see. Yes, yes, *gloves*!" she burbled, feeling happier.

Priscilla had never been summoned to the Headmistress's office for a serious misdemeanour during her whole school career, but she knew it would have felt like this.

"*Absolutely*, old boy! Gloves on *all* the time!" said Walls.

"*Thank God!*" said Flipper, fervently and sincerely, without any degree of blasphemy.

He opened his eyes and sat up. He had recovered. His voice had a tone of command.

"Now, one, keep the gloves on; two, get hold of that 'packaging'; three, shove it back inside the buddha; four, put the head back on again; and then, five, put it down on the hall table; and, six, stand well back and leave it alone. Thank you!"

He collapsed back onto the stairs. Antholian and Flipper looked like discarded fashion dummies in a shop window that was being re-dressed, thought Priscilla, although that might be due to the weird effect of those blond wigs as well as the careless disposition of their tired limbs.

Walls and Priscilla scrabbled quickly under the hall table and re-stuffed the buddha. Pippy, realising that her new toys were being removed from reach, darted out from the lounge and growled at them before retreating back to her own secret jewel collection. Nobody took any notice of her. Pippy's earlier theft had been temporarily obliterated from both Walls' and Priscilla's short term memories by subsequent events.

They finished cramming the packets back in and carefully screwed the head back on.

"I don't understand though," said Walls. "I thought this type of, er, *packaging*, originated in Africa. Why a buddha?"

"Blood diamonds banned in China. Lots of demand for diamonds there. Smuggled in through Tibet and Nepal. Needed proof to break the supply chain. Buddhas go out, straight export, returned to source as supposedly defective, all filled up nicely! And I shouldn't have even told you that. Kindly forget it again!" said the still motionless Flipper, without opening his eyes.

"Shall we wrap it up in the brown paper again as well?" asked Priscilla, hoping to remove *all* the debris from her hall carpet.

"You might as well!" replied Flipper, suddenly hoisting himself into a normal sitting position. "It should all be OK. Your floor dust will be all over everything but there should still be some good evidence somewhere on there. Thank heavens! I thought... all wasted... I thought!"

Priscilla wondered whether to point out that her floor was *spotlessly* clean as she had an *excellent* cleaning lady, but she decided to refrain.

Flipper straightened up and looked fully awake and entirely in charge again.

"Now!" he said. He stood up and took a pair of scissors and some plastic bags from the front pocket of his rucksack. "I just need some of your hair."

"Hair!" said Priscilla. "Not *much*, I hope!"

"Just for your DNA! Your DNA is bound to be *all over the thing*," he explained.

"My *hair*!" cried Priscilla, putting her hands over it.

"I could take your finger instead, if you would prefer!" joked Flipper. "Shut your eyes if it worries you."

She closed her eyes and screwed her face up and Flipper, fishing out a large lock from the back of her head, carefully clipped it off and sealed in it a bag.

"Have you finished?" asked Priscilla, opening one eye.

"Finished!" said Flipper cheerfully, palming the bag.

"It's OK!" said Walls, comfortingly. "It's only a *little* bald patch!"

"A *bald patch*!" squawked Priscilla, rushing over to look in the mirror, "Walls! You *liar*!" she added, when she had checked the reflection of her face.

"Don't tell her the bald patch is at the *back*!" whispered Flipper in Walls' ear.

Walls giggled, but he had to endure the scissors next, and since his hair was so short he had a more

316

pronounced bald spot on the back of *his* head. He felt it with his fingers, ruefully, and sighed. Flipper labelled both bags carefully.

"Do you want some of mine?" asked Antholian facetiously, straightening up and offering him the blond wig.

"Good thinking," said Flipper, perfectly seriously. "The wig should have plenty of your sweat and skin stuck on the inside of it. Of course you only touched the *outside* of the buddha when it was in your shop, as far as I know, but better to be safe than sorry."

He found a larger plastic bag, put the wig carefully into it and labelled it.

"They should be able to tell if it's *dog*'s DNA; I don't think I need worry about that," he continued. "Of course I *ought* to collect every type of DNA on this carpet, or *possibly* take the whole carpet. Bother! If you should find that your hall carpet's missing in a day or two's time just don't mention it to anyone. Forensics really – not my field. Not sure whether… No, I don't think I need to collect it myself right now!

They'll send someone round if they need to, when you are out, naturally! They might just need to take samples, if you are lucky!"

Priscilla was now feeling very nervous on behalf of her hall carpet. Fortunately Flipper himself seemed to have stopped his own cavalier acquisition of 'samples'.

"Wilton Ashford Berber in Spice, almost new, *as* new, I would say," he added, apparently talking to himself. After everything else this statement did not strike the other three as remotely odd.

"How did you know that?" asked Priscilla.

"Carpet designs are just one of my many specialist subjects!" said Flipper.

Flipper had reinstated himself fully as Major-General in charge of this operation. He now turned directly towards Priscilla and continued, with the voice of one who expects to be instantly obeyed.

"You and Tony go into the kitchen and make some hot drinks. Put plenty of sugar into them – very good for shock! Keep out of the way for the next few minutes. *Another* visitor is due at any moment! Walls and I will deal with that problem!"

Priscilla was miffed about being relegated by this arrogant young man. Being sent off to her own kitchen! This wasn't Flipper's house, it was *hers*! But as Antholian obediently forced himself upright Priscilla finally noticed how exhausted he was and decided that perhaps Tony *did* need a reviving drink. She did not want to have to make a trip to the casualty department, especially at this time of night! But Priscilla had every intention of returning to the hall once she had revived Tony, and finding out who the visitor might be and what was happening.

Antholian realised how offended Priscilla was. He put his arm round her, ostensibly to support himself, hobbled into the kitchen with her, and lowered his stiff limbs carefully onto a kitchen stool.

"He's right, Aunty Pris – stay out of the way, *with me*! You don't understand *what he is*! You don't understand how *dangerous* this is! If you had had the evening I have had…!" His voice wobbled.

She looked at him with concern. Where had the calm philosophical Buddhist gone? He was, she thought, still very young, and John and Elodea were both far away in Japan. She felt responsible for him.

"I daresay this isn't what you are *supposed* to give people in your state these days," she said, "but here you are. Have a tot of cherry brandy while we wait for the kettle to boil!"

She poured him a generous tot into a little spirit glass.

Antholian, the abstemious, drinker of only water and tea, grabbed it and knocked the lot back in one gulp. Then he laid his head down on the work surface, resting it on his folded arms, and went instantly back to sleep.

Meanwhile, back in the hall, Flipper was giving Walls a few quick whispered instructions.

The doorbell rang.

Walls opened the door.

"Yes?" he said.

"I'm coming straight in!" said the young lady.

As she stepped forwards and kicked the door closed behind her with her foot she looked more attentively at his face.

"*Sebastian*!" she squeaked in surprise.

"Hello, Audrey!" he said, sounding equally amazed, but with a note of horror. "I suppose you are an emissary from Flic! Freaking dames! Has she traced me?"

"Flic? That useless clothes-horse! I haven't *seen* her for months and months!"

He noticed her Coromandel scarf.

"You aren't one of Priscilla's *students* these days, are you? I had no idea! How did I miss that? I would come back in the morning, if I were you! I don't think she likes being disturbed at home at this time of night!"

"What? Oh! The scarf! Bought this in town today. Don't you just love the dagger dripping blood, and the rose? Cool or what? I bet people queue up to go to this college!" she giggled.

"No, I don't think it's at all cool because I went to Kings, but you won't understand that. Let me explain. The whole scarf is a testament to the brazen delight with which Coromandel College hero-worship their dastardly founder. It's also a tribute to their shocking historical inaccuracy. It should be a *pillow*, not a *dagger*! Although I daresay their villainous founder probably stabbed people as well! But what on earth are *you* doing *here* at this time of night? Have you come to the wrong house?"

She reverted instantly to her original intention. She flashed an identity card at him while reaching in her belt for her gun with the other hand.

"Hands up!" she barked. "You are a suspected international criminal! Don't move or I shoot!"

"And what are you going to shoot me *with*?" asked Walls, trying to keep a straight face. He had known Audrey far too long to be able to take her seriously in this role. He would still have been laughing even if she had actually shot him. Childhood friends and siblings never look very important when we meet them as adults, even those who have taken up careers such as prime minister or president. It is as though they are only playing at being grown-up.

Audrey had already realised that her reaching hand had found no gun. Her face fell. She whisked around, but it was too late.

"Audrey, Audrey!" said Flipper wearily. He was standing behind her with her own gun in his hand, trained on her. "All that effort to school you and improve you, for *nothing*! I'm sure your basic training included all this! And then I taught it to you, with added and improved details, *all over again*! And *still* you forget! One – check the total number of people in the house and their exact positions in the house before you enter. Two – always, always check behind the door as you walk in. Three – don't pose as someone who attracts attention: drunken, singing tramps are completely out. Four – always chase the *criminals*, not fellow defenders of the law. Five – never, never blow your cover, Walls knows who you *are*, so invent some other reason for your visit and collect as much evidence as you can *before* you make any move! Words fail me! I don't know why I bothered to try to improve you!"

Audrey rather wished that words *had* ailed him – there seemed to be no stopping him. He continued onwards in an exasperated flow.

"Let us review matters! Did you get *anything* right this time? I suppose you planted a tracking device on Tony while you were buying something in his shop this afternoon. You watched me go in there this morning. Well done on that bit! Very bright! Also, well done about having no scruples at all in attempting to arrest someone who is your old friend and almost a relative. Excellent lack of milk of human kindness! Very commendable in our field of work! And don't try reaching for your second gun.

Why would you imagine that I had left any other weapons on your person?"

He finished his lecture, produced her second gun from his pocket and twirled it round in his hand.

"International criminals don't deserve any human kindness! Blood diamonds are a disgusting trade! And I spent *ages* outside checking who was in here before I entered! I was just *wrong*, that was all! Could have happened to anyone! And I don't *know you*. I've *never* met you. You are just speaking complete nonsense!"

"You look so cute when you are cross!" interjected Walls. "If you weren't my affianced's big sister I would kiss you right now!"

"No, you *wouldn't*!" said Flipper, with a sudden angry edge to his voice, moving between the two of them.

All Walls' friends were inured to his predations upon every female in the room, even with girls who happened to have their partners standing right beside them. On the whole they tolerated him. You couldn't really be angry as he did not mean anything by it. It was like trying to rebuke a puppy. But Flipper did not want Walls to kiss Audrey, at the very least not before he had done so himself.

Audrey, who had known Walls for most of his life, completely ignored him and concentrated on Flipper.

"Who *are* you? Other than *another international criminal*! You claim to know me but I've never seen you before in my life!" She glared at him, thoroughly shaken but still feisty.

"Your lot's face recognition software is pretty pants, isn't it?" said Flipper, lightly, then changing to a more serious, pleading tone, "But *you*; don't you *remember* me, Audrey?"

"Not at all!" she declared.

"Audrey, how *could* you forget me? Look in my *eyes*!" begged Flipper.

He put the guns into his pockets and gathered her in his arms as he spoke.

She furiously beat on his chest with her hands.

"Unhand me at once! Before I *make* you!"

Her angry eyes looked directly into his. She relaxed, amazed.

"*Zigsa!*" she cried. "But you are *Tibetan*! What are you doing here? Why are you in disguise?"

"*You*, Audrey, are an *idiot!*" said Flipper. "Very beautiful, but still an idiot! Just as well Walls has bust your cover! You will have to give up this job and then you can go and find a new identity with me! I'm *dead*, you see. Unfortunate but true. I need a new identity!"

"What?" asked Audrey, confused. The end of the word ended in a muffled noise as he kissed her.

"Ah!" sighed Priscilla, with deep feminine satisfaction, from her vantage position in the kitchen door. She was not so much of a feminist academic that she could not appreciate the romance of this moment. "It's just like a film!"

Priscilla and Walls looked at each other. Both their eyes filled with tears of emotion.

"Back-up will be here to pick me up very shortly," said Flipper, emerging from the embrace, putting Audrey, rather hastily, back down on the floor and returning to his businesslike persona.

"How do you know that?" asked Priscilla, feeling that now that she had seen his romantic side she could be cheeky and ask questions.

"Micro-sized two-way radio in my ear!" he replied. He had just had to endure a barrage of wolf whistles and groans down it while he was kissing Audrey.

He removed Audrey's guns from his own pockets, reversed them both and handed them politely back to her, with a bow. She snatched them from him. Although she had returned his kiss she was still clearly enraged, and stamped her foot on the carpet.

"You didn't *have* to *take* them!" she spat at him. "You didn't have to score points like that!"

"Be fair! I *did* have to! I didn't want you to *shoot* me by mistake!" replied Flipper.

"And you were quite wrong about all those *so-called* mistakes I am supposed to have made! I *had* checked who was in the house – house owned by harmless academic don! See! And if I had known it was *Sebastian* who was the second 'harmless academic' currently residing in the house with her I would have been even *more* sure that it was completely safe to just walk in. He doesn't believe in even having rights to bear firearms so he wasn't likely to be much trouble. He had been checked off, although the reason for his presence in the house was unclear. *Usual* second inhabitant a waitress at the Maitre, also judged to be completely non-threatening. See! Entering this house was an entirely safe procedure and anyway, *my* back-up will be here shortly too."

"I won't ask what your 'prior intelligence' said about Antholian and myself, in case it damages my ego permanently! But I repeat, Audrey, you are an idiot, even if I love you! And *your* back-up isn't on the way because, having more sense, it has gone in entirely the opposite direction, after the *actual* criminals!"

"*What?*" said Audrey. "How do you know?"

"*We* know *everything!*" retorted Flipper, in a very superior way.

"You *don't* know everything! You don't seem to know that I don't love you! Not at all! Our love affair was purely for *work* purposes! And *you* are supposed to tell *us* when you are operating in the same field!" came the riposte, and Audrey subsided in silent fury.

"And vice versa!" retorted Flipper, very annoyed now. "Presumably *you* didn't tell *us* for the same reason. This entire field of operation is so damn *corrupt!*"

"A *harmless academic!*" squawked Walls, cutting in. "How could *anyone* call *me* a harmless academic?"

"Of *course* you are, Walls!" said Priscilla, in a cooing voice. "You know you're just a *little academic lamb!*"

"*You* can't say anything! So are *you!*" retorted Walls. "She said the *same* about *you!*"

"Yes, but I don't pretend to be *a big, tough, rowing dude!*" said Priscilla. Surprised at her own modern turn of phrase she added to herself, What sort of vocabulary am I picking up from Angel and Barnabus?

Then Priscilla turned her attention to Flipper.

"Tell me," she said, genuinely annoyed by his recent academically absurd statement, "how can you claim to have achieved the impossibility of knowing everything? *Scio me nihil scire!*"

Up till now she had only seen his face with an expression that was serious, annoyed or teasing. Now he turned from Audrey, who was sulking and refusing to look at him, and flashed the full sun of his most radiant smile on her. She felt herself melting against her will. *Another* charmer!' she thought to herself, with a sigh. Are *all* Kings rowers such *hommes fatals*?

"*Si hoc legere scis nimium eruditionis habes*," Flipper responded, still looking at her with the same beautiful smile, which took the sting from the words. "As for how to know everything," he continued, "in my *own* case I was educated at New College School, Winchester and then Kings. That just about covers 'everything', I can assure you! But as for *our* sources of *all* knowledge we use Wikipedia, and if that fails we hack into the Amazon database. That way we not only know what our suspects have just bought but have a full profile of their possible future purchases. You know, people who bought nitro-glycerine and petrol often also looked at enriched uranium!"

"Very funny, I *don't* think!" said Priscilla, but she smiled back at him, all the same.

She found herself wondering whether Audrey was quite right in the head. Audrey seemed to be *spurning* Flipper's love! Clearly completely insane! How could anyone turn down someone with a smile like *that*?

Walls was devising a secret plot to learn Klingon so that *he* could speak a language that *no one else in the room understood.* He was tired of always having to look as if he could follow the joke when they spouted phrases in Latin and Ancient Greek. No, he thought, sadly, learning Klingon would *never* work: at least *three* of his friends would be bound to turn out to speak it fluently themselves!

Flipper turned again to Audrey, very wistfully now. He was no longer lecturing her or teasing her, not at all superior. He was just a young man hopelessly and desperately in love.

"*Please!* Come with me! Come with me to the safe house! Will your seniors let you go?"

"Come with *you*?" Audrey stamped her foot again, and then gave a doleful sigh. "But I don't know that I have a lot of choice about being *let go*. I fear I may have to quit. I have a two-way radio attached as well and your recital of my errors being transmitted through it, combined with the fact that Sebastian has bust my cover, is likely to be the end of my career!" She brightened slightly as a thought occurred to her. "I could kill Sebastian, of course, and maybe all the rest of you. Then my *cover* would be preserved!"

She paused for a moment, as if considering whether this plan was worth pursuing.

"I really *don't* feel that would be a good idea!" said Walls, hastily, while Flipper simultaneously said, "Don't be daft; you can't do that! You can't just kill innocent civilians. *Definitely not allowed*!"

Audrey spoke again, her voice becoming rapidly more and more hysterical. "My career is washed up then! You are *horrible*, Zigsa! I *liked* my work. You didn't have to trick me like that! You didn't have to say all those things! And you didn't have to lure me into a house that had Sebastian in it! Did you do that on purpose? I bet you did! You did it to make me look stupid! I had done really well up till then! I won't come with you! I will go somewhere where people appreciate me! I *want to go home*!"

The final sentence was pronounced in a childish wail. She burst into floods of tears.

"Come, come!" said Priscilla, putting her arms round the girl. "Things won't seem so bad in the morning!

Being sacked happens to lots of people! And you could do worse than take Flipper's offer; he's quite a nice young man really! He even has an Oxford degree in, er, in, um…"

"PPE," put in Flipper, "from *Kings*. Expert in philosophy, politics *and* economics! And I speak ten languages, all fluently, some with several additional regional dialects!"

"And I expect *you* only got the job in the first place because your daddy pulled some strings, Audrey," soothed Walls. "It's not even as if you're *good* at it!"

"For heavens sake, Walls!" said Priscilla, who had just been guilty of thinking the same thing herself. "Can't you see *she's understandably upset*? You are not helping at all! Poor child! What she needs is a *lovely cup of tea*!"

"Not *tea*! I hate tea! *Coffee*!" Audrey hiccupped through her tears. She had experienced English tea in the past. "And you know perfectly well, Sebastian," she added, rather incoherently, through a crumpled face and red nose, "that you can't get in like that! I was in the Air Force first; you *know* I was! I *hate* you! *I hate you! I hate you! I hate Zigsa! I hate men!*"

"Adventure-filled, *your* Air Force career, *sure*. Your *desk* tried to kill you *many times!*" said Walls, quietly and mischievously. He could not seem to stop himself from ragging Audrey.

"*Coffee* then, dear, *not* tea!" said Priscilla, quickly, before Audrey could really grasp what Walls had just said. Priscilla had encircled the distressed Audrey with her arms at the end of Audrey's last speech and was soothing her against her shoulder as if Audrey was a colicky baby. "Come on, come with me, come and have a lovely cup of coffee in the kitchen! You'll feel a lot better!"

Audrey stopped sobbing for a moment, and blew her nose.

"*That's* right!" said Priscilla, who had had a lot of practice with crying females since Angel had moved in with her. "Come on into the kitchen with Aunty

Priscilla! You'll feel better when you've had a hot drink!"

Walls and Flipper were both expecting another explosion of wrath from the independent and strong-minded Audrey but to their surprise she put both her arms round Priscilla and told her how wonderful she was and that she would never, never forget her. They went out to the kitchen together, arms entwined.

"Perhaps *we* should have offered her a *cup of coffee?*" whispered Walls to Flipper. "All the same, if I were you I should *stand back a bit*! She doesn't seem that keen on you so *take the opportunity to get away now*! She really *isn't* what you think! Consider this: she just tried to arrest me and even considered killing me, you know, and I'm *pretty well a relative* – I am her *sister's fiancé*. She's Flic's sister, although I daresay you already know that because you must have background-checked her! But, if she does that to *me*, imagine what she might do to you when you aren't even related in *any way*! Also, remember, I'm engaged to *her sister*! I know the family; I've known them since I was tiny! Seriously, step back quickly!

This one is from the same stable as her sister, old boy! Keep away from her!"

"I'll bear what you have said in mind, old chap!" Flipper whispered back. "But I regret, I'm a lost case! I am so in love with her, truly, deeply, madly, just like the storybooks! I don't really care!"

There were more wolf whistles and jeers in Flipper's ear.

"Oh do shut up!" he said.

Walls looked hurt.

"Not you, Walls; the lot in my ear! I've a good mind to take the damn thing out!"

"Don't you want us to take you to the safe house then? I'd be more polite to us if I were you! Especially if you want to take an unauthorised extra person with you!" breathed a dulcet voice in his ear.

"OK, OK!" he said. "Keep your hair on!"

"Do you have to talk to your imaginary friends in public?" asked Walls. "Come on, we'd best get into the kitchen. The females will already be friends for life on Facebook. We had better go and intervene before they decide to go away with *each other* instead of us, and eschew all males for ever!"

"*You* don't want to go away with *Priscilla*, do you?" said Flipper, much surprised at this suggestion.

"No, I don't!" said Walls. "I didn't mean it like that! It came out wrong! But, I'll tell you what, I *don't want to go away with Flic either*!" He had a hopeful idea. "You couldn't *arrange* things so that *Flic* would have to take a new identity, I suppose? *No*? Darn!"

They progressed together into the kitchen. Antholian was still fast asleep, still sitting on the stool with his head resting on the work surface. Audrey and Priscilla were leaning on the opposite work surface drinking coffee and, although Walls and Flipper found this difficult to believe, they appeared to be discussing the merits of various skirt hemline lengths. The atmosphere was peacefully domestic.

Walls and Flipper, feeling that they had wandered into something a little surreal, poured themselves black coffees and attempted to join in the polite small talk for a few moments.

Then Flipper remembered he had something important to say.

"You must go to my funeral!" he said. "Not you, Priscilla – you don't know me – but Tony and Walls will have to go!"

Antholian woke up as his own name echoed through his dreams. He stretched, stiff and uncomfortable, and looked round, a little puzzled.

"Did someone say something to me?" he asked.

"Funeral, mine. You and Walls have to go to it. Might blow the cover otherwise!" explained Flipper, helpfully.

"Why do folk keep calling you *Walls*, Sebastian?" interjected Audrey.

"For the same reason they keep calling *him* Flipper!" said Walls. "I could tell you his real name but he's just about to change it so there's not much point. Walls and Flipper are our *rowing tags*! But please feel free! Call me Sebastian and him Zigsa – whatever makes you happy!"

Antholian, still half asleep and very confused, focussed on Audrey.

"Weren't you in my *shop* this afternoon?" he asked. "I do hope your, er, medical condition, has improved. Was, you know, the *remedy* successful?"

"Worked like a dream!" said Audrey.

Was she being sarcastic? Antholian wondered. Was this the person that Flipper had been expecting to call here next? What was going on? Who was she? Why was she here? Why did she know Walls?

Walls turned back to Flipper.

"I'm absolutely *not* going to your funeral, Flip! I never attend funerals; they are simply *too sad*!"

"That's a bit much! *I'd* go to *yours!*" replied Flipper. "I'd even give a eulogy!"

"Yes, but if it was *my* funeral *I'd* be *dead.* You're not dead; it's not reasonable to expect me to go to such a distressing occasion under the circumstances! As a single male I exercise my right to *never* go to upsetting or distressing events!"

"But if you *don't* go other people might suspect I'm *not* dead! You *have* to go!" protested Flipper.

"*Have* to?" asked Walls, becoming quite cross. "I sure don't! I've told you, I never go to *real* funerals unless absolutely forced to do so by my parents. Damned if I'm going to a *fake* one! Everyone else crying, miserable looking funeral directors, a coffin… Coffins freak me out. *No,* I tell you!"

"I *could* go to the funeral and sit there *meditating* and then announce that I had had a vision to tell me that you had been reincarnated as a *dolphin*! But I'd just as soon *not* go. I'm right with Walls on that one. I hate going to funerals!" said Antholian flippantly.

"I'd go to *your* funeral as well, even though I don't know you very well, because you are Buffy's brother, and also as a gesture of solidarity with other small shops in the Cowley Road! Attendance at funerals is *most important* as a *mark of respect*! I just got blown up by a faulty gas cooker, blown up with my entire shop. Tragic – a young life, cut off in its prime! And you two can't even be bothered attending my funeral in case it *upsets you*! I'm really hurt by both your attitudes!" said Flipper, sounding genuinely ruffled.

"But you *aren't* dead!" protested Walls.

"Precisely!" said Antholian.

"Do stop making excuses, you two!" said Priscilla, speaking in a voice of authority. "Of course you *have* to go! You will upset Elodea and Barnabus if you don't both turn up, and they are going to be upset enough about Flipper being dead anyway!"

"Are you sure?" said Walls and Antholian in chorus.

"Absolutely!" said Priscilla. "Of course I don't have to go myself because," she added, with a note of triumph, since she didn't like going to funerals either, "I *never met Flipper when he was alive*."

"Bother!" said Walls. "So you didn't! Good of you to advise Audrey to take up an offer of love from someone you only know as a zombie!"

"You know," said Antholian, thoughtfully, "I can't help thinking that your entire plan was *unnecessarily complex*, Flipper!"

"My plan! My original plan for today was perfectly simple – it just involved a controlled explosion to destroy my shop and kill myself. Until you three joined in! No, not *you*, Walls; I'll let you off in this case! And Buffy – it was his fault as well! You three *and* Buffy! What with aunts borrowing buddhas and Tony and Buffy sending texts and then Audrey showing up in the street today so I had to rescue her as well as myself and Tony! *My* plan – *complex*! I like that!"

"I didn't need rescuing! And I agree with whoever this is!" said Audrey, rather cockily. "And things were already going wrong with your *original plan*! What do we learn in training? 'As a last resort consider faking your own death' – as a *last* resort!"

"I think you have confused secret missions with how to avoid grizzly bears. My self-destruction was a *planned event*!" replied Flipper, in a light tone. He continued more seriously, "In any case I like *that little speech*, coming from *you*, walking hazard of the year! If it wasn't for me you'd have been *really* dead in *Tibet*, let alone today! You are all so damned ungrateful! You, Audrey, I had to lure you away from danger on top of everything else I was already doing today! You, Tony, would be dead if it wasn't for me! Honestly! I save at least three of your lives and I get a lecture! Gratitude!"

Antholian decided not to point out that the buddha would never have been in his shop and consequently he would never have become involved in any of this if it hadn't been for Flipper. He subsided again.

"I didn't *need you*! I was fine! Even *you* said that! My attachment of the tracker to Tony was *faultless*! My tracking was *faultless*!" retorted Audrey.

"That statement is simply *ridiculous*! Tony wasn't an international criminal! Nor am I! You were tracking the wrong people!" said Flipper.

"*Whatever*!" replied Audrey.

"I should have left you to get killed!" said Flipper.

"I told you already," said Walls, "close acquaintance leads to discovery of the horrible truth about that family. Take my advice! Keep away! Run now!"

"What business is it of *yours*?" demanded Audrey.

"I'm *nearly* your brother-in-law!" said Walls.

Flipper, Audrey and Walls all glared at each other.

Then Flipper gestured at them all to be quiet; he was listening to his ear again.

"The car's nearly here. I must make my final farewells," he said. "This is where I become *really dead* as far as you are concerned! I'm going to miss all my friends! Especially you and Buffy and Finn, Walls! And you, Tony, I'll miss you too. I haven't known you for long but we had a great run, didn't we?"

He looked very lonely suddenly, and only about twelve years old. Priscilla felt a pang in her heart. What a terrible thing his superiors had required him to do, and he was doing it willingly! Just to stop some diamonds being smuggled!

Flipper looked at her. "It's not just the smuggling or the smugglers. People are dying. The people who work to produce the diamonds in such dangerous conditions to make them cheaper for the very rich – *they're* what matters!"

"How did you know what I was thinking?" she gasped.

"I knew because I have to keep reminding myself of why I am doing this too, especially today! And I saw your thoughts on your face!" he answered.

Priscilla was not keen on being hugged or hugging, although she had been forced to take up the practice first with Angel, and now Audrey. But she stretched her arms out willingly, put them round Flipper and gave him a big bear hug. He smiled down at her.

"I'll be OK. I *choose* to do this. Don't worry about me! What other job could be this much fun? I won't be giving my job up because I'm dead! Just be doing it as a new me!"

Then he detached himself and turned to Walls.

"Tell Buffy, tell him, tell him *Finn's back*! *He'll* be at my funeral!"

"Would you stop going on about *your funeral*!" said Walls. "It gives me the creeps! But Finn's back? That's great shakes. Good old Finn! I'll look out for him!"

"Finn's back from the USA? Has his bank transferred him to Britain?" asked Antholian.

"Yes, yes. Transferred to working in a branch over here!" said Flipper.

Walls caught Flipper's eye. His own eyes had a question in them. Flipper's eyes laughed in return. He and Walls exchanged a secret smile.

"*I* didn't tell you!" Flipper mouthed to Walls.

"*Quite so!*" Walls mouthed back.

"I'm glad he's back!" said Walls, aloud. "I'll tell Buffy. Anyway Buffy'll see him at your, your, er, your *you-know-what*! I s'pose Finn will be attending that as well?"

"Most likely! Now, I know I don't need to tell you all to forget *everything*. You mustn't breathe a word about any of this! Not soon! Not ever! Today was an *ordinary day*! Nothing unusual happened *at all*. Tony has been meditating and then went straight to sleep in bed. You and Walls proofread and went straight to bed."

"Quick question! Did your shop blow up or not?" asked Walls.

Flipper cuffed him round the ear.

"You know it did, you fool! OK, *nothing unusual* happened today *except* that my shop blew up and I died. OK? Not a word! Don't even keep a memory; wipe it from your minds! Oh, and, 'they' say that, just to make sure…" – he fished in his rucksack – "…all three of you need to sign one of these."

Each of 'these' was an agreement to abide by the Official Secrets Act.

"You are legally bound by it whether or not you sign this anyway," Flipper added, helpfully, fishing out a pen too, "so you might as well!"

"No wonder your rucksack was bulging!" said Walls. "How many copies of the Official Secrets Act do you keep in there?"

"It isn't the actual Act – only an agreement to keep to it!" said Flipper. "I can fit a lot of these in, I assure you! And, as I said, you can be done for breaking it whether you sign or not! So…"

They signed. There seemed no point in quibbling.

"I won't say a word," said Walls. "With my complicated love life I'm used to keeping secrets. I'm very good at it, assuredly!"

"You know we won't say anything! Not a word! Ever!" said Antholian with great confidence. He was not sure who he could possibly have told anyway. Not the sort of story to share with total strangers. He would be unlikely to confide in either of his younger brothers or his father about anything much normally. It was rather a shame not to be able to tell Elizabeth or Mama though. It would be so wonderful to be able to *impress* his *big sister* with this story! And it was the sort of story that Mama *really enjoyed*! It would be hard not to be able to tell her! His face fell.

"And you, Priscilla, you know not to say a word! You *can* tell people after   twenty-five years. Till then, after tonight, don't breathe a word about it, not even to each other. You never know who might be listening!"

Priscilla had a vision of the old wartime poster and struggled not to giggle. Walls answered for her.

"Naturally none of us will say anything!" said Walls. "Who do you take me and Pris and Tony for? *Silent to the grave*, that's us!"

"Absolutely!" said Priscilla, having got past the desire to laugh. She tried to look thoroughly insulted at the suggestion that there would be any risk of her ever telling anyone about it. All the same she would have loved to tell *Elodea* all about it! Such a wonderful story! Now Priscilla would just have to listen to Elodea raving on and on and on with uninteresting facts about Japan, and she would never be able to take up this amazing once-in-a-lifetime opportunity to out-story her! Or Charles! She would have loved to tell Charles!

"It doesn't have to be to the *grave!*" said Flipper. "I already said! Just twenty-five years! You can talk all you like about it then!"

"Twenty-five years!" said Walls. "We'll *all* be *dead* by then, or if not literally *in the grave* I'll be *over* fifty, which is the same thing!"

"No it isn't!" said Priscilla, very annoyed. "Fifty is *not* dead! I myself have *every* intention of being around in twenty-five years' time and I expect you and Tony to meet up with me on the twenty-fifth anniversary of this day so we can have a good laugh about the whole episode!"

"Are you *quite* sure? About still being alive in twenty-five years?" said Walls, very naughtily.

Priscilla hit him with a handy fish slice. She was already planning to meet Elodea for tea in twenty-five years' time and tell *her* all about it. She would be truly amazed! Priscilla could already imagine Elodea's face! Very, very satisfactory!

"Something to tell your grandchildren, eh, Tony?" said Flipper to Antholian.

For Antholian was now smiling to himself, daydreaming happily. He would write it all down and store the notes in a bank deposit box or with a solicitor in an envelope marked 'not to be opened' till the correct date. *Then* he could impress the world! How old would he be? Well past fifty! Very, *very* old! As Flipper said, a tale with which to impress his *grandchildren*. He imagined them, small versions of himself, clustered around his knees. Then he remembered that his own grandparents had told him stories from their youth that they thought were impressive but he also remembered that he had never been impressed! The stories were all very boring. He also recalled that he did not intend to have children or grandchildren as increasing the population of the globe further would be immoral, especially as his siblings had already reproduced and thus continued his genes for him. He sighed!

"What about *me*?" said Audrey. "Am *I* allowed to talk about it? Shouldn't you be getting *my* signature?"

"Not necessary. You are a highly trained operative!"
replied Flipper.

Audrey was not impressed. "You didn't seem to
recollect that *before*!"

"I'm sorry," said Flipper. "You know I know you are
highly trained. *I trained you in Tibet*! It's just that you
go and forget it all so fast. You can't help it, but you
really aren't safe to be let out! You *should* be sacked,
really you should, because you are going to have a
very short life otherwise! You're too cute and trusting
to be a spook!"

Audrey made a huffing noise and wandered off into
the hall on her own.

Cute and trusting? thought Walls. Flipper *must* be
besotted, Audrey would have been quite happy to
shoot me, her prospective brother-in-law, earlier! Not
much he could do! He had already made *every* effort
to warn Flip about Audrey! If Flip persisted in
adoring Audrey despite this, the outcome was now
entirely Flip's own responsibility!

Flipper ignored Audrey's departure into the hall and turned to Antholian.

"I forgot to say, the people who broke into your shop, Tony – they'll be dealt with. They are being tracked down. There was a tracker hidden in the fake diamonds in the substitute buddha. They should have noticed that themselves but criminals are so sloppy when they think they are winning! Someone will pop in to check that your shop and Boris are both A-OK shortly. I expect Boris will just have a bit of a thick head in the morning. When you go back tomorrow the shop should look just as it was before, but buddha-less. Only remember this as a bad dream, passing and forgotten in the morning!"

"I am going to do so, I can assure you of that!" said Antholian. "Furthermore, I am never, ever, again going to let *anyone* enter my shop while carrying a buddha statuette of any shape, size or form whatsoever! And if anyone comes in and asks for one I am going to throw them out, yes, Aunty Pris, even if it's you!"

He added, somewhat inconsequently, as his tired brain ran on, "As Octavio Paz says, 'Modern man likes to pretend that his thinking is wide-awake. But this wide-awake thinking has led us into the mazes of a nightmare in which the torture chambers are endlessly repeated in the mirrors of reason.'"

"Eh?" said Walls.

"Sorry." said Antholian. "Not really awake!"

"Wish I could remember quotes that long when *I'm* half asleep," said Walls, enviously.

"Probably why you took History and not Philosophy!" said Flipper helpfully.

"History needs an *excellent memory*!" said Walls, indignantly.

They were all waiting, ears alert, to hear the sound of Flipper's car outside. Their speech was now reduced to random statements, simply to fill the time gap. The last moments before departure, that awkward final parting time that always happens when people are waiting to begin a long journey, to go to hospital, to die. Seconds in reality and yet, when filled with the awkward discomfort of imminent departure, seeming an eternity. Yet eventually the end arrives, startling and far too soon.

"They're only a short way away!" announced Flipper.

He shook hands with Walls, Tony and Priscilla.

Audrey had reappeared and was standing, rather aloof, in the doorway from the hall.

Flipper turned to Audrey and, taking her hand, he got down on one knee.

"*Please*, Audrey, I should have said this before. I hope I have enough time now! I have wasted so much time already and now it is nearly too late! Say it's not too late! *Please* come with me! I *love* you! Please say you love me! Or at least say you will come with me! If you don't come with me now we may *never* see each other again! *Please*! I'm *begging* you, beseeching you, *pleading* – "

"Don't be silly. *Naturally* I'm coming with you!" she interrupted him, but she said these words in a very casual and offhand way.

"You *are*?" gasped Flipper. "You *are*? I might *really* die, from *happiness*!"

"*Men* never understand *anything*!" she replied. "How could you imagine that I *wouldn't* come with you? But note that I've only got a couple of weeks' leave of absence from duty. My superiors did not rate my performance as low as you did! However, I am granted a two-week leave on compassionate grounds because of proximity to scene of explosion in which a previous collaborative colleague was killed! So don't think I *have* to come with you because I lost my job! This is *my choice*!"

Somehow the way she said 'my choice' did not make it a statement of her capitulation to Flipper's charms, but a statement of her complete independence.

A voice in Flipper's ear said, "Message from the other side. They say don't worry about the fortnight too much; she can stay for as long as you like, preferably permanently!"

It is a measure of Flipper's devotion to Audrey that his facial expression never flickered when he received this piece of information although a very close observer might have seen a momentary twinkle in his eyes.

"But," added Audrey, melodramatically, "I *preferred* you when you were *Tibetan*!"

Walls found himself wondering about Flipper's hopes of future bliss.

As some native North American chief was supposed to have said, "It's as well we don't all have the same taste or everyone would want my squaw," Walls murmured to himself.

Flipper took Audrey's hand and looked into her eyes and recited a quotation from Buddha: "I have shown you the methods that lead to liberation. But you should know that liberation depends upon yourself."

"*Ah!*" cried Audrey. "Why couldn't you *really* be Zigsa?"

"I *am* Zigsa! He is me and I am him just as surely as I am *me!*" said Flipper, cryptically.

"I say, Flipper, that reminds me of another good quotation," said Walls, making a final desperate attempt to, as he perceived it, save his friend from himself. "As the Dalai Lama said, 'Remember that not getting what you want is sometimes a wonderful stroke of luck!'"

Flipper glared at Walls, then topped his efforts with another Dalai Lama quote: "I believe that the very purpose of our life is to seek happiness. That is clear."

Antholian, dreamily, continued this quotation. "Whether one believes in religion or not, whether one believes in this religion or that religion, we are all seeking something better in life. So, I think, the very motion of our life is towards happiness!"

Audrey gave a gasp and hurried over to Antholian, stroking him gently behind the ear.

"I nearly forgot! There you are! All gone!" she said, sounding pleased.

She took a tiny plastic bag from an inside pocket, popped something minute into it, sealed it and replaced the bag inside her jacket.

The removal of something invisible from behind his ear, thought Antholian, was the last straw in this puzzling chain of straws. Perhaps Walls could explain it to him later, except that he supposed that they weren't allowed to discuss it. Perhaps it would make sense in a few days' time when he had thought more about it?

Audrey turned to Walls next.

"Sebastian, if you blow my cover to Flic or the parents or anybody else, I can assure you that you will *never* marry Flic!" she pronounced sternly.

Walls' face flickered with hope for a millisecond and then he subsided, merely mumbling "Get thee behind me, Satan!" under his breath.

"And," added Audrey, "whether you tell Flic or the parents *before* or *after* you are married, I will make certain sure that *both* the pa's cut *both* of your allowances off."

Walls looked crestfallen.

"Ah well, *temptation removed*!" he said.

"Eh?" said Audrey.

"I mean, you *know* I wouldn't blow your cover, Audrey, not ever! What do you take me for?" said Walls.

"Time to go!" said Flipper.

Audrey turned her back on Walls and held her hand out towards Flipper.

"I wasn't going to say this but, before we go, just in case of, you know, mishaps, I think I will. Balancing everything out, I quite probably love you too! There you are! Now get a move on before they go without us!"

"*Audrey!*" breathed Flipper ecstatically.

Flipper and Audrey looked into each other's eyes for a moment and then he bent quickly to kiss her hair. Flipper's current situation, particularly that of being dead, could have been regarded as tragic but he now looked jubilant. He collected the brown paper parcel from the hall table and they both disappeared through the front door together, quickly and silently, like two shadows.

Walls was going to call "I'll miss you! Best of luck!" after Flipper but decided he had better not advertise their departure. He wished he could do so, though he thought to himself that Flipper was going to need a lot of luck if he was thinking of spending the rest of his life with Audrey!

Antholian, who had also wandered into the hall behind the two lovers, sat down heavily on the third step of the stairs. He felt rather flat and empty now all the excitement was over. He yawned, and realised that he was still extremely tired despite having had a couple of naps. On the following evening he also realised that Flipper had taken his Boris-exercising outfit away with him. The rowing lycra was really not a good substitute but it would have to suffice until Antholian could cycle over to Little Wychwell and find an alternative outfit lying around in his old bedroom. He was not going to bend his rules about buying unnecessary new clothes just because he felt embarrassed wearing tight rowing lycra that belonged to a college which he had not attended! But, for now, unworried by these future problems, he turned, curled his limbs round on the lowest steps of the staircase, and fell instantly asleep again.

Priscilla, peering cautiously through the kitchen window, was just in time to see a large black anonymous car purr up the street and disappear in the darkness.

She felt tearful.

"Will we ever see them again?" she asked Walls. "They were both *so sweet*! Poor Flipper! *Quem di diligunt, adolescens moritur*!"

Another fool, thought Walls. Flipper thinks Audrey is *cute*. Priscilla thinks they are *both sweet*. Walls felt he would not have described either of them in this way!

"*Sweet*?" he said. "I don't think either of them are either cute *or* sweet. One of them has just blown up a shop in the Cowley Road and there is an exploded dead body in it, supposedly his, but given that it isn't his then he must have obtained a corpse from somewhere. Maybe he killed someone? Have you considered that? Very sweet! And *Audrey* wanted to shoot *me*! I can see the recruiting advertisement now: 'Are you a sweet and kindly person? Become a Secret Agent – it's a job for sweet and kindly people!'"

"Audrey didn't want to *shoot* you; she only wanted to *arrest* you!" rebuked Priscilla. "And they are *both* sweet!"

Priscilla could hardly believe that she could hear her own voice speaking such arrant nonsense. Either it must be the lack of sleep, or else sharing a house with the very over-sentimental Angel was having a worse effect on her than she had thought. She really must encourage Barnabus and Angel to get married as soon as possible so that Angel could *move out* before Priscilla's feminist pacifist standpoint lost *all* credibility!

Walls completely ignored everything that she said except for the sentence about Audrey.

"You forget! We're American, Audrey and me! 'Shoot' and 'Arrest' are pretty much the same word. Especially if you are a young, black man."

"Really, Walls! It's not that bad these days! The *President*, you know!" suggested Priscilla.

"As far as I am aware the President hasn't often been in trouble with the law. Come to that, nor have I! She had the nerve to think that *I* was a blood diamond smuggler! *Me*! As if I would! Someone I have known from childhood and she still thought I could be a diamond smuggler!" grumbled Walls. The late hour and the excitement had thoroughly upset his usually sunny outlook on life.

"Yes, but consider what a very, very bad thing it would have been if you had been. Understandable that she felt you should be arrested under the circumstances. Dear me! Both so young and so pathetically vulnerable and it's all so romantic! Meeting again like this!" sighed Priscilla, entirely lost in the romance of it all.

Her feminist standpoint made a brief protest in one corner of her mind and then went into a coma with shock. She fancied she heard it say it would recover when she was *properly awake* just *before* it fell into an apparently lifeless heap.

"You don't understand at all. *Not* being sweet is dyed into Audrey's blood! Just like her little sister! And it's not just Flic and Audrey, it's the *whole* of their pop's family, you know! Republican Tea Party supporters *and* gun toting lunatics! 'Rights to carry arms', and all that. Flic has a cute little set of *pink* handguns. Can you believe that? *Pink* handguns! Do you know that Audrey and Flic's grandmom shot their grandpop? Shot him *dead*! It all got hushed up somehow because they are so rich, so there was no court case, but she did; everyone knows she did. She caught him in bed with his mistress and shot him. See? That's what they are like!" ranted Walls.

Priscilla was so concerned for her feminist standpoint that she had stopped listening and thus only returned to his impassioned speech from the words 'cute little set of pink handguns'. She thought that from the feminine perspective Flic's grandmother had a point. Her feminist standpoint quivered back to life and raised its head again. If she took a professorship at an American university she herself could have lots of handguns. She could have a different design for each of her handbags! But she would probably still not be allowed to shoot inattentive students. Many of the classical civilisations would have approved of such a strategy if guns had been invented at the time! The Spartans would most *definitely* have approved of shooting students who *might get Thirds*. What was Walls going on about now? Perhaps she should listen. He seemed to be getting rather emotional.

"I keep out of their way. I keep out of their way," Walls was muttering, apparently to himself, "and then they turn up *here*! It's not endurable! It's *not* endurable!"

"But, Walls, why does *Flic* want to marry *you?*" interrupted Priscilla.

Walls looked flabbergasted. He replied, in a genuinely astonished tone, "Why does *she* want to marry *me?* Rich, intelligent, good looking, hot! I'm a wonderful catch! Why wouldn't she?"

"I thought you said your *fathers* arranged the match! What about them?" continued Priscilla.

"Oh yes, our parents are all rich, good looking and hot too!" replied Walls, somewhat absent-mindedly. He looked at her face. "Look, I try never to discuss issues like this! I try never to talk about my disastrous engagement! I keep out of politics and business issues, especially anything with vaguely racist connotations. Just don't go there and it doesn't exist. People get too hung up on the whole thing! Ignore it all; it will go away! But, if you insist on talking with gloves off, let's start with the pops! They want the two businesses to be linked more closely for purely financial reasons, but there is more to it than that! Flic's pop is a Republican senator and someone with my ethnicity in his family would do a lot for his ideologically sound credentials. Then her mom isn't a Republican, she's a Catholic Democrat, same as my family, see, so that makes *her* keen on the match too. Flic's mom's actually a great person, although she looks a lot like Flic. Audrey looks like their pop. But her mom isn't as lovely as Flic! Not nearly, never was, even when younger. Ah, you should *see* Flic! She is the loveliest girl you ever saw! I thought she was utterly gorgeous when I was younger! I didn't propose entirely due to family pressures; I was a willing victim to the deal! She's the sort of girl that teenage guys dream of *seeing*, let alone having the opportunity to marry! Blond, blue eyed, tiny, lovely figure... Faultless appearance in every way! I didn't wonder too much about her *mind*; I was just looking at the wrapping, you know! And every time I see her again she is so magically lovely, it's hard to know sometimes, sometimes even now, I still want her real bad and..."

He faded into his own thoughts.

Priscilla had not listened to most of this speech. She was thinking about the fact that she had, yet again, *lost the buddha before Charles' visit.* She could get *another* one from Flipper's shop. She wondered why she had not thought of that before. Then she remembered that the shop and its stock were either blown up or severely damaged or probably carted away as 'evidence'. She reached the end of this train of thought and returned to listening to Walls just as Walls reached the words 'willing victim'. As he finally ran to a halt she thought that Walls *still* never looked further than the wrapping on his female acquaintances – at least he never showed any sign of doing so. Perhaps he would one day, when he was older! She felt sorry for Audrey: having a younger sister quite so beautiful must have been very trying for her! No wonder she had grown up strangely violent!

Walls' thoughts had swung suddenly to a completely different topic. Something truly awful had occurred to him too.

"Poor Buffy!" said Walls. "Flipper – one of his best buddies, you know! I suppose *I* have to tell Buffy that Flipper's dead? I would hear it on the local news, wouldn't I? I don't want him to read about it in the national newspapers without having someone break it to him more gently."

"Don't worry!" said Priscilla. "I'm sure Elodea will tell him. Oh! Blast and botheration! I suppose *I* have to ring Elodea in Japan and tell *her*! That *will* be awful. She is going to be in *absolute floods*! I don't have to do it yet though: I wouldn't know, yet! I don't have to ring yet! Come to that, I *don't even know Flipper*. I wouldn't realise it was him if I did hear it on the news! Oh yes I would, because Tony told me about him this afternoon and that bit is allowed to have happened. But not the buddha! This is all so complicated! Why on earth would I have gone to visit Tony? I'm bound to let that slip out! Lying is so complicated! Of course, I went to see if he had a buddha, but he didn't! Got it!"

She paused to consider whether and when she *would* have to ring Elodea. Then she had a truly wonderful thought which would get both herself and Walls out of having to hold painful conversations about death with distressed people!

"Wonderful! Wonderful! Neither of us have to do it! Tony will obviously know about Flipper's demise first, his shop being situated where it is! *He* can tell Elodea and Barnabus! In fact, *he* probably has to tell *us!*"

"Brilliant!" said Walls. They both smiled conspiratorially at each other.

"Perhaps, perhaps Flipper will get in touch with Barnabus again once the fuss dies down, even if his identity has changed. But if Audrey stays with him and changes her identity, what about poor Flic? And their parents? Won't they miss Audrey?" Priscilla found all the possible terrible consequences rising up in a jumble in her mind.

"Audrey won't have to change *her* identity, even if she marries Flipper. She can just marry his *new* identity," said Walls, helpfully and with wonderful confidence.

"Do you know that or are you just guessing?" asked Priscilla.

"I'm just guessing! *I'm* not a spook! I have absolutely no knowledge about what happens when spooks reincarnate or regenerate or whatever they might call it! Bit like Doctor Who! But Flic would never miss Audrey in any event! They *hate* each other, always have! Flic's much prettier than Audrey and Flic toes the family line, always. Audrey's the rebel. She hasn't lived at home for years. We used to all play together when we were kids but I hardly ever see Audrey these days. It's a wonder I even recognised her!"

"You hardly ever see Flic either!" Priscilla reminded him. Then she thought of something. "Flipper's mother! And his father! And it's *her birthday today*, her *birthday*, and she is going to think he has been blown up!"

"It's not her birthday!" Walls exclaimed. Really, he thought, women, even academics, not ever really quite with it! "Flipper was just inventing all that stuff about her birthday, you know! He doesn't even *have* any *parents*. They are both dead – really dead that is – not like Flipper. His mother died falling off a horse on a hunt quite a few years ago. His father died in a car crash near Monte Carlo. He was driving round those twisty little coast roads, with his mistress, in an open top sports car. Rumour has it that Flipper's mother had cut the brake cables but I think his father was probably just driving too fast. He died when Flipper was only five."

"The poor little boy!" cried Priscilla. "No wonder he went right off the rails and took up such an *odd* career!"

An interesting perspective, mused Walls to himself, but he felt he should correct Priscilla's view of Flipper's life.

"No. He was fine. He wasn't that attached to his parents. He didn't really know them all that well. He was brought up by nannies, prep school and public school, see! He's had a pretty good life so far, *believe*! He's a great guy, rows really well, very intelligent, works really hard, succeeds at everything. Ten foreign languages! Did you hear that? I can barely speak *four*! And two of mine are East Coast American and Upper-Class English! I'm going to really miss him! Do you think he'll call round when he's *someone*

376

else? Maybe he'll let me know who he is? Will I see him again? What do you think?"

Priscilla ignored the end of his speech. She had not been listening to any of it past 'good life', which was where her thoughts had wandered, but she had been much struck by the beginning of his speech.

"Wasn't attached to his parents! Didn't really know them? Poor thing!" sighed Priscilla. Something about Flipper's boyish face, his brilliant academic mind and his, in her eyes, most regrettable profession, had touched her heart. She felt tears fill her eyes. If he had been *her* son…!

"There's nothing wrong with being brought up by *nannies*. My nannies were great!" expostulated Walls.

Priscilla realised her mistake. She had forgotten Walls had had much the same background as Flipper, even if it was in a different country.

"But you *know* your parents!" she protested.

"Yes, yes. See them at least once a year. Always have!" said Walls, half joking. "Hey, you know what?"

"What?" asked Priscillla, but she had little interest in prolonging the conversation any more. Her desire to go to sleep was growing stronger as the adrenaline rush faded.

"If whoever Flipper becomes is Audrey's partner, then when I meet Audrey's partner obviously I will meet Flipper again! But what if I can't tell? I mean Audrey might decide *not* to stick with Flipper, or, if he has any sense at all – and I did try to warn him, I really did; you know that – Flipper won't stick with *her*. Well then, if she goes off and finds someone else, how am I meant to tell whether Audrey's partner is *Flipper* being someone else, or *actually is* someone else?"

Priscilla considered the tautology briefly but abandoned hope of unravelling it before she had had some sleep. She was beginning to reel with exhaustion. Walls still seemed to be bouncy enough but he then he was more accustomed to staying up all night, either working or partying, and then doing early morning rowing afterwards. Priscilla remembered Tony, fast asleep on the stairs.

"Should we get Tony to bed? It's going to be difficult to go up and down the stairs with him where he is. Maybe we should just pick him up and dump him on the lounge floor? Or shall we leave him there? *Quieta non movere*?"

She looked at her watch and sighed! She wanted to go to bed right now without worrying about Tony! Such a bother, all these grown-up children! She had never wanted all this parental responsibility! Barnabus! Angel! Walls! And now Tony! Just as well that Flipper and Audrey had gone *somewhere secret*! Even worse was the fact that Priscilla felt that she never got any appreciation for looking after all these wayward children because they all *thought* that they were *adults*!

But before Priscilla and Walls could decide on what to do with Antholian's sleeping body, the doorbell rang…

hapter 9

Walls and Priscilla both stared at the door. Who could possibly be ringing the bell at this time of night. There was only one answer in both of their minds.

"The *bad guys?*" whispered Walls, voicing their fears in a low, horrified hiss.

"It could be *Flipper*. Maybe he *forgot* something?" whispered Priscilla in reply, trying to sound cheerful and bracing but expressing this idea more in a spirit of wild hopefulness than actually expecting herself to be correct and Walls to be wrong. She shivered.

"*Don't* open it!" hissed Walls.

"Absolutely *not!*" replied Priscilla, *sotto voce.* "What do you think I am? *Timidi mater non flet!*"

The doorbell rang again – a long trill.

"Keep down on the floor," gasped Walls, throwing himself down and yanking Priscilla down with him. He continued, directly into her ear, "Not that this will help us much! They could shoot the lock off the door! Or fire an automatic *through* the panels!"

"So why lie on the floor?" asked Priscilla in a sibilant whisper.

"It's safer! People always lie on the floor in these situations!" answered Walls. "Quiet! I'm listening!"

They both listened. There was silence except for their own breathing.

Priscilla reflected wearily that she wished that Barnabus and his friends did *not* see lying face downwards on a carpet as the answer to all emergencies. Possibly if they were older and stiffer they might all find it as unattractive as she did. Bomb in the kitchen? Lie on the hall carpet. People likely to shoot the lock off the door? Lie on the hall carpet. She felt how calm she was compared to the *first* time she had nearly been shot, by Big Frank. On that occasion she had 'fainted dead away', whereas now she felt remarkably relaxed about the whole thing. One can get accustomed to anything, she thought. *Damna minus consulta movent.*

The bell rang again – a long, slow, press on the button. There was another pause.

Priscilla found she was reciting Donne to herself. "Ask not for whom the bell tolls, it tolls for thee!" She had a job not to giggle. She reflected that such incidents in her life never happened except when she was being vulcanized. But Barnabus and Elodea were not even in the country! Could Walls' *surname* be *Smith*? Then she realised that she still had *Tony* here in the house! There was a Smith present and correct! No, there were *two*! She had forgotten that she was still being vulcanized as a Pippy-minder.

Priscilla had never expected her life to turn out to be so exciting or to have such a potential to end suddenly and unexpectedly. The words 'shoot the lock off the door' began to register their full meaning in her brain. After shooting the lock off, what happened next?

What else had Walls said? "Fire an automatic." An automatic? Some kind of gun, she believed. They were going to be *shot*? She began to feel a whirling in her brain. She needed to produce immediate calming thoughts to get it under control.

It occurred to her that she hadn't seen Pippy for ages. She wondered, in an uninterested way, what she was up to. *Cave tibi cano muto*! But if they were all about to be massacred it hardly mattered what Pippy was up to right now. She wondered if Elodea would be saddest about her death or Pippy's. She did hope it was hers! The whirling increased. To try to regain a sense of calm she began to plan her own funeral. It would be in College of course, and *everyone* would say what a *wonderful* person she had been, *de mortuis nil nisi bonum*. She wished she had thought to put in her last will and testament that she wanted the whole service taken in either Latin or Greek. Charles would be there – it would fit in so conveniently with his visit. She felt tears of pathos gathering in her own eyes over her sad and early death.

But the person or persons outside had still not forced the door or shot the lock or done anything at all other than ring the bell. The fact that this behaviour seemed rather strange for violent criminals occurred to both Walls and Priscilla at the same moment. They looked at each other, a question in each set of eyes.

At that very moment they heard the outside letter flap being lifted up.

Thank goodness, thought Priscilla, that I have an *inside* flap, so that they can't see straight in.

They are going to shoot us *through the mail slot*! thought Walls. He wondered if he should throw himself across Priscilla to protect her – women and children first and all that – or whether if he leapt up from the floor and sprinted, right now, abandoning Priscilla to her fate, he could make it up the stairs *before* they fired.

"It's no good hiding!" called a shrill female voice. "I know you're in there!"

Priscilla had a moment in which her feminist perspective had to be readjusted. She had been imagining the criminal, or criminals, outside her house to be *male*. How *very shockingly sexist*, she scolded herself!

"*Don't* answer it!" she whispered to Walls, desperately, as he groaned and rose to his feet.

"I think we *have* to!" sighed Walls, equally quietly, grabbing her hand. "Audrey has *betrayed* me! The *double-crossing rattlesnake*! Come on, ups-a-daisy! Can I suggest you climb over Tony and go and do something with your hair?"

"Why bother about my hair?" whispered Priscilla. "If Audrey is a double agent they are going to kill both of us and then go after Flipper!" Then she added, "Although it might be better to die with tidy hair – the newspaper photos of the body, I suppose – but have I got enough time to do my hair before they kill me?"

The voice came through the flap again. It was whining this time.

"Hurry up, Sebastian, I'm getting *cold*. You wouldn't want me to get a chill now, would you? It's only making me cross, keeping me out here!"

"Not *that* sort of double-crossing rattlesnake! *Much worse!*" groaned Walls. "Look, just go upstairs and tidy yourself up! I have to deal with this myself!"

What could be worse than being killed, unless it was being tortured for information first and then killed? Priscilla was now not only terrified but also now baffled. Due to this she had not even registered the *exact* words floating through the door, or 'Sebastian' might have given her a clue to the doorbell ringer's identity. Walls was propelling her firmly towards the stairs and shoving her upwards and over Tony's prone form.

Priscilla had a vision of Walls, heroically opening her door and striding out to meet the foe, like a showdown on a cowboy film.

"I'd better stay. You might *need* me!" she continued to protest.

"No, no. I can cope!" he whispered and then, raising his voice and turning towards the door, he called out, "Just coming, Flic, *darling!*"

At last Priscilla understood! Not dangerous armed diamond smugglers at all! It was Walls' dearly loved fiancée! *Audrey had told her sister where to find Walls*! Priscilla clambered with difficulty past Tony's last limb. Tony seemed to have developed limbs in equal number to those of an octopus while he had been lying on her stairs! She gave this one quite a hearty kick by mistake. Tony groaned and turned over. Then he smiled in his sleep and settled down again.

Priscilla, her brain moving into gear, was fleeing up the rest of the stairs. This was a fashion emergency of the most extreme! Flic, the fashion connoisseur, the example of designer dressing, a woman who frequently featured in glossy magazine articles! Priscilla decided she had better get *completely* changed and *entirely* redo her make-up. Flic would certainly be dressed like a mannequin.

On the landing, however, Priscilla paused. Perhaps she had better not bother to make too much effort because it would take too long. She considered what John or Charles might do in a similar situation to that of Walls, not that they had unwanted fiancées. Men always took the easiest route out of a problem! Walls was likely to get rid of the girl back out of the front door as fast as possible. But if he did it very fast she might not even *see* Flic, and that would be so disappointing. She and Angel had several times debated on whether Walls might actually love Flic despite his claims not to do so! The opportunity to find out had arrived. But if Priscilla overdid her changing and primping the opportunity might already have been shoved back out of the house!

Satisfied that she had a valid reason for her own curiosity – that of Angel's disappointment if she did not observe this interesting event – Priscilla entirely abandoned her titivation scheme. Instead she leant forward over the stairs as far as she could so that she could listen to the conversation below. If they seemed to be kissing passionately, she reasoned, she could go and get changed and give them some privacy, although, she reflected, in Walls' case the fact that he was kissing someone passionately usually only indicated that they were female and under thirty, and not that he was in any way whatsoever attached to them!

Walls had opened the door.

A vision of female beauty, trailing expensive perfume, tottered in on very high heels.

"Sebastian!" she cried!

"Flic!" he cried, leaning towards her.

They both kissed the air just above each other's cheeks.

"I gather," she said, sarcastically, "that you cut your vacation in the Pyrenees short! I called round at this early hour to *catch* you, I mean, to *visit with* you, because I thought you were bound to be in from last night's date by now and not yet departed on your early morning jog!"

"Did *Audrey* tell you that I was here?" he demanded.

"Audrey! Why would she know where you were? She's travelling again, you know, having another gap year to go round the world or whatever she does!

Helping orphans in a foreign land, I suppose! Haven't heard from her for months! No, silly! *Angel* told me, of course!"

Fortunately Flic never investigated Walls mention of Audrey further and, equally fortunately, Walls was too devastated by the news of Angel's treachery to notice his own slip and draw further attention to it by trying to cover it up.

"*Angel*! I can't believe it! How could she! I thought she was my *friend*!" Walls exclaimed.

"Oh, she *is* your friend! It went like *this* you see, honey! I was shopping yesterday in those glorious clothes shops at the end of your high street and I had to find a rest room! So I popped into the Maitre and, would you credit it, there were two waitresses who just happened to be discussing Angel and Buffy being on vacation. I couldn't avoid hearing them so, when I had been to the rest room, I stopped one of them in passing and, er, *acquired* Angel's mobile number!"

"Bribed, I presume!" said Walls crossly.

"The poor mites – they live in poverty. It was just a *charitable donation*! Also you seem to have taken Rebecca – that's the waitress's name – out on one date, and then forgotten all about her afterwards! So careless, you are, my baby! Rebecca was very amenable to helping me!" cooed Flic. "Once I had Angel's number it was simple to trace you. Your friend, Angel, has a heart made of very soft candy!"

"I suppose you told her a sob story and made her cry! Not that making Angel cry is exactly difficult!" mourned Walls, adding something about Women! Always stick together! under his breath.

"I was so *moving*, Sebastian, even you would have been swayed! She was entirely impressed by my *broken-hearted tale*! It's your *own* fault, you know! I was only ringing her to see if her phone had reception in the Pyrenees, *unlike yours*, so I could talk to *you* on *her* phone! But once she realised how *distressed* I was, not to be able to find you, she was so helpful. She even told me the time of day you were most likely to be in the house. Calling at this hour was *her* idea, you see."

"OK, OK, *whatever!*" said Walls, thinking that Angel was such a silly softie that she wasn't really responsible for what she did sometimes, but that all the same he *was* going to tell her what he thought of her when he saw her even if this made *Buffy* cross! "Just tell me why you are so keen to track me down and get it over with! Couldn't you have just sent me an email?"

"No, Sebastian, honey babe! Not with something *this* important. I wanted to tell you *myself.* With my own lips and with you in the *same room!* Just to make absolutely sure you couldn't claim I didn't tell you! You are going to be enchanted with this news! I have *set the date!*"

"The date for *what?*" he said, desperately stalling.

"For our *nuptials*, honey! Such a *long* engagement for us both! So far apart for *so* long! I have booked the most *wonderful* venue; I've set the *guest list*; I've booked *Hello* to cover it! *Exclusively*, of course! All you have to do is *be there!* April tenth, next year. All set! Oh yes, and I believe I *may* have asked your little friend, Angel, to be one of the *bridesmaids!* It wasn't difficult to convince her that I needed to speak to you directly after that!"

"You are the devil in human form!" said Walls. "Well, you've said what you wanted to. I agree. *Anything you say*. You'll be off, then! I don't want to keep you from getting to your next spa appointment or whatever other important business you may have today! No point in offering you breakfast! I can see from your ridiculously skeletal figure that you still don't eat!"

He opened the front door and bowed.

"I charmed you noticed that I'm still as trim as I always was!" she purred, looking genuinely pleased. "But," she protested, "I haven't told you the venue yet!"

"Email it to me! Then I'll have it in *writing*!" he said. "*And* the date! I've *already* forgotten when you said it was! No, even better, invite me to the event through Facebook! Then I'll get a reminder on the day!"

393

He nearly managed to shovel her through the door at the end of this speech and thus be able to retire to bed, defeated but unbowed. But he had reckoned without Priscilla. She came sailing down the staircase in as stately a fashion as anyone can possibly manage when one has not slept all night and one's hair and clothes are terribly dishevelled and one has to finish by climbing over a prone man on one's stairs. Elodea, Priscilla felt, would have been most impressed with her knowledge of human nature in this instance, and Elodea would *also* approve her behaviour in stopping Flic's rapid departure. Elodea would *certainly* want to know every detail of this exciting visit as well as Angel!

"Where are your *manners*, Walls, dear?" she asked. "Are you not inviting your *fiancée* to *stay for breakfast?*"

Priscilla felt she couldn't call the girl Flic, which she *hoped* was a ridiculous abbreviation of another name, probably Felicity, but she did not like to risk 'Felicity' either in case Flic's actual name *was* something else.

"I don't have *any* manners: I'm an *American*! And she doesn't *eat* breakfast! Look at the size of her! She doesn't *eat*!" said Walls, thoroughly nettled at Priscilla's frustration of his plans to get Flic through the door.

"Not your *usual* style!" said Flic, goggling at the sight of Priscilla and at the same time noticing that there seemed to be a lifesize dummy of a man lying on the stairs, which was odd. Then she regained her usual society poise and stepped forward politely to shake Priscilla's hand in a formal 'English' way.

"Enchanted to meet you, Ma'am!" she added, formally.

"And I you!" said Priscilla, equally politely, but feeling at a slight disadvantage due to being balanced on two steps with her feet in the narrow gap between Tony and the wall.

"Many apologies for disturbing your *sleep*!" added Flic, with just a slight emphasis on the word 'sleep'.

"That is all right!" replied Priscilla, with a degree of majesty that Queen Victoria might have envied. "I have always been an early riser! Walls had not yet retired to bed as he and *my nephew* have just completed a night run as part of their *marathon* practice."

Priscilla crossed her fingers hastily and surreptitiously as she said 'always been an early riser' in order to avert the lie.

"*She's* not my *girlfriend*, Flic!" said Walls, nettled by the very suggestion. He then added sarcastically, "How could she be when you are my *fiancée*?"

He continued, "This is *Priscilla.* She's," – and here a wonderful inspiration occurred to him – "she's *my Classics tutor and temporary landlady.* I am taking a crash course in Classics with her. It's a condition of my Research Fellowship award. I didn't want *everyone* to know I was having to do a crash course in Latin and Greek, so I told them all I was on vacation! And I'm practising for a charity marathon with Tony here as well, when I'm *not* studying! *Mens sana in corpore sano!*"

"*Really?*" said Flic sarcastically.

"Yes, indeed! And I am getting on very well with this wonderful lady as a tutor!" said Walls, who had taken an opportunity to study his palm while the other two were shaking hands. He had no idea what the phrase he selected meant, as the English translation had become a bit smudgy. Here goes, he thought to himself, and launched into "*Arma virumque cano, Troiae qui primus ab oris Italiam, fato profugus, Lavinaque venit!*"

"Really, Walls, you are making splendid progress but your pronunciation is *appalling*, and I have already told you about *mens sana in corpore sano* once already! However, I can't take all the credit for the speed of your learning; you are an *apt* student!" complimented Priscilla, wickedly continuing his quotation, assuming that neither Flic nor Walls would have any idea what she was saying! "*Litora, multum ille et terries iactatus et alto vi superum servae memorem Iuonis ob iram, multa quoque et bello passus, dum conderet urbem, inferretque deos Latio, genus unde Latinum, Albanique patres, atque altae moenia Romae.*"

Priscilla was about to receive a surprise!

"*Musa, mihi causas memora, quo numine laeso quidve dolens, regina deum tot volvere casus, insignem pietate virum, tot adire labores impulerit Tantaene animis caelestibus irae?*" said Flic, ending with a flourish and then, "I really love that *Virgil*, you know, his *Aeneid* – quite something! I studied Classics at Princetown!" she added to Priscilla. "Love it!"

"And if they didn't take such a dim view of *cocaine possession* you might have *graduated* as well!" interposed Walls, who could see Priscilla changing sides if he didn't do something desperate. He had no idea that Flic had ever done that much studying, bother her!

"You know that wasn't *my* cocaine, Walls. It just *happened* to be the *trunk* of my car! *Anyone* could have put it there!" protested Flic in a whiny little voice.

"Let's not raise old scores!" said Priscilla, hastily. She felt herself that Walls was washing dirty linen in public unnecessarily, especially as the girl was a *classicist*! Although it was a shame that one so potentially talented had not *completed* her studies!

Walls felt the ground slipping from under his feet. If Priscilla and Flic colluded he might find they had reset the wedding date for tomorrow and he was being forced into a suit and heading for the altar at any second!

"Flic," he said firmly to Priscilla, "is just *leaving*!"

"No, no, Walls," said Priscilla. "I'm sure she would like to stay for breakfast! Go and cook a *lovely* plate of bacon and pancakes for us. Oh, yes, and for Tony, too!"

"I've told you once. You don't imagine that someone with Flic's figure *eats*, do you?" said Walls. "I've agreed to the date for the wedding! Whatever it was! Isn't that enough?"

"*I* eat!" said Priscilla, bodily propelling Walls in the direction of the kitchen. "And I'm very hungry! Off you go!"

"Let me show you into the lounge!" she said to Flic, and having waved her through the door she dashed back to the kitchen to mollify Walls. She didn't quite know why she had asked Flic to breakfast except that it was the only delaying tactic she could think of at the time and she herself was starving hungry.

Flic wandered into the lounge. She was momentarily taken aback by the fact it seemed to be a gymnasium but thought that perhaps this was a strange English eccentricity. She leant politely against the exercise bicycle, waiting for guidance on where to sit.

Pippy had grown tired of pretending to be a dragon under her armchair, and was curled up in the middle of one of the exercise mats in a tight, miserably neglected coil. At the sight of a potential friend Pippy arose, trotted over and reached up to pat Flic's knee, looking up at Flic with big, pleading eyes. Flic bent over – a difficult manoeuvre in a very tight skirt and very high heels – to rub the cute little dog's head gently. At least, Flic thought, wallowing in the pathos of her situation, *someone* in this house liked her, even if the someone was a dog! Sebastian! Was he for *real* sometimes? He knew they *had* to get married. He might at least behave nicely about it! He *knew* both their fathers were forcing closure on the event with threats of terminated funding. What the hell! Men always got over sulks in the end. After all it wasn't as if *she* wasn't a class A bride. Most men would love to marry her!

Flic decided to sit down and take a rest. She had had to get up so very early to catch Sebastian and she was dreadfully tired. She looked round the room again, with myopic puzzlement. Where *were* the chairs? Perhaps she would just perch on the *exercise bike*? Then she noticed something most unfortunate beside it.

She drifted out, across the hall in the direction of the kitchen.

Antholian, already half awoken by the animated conversation taking place in the kitchen, combined with a crashing of frying pans and plates, opened his eyes. A vision of unexpected loveliness crossed the hall in front of them. He rubbed his eyelids but the now departing figure was still there. He rose to follow it towards the kitchen.

Walls and Priscilla had descended, in their states of complete exhaustion, to a nursery level argument. Having begun with:

"You didn't have to invite her for breakfast."
"Yes, I did! It was only polite!"

they had now descended to simply saying "Did!" or "Didn't!" alternately.

"I say," said Flic politely, raising her voice to interrupt their exchanges. "I say, could you call your *maid*? Your cute little doggy seems to have made a poop on the bench press!"

"Aaargh!" screamed Priscilla. "We forgot to take the little blighter out!"

"Regrettably," said Walls, speaking loudly and clearly as one might to a toddler, "Priscilla doesn't have

402

servants but she does have *cleaning materials*! Perhaps *you* would deal with it since we are both busy *cooking*!"

"It's all right!" said a voice behind Flic.

She jumped and turned.

"*I'll* deal with it!" said Antholian. "She's my dog, or my family's dog anyway!"

"I thought you were a *dummy*!" said Flic.

"No, no. Quite intelligent really!" said Antholian, wondering what Walls and Priscilla had been saying.

"No, a *shop mannequin*, you know!"

"No, absolutely alive!" he said, and smiled at her.

She smiled back, radiantly. He was instantly and completely smitten.

"It's *Flic*, my *fiancée*!" said Walls, wearily, recognising the signs and hoping to save Tony from himself in time. Flic was clearly having her usual effect – the one she had on all males who were not himself – and he *liked* Tony! Then he added helpfully, not really to inform Flic but more to fill Tony in on what he needed to know: "Flic, this is Tony, Aunty Pris's nephew. He and I have just done a night marathon practice together!"

"Antholian, not Tony!" corrected Antholian, automatically, and he shook Flic's hand formally. He was confused but he assumed that Flic had only just arrived in the UK from America and that this explained her early morning visit. "Charmed to meet you! If I could just get into the kitchen for cleaning materials I will correct the situation in the lounge and then I can go and find you a chair to sit on. I hope you are not too exhausted from your long flight!"

He went so far as to bow to Flic and give her a rare but very enchanting smile of his own.

"If you don't keep at least three rooms away from her, let it be on your own head!" said Walls, but under his breath. He turned his back on Flic and concentrated on his frying pan.

Walls was happy cooking. It soothed him, he found. Priscilla was watching the cooking with equal concentration, looking at his glorious creation in the pan. Her stomach had rooted her to the spot. Her saliva was flowing freely in happy expectation. She feared she might start dribbling in a minute!

Flic, feeling ignored, wandered into the hall and sat on the stairs until Tony finished his deep cleansing of the lounge. He went past her with Pippy in his arms, vanished into the garden for a few minutes and then returned, once more carrying the little dog, who was trustingly nestled against his chest. He and the dog made a very cute combination, thought Flic, especially in that *lycra*! Clearly another exercise freak! Somehow she had expected people in Oxford to be more academic than athletic! No wonder Sebastian liked it here: he always had been keen on sport!

By the time Priscilla and Walls entered the lounge with two trays of food, plates, coffee and cutlery, they discovered Antholian and Flic sitting side by side on the settee, with their knees bent up because it was crammed behind the gym equipment, holding a deep conversation.

Priscilla and Walls had made up their own differences. Walls had looked at Priscilla, sleepless and exhausted, as she bustled around getting out her best china and cutlery for the guest, and decided that not only had he been unfair to Priscilla but that perhaps he was being churlish and inhospitable to Flic. She had come a long way to visit him, and gone to all the trouble of finding him here. So Walls had apologised to Priscilla for his discourteous behaviour and then used his usual method to pacify females, although in Priscilla's case he had kissed her on the cheek and not the mouth. Even so, Priscilla found she was blushing and giggly afterwards. They finished preparing the huge breakfast in peace and harmony.

"You didn't tell me that Flic was so interested in Buddhism!" said Antholian, eagerly, to Walls as he and Priscilla came into the lounge.

Walls had, until then, decided to behave himself until Flic left, and manage *somehow* to *only* be polite and kind. After all she was stuck in the same contract as him and for the same reasons: firstly, youthful stupidity; secondly, spinelessness; and thirdly, fathers who really were prepared to cut off their allowances. But this deception on her part about Buddhism was too much!

"Yes, yes, she *always* has been! I'm sure she *should* really convert! Although, no, *don't*! You see, we would have to break our engagement if that happened as I would rather marry another Catholic, but at the very least it has to be another *Christian*!"

"Oh, but Buddhists *tolerate other faiths*!" said Flic. "I could be a *Catholic Buddhist*!"

Walls glared at her and then ferociously shovelled a gigantic pile of pancakes and bacon onto a plate and handed it to her.

"Oh, Walls! You *shouldn't* have! So generous!" she said. Her face, as she looked at the pile of dreaded calories, was a wonder to behold. She broke off a tiny piece of pancake and nervously introduced it to her mouth.

"No bacon, Walls: not vegetarian!" said Antholian. "But pancakes, please!" he added, telling himself that it would be wickedly wasteful not to eat this food when it was already prepared.

"Coffee?" said Priscilla, rather louder than she needed to. Fussy eaters, as she designated Flic and Antholian, always annoyed her!

"Yes, yes, *coffee!*" said Antholian, trying to make up for his transgression.

"Yes, please!" said Flic, also very politely. "Black, no sugar!"

"I suppose it *would* be!" said Priscilla, looking at Flic's almost untouched plate and her size zero figure.

Priscilla seized her own plate from Walls, poured maple syrup over everything, wrapped up two large rashers of bacon in a pancake and stuffed it into her mouth. Maple syrup dripped off her chin onto the plate. Quite delicious! Priscilla usually ate extremely politely – if anything she was what Elodea considered to be an irritatingly finicky diner – but in the face of these two picky eaters she had decided to gorge herself as fast as possible. She did not want the chef to feel unappreciated.

'Bless Walls!' she thought, forgiving him everything as she stared at the mountainous pile on his own plate. At least he *ate properly* and didn't make other people who ate *sufficiently and properly* feel greedy or overweight!

Antholian suddenly looked at the clock. He sprang off the settee and climbed over the gym equipment.

"I have to go! Walls, can I borrow your bike? I'm not going to make it! I'm going to be too late!" he wailed.

"Too late for what?" asked Walls. "The shop won't open without you and you surely don't open it yet?"

"Not the shop!" said Antholian. "*Boris*! If I don't get him back next door before six a.m. then Mr Fisher will decide that Boris and I have both been killed by unknown dangerous invaders, and break the back door down with an axe to rescue us! He is totally paranoid.

409

He axed the door down once before when I overslept by mistake!"

"You wouldn't *need* rescuing if you were *dead*!" pointed out Walls.

"I know, but Mr Fisher doesn't think; he just does things! It's not a good end to accidentally oversleeping, waking up to the sound of your door being demolished, I can tell you! I don't want to have to write to the insurance company about having had my back door accidentally demolished with an axe *again*. I shall have to tell Mr Fisher I was meditating and didn't hear the, er, you know..."

He trailed off, remembering that Flic was there and that now *she* would know that *he* had been here for the *night*. They were all screwing everything up for Flipper! Antholian looked and felt suddenly very miserable. He had just met a wonderful woman but she had turned out to be engaged to Walls, who didn't even appear to appreciate her, and he was facing the prospect of arriving home to find a psychotic next-door-neighbour rampaging around his shop and flat, with an axe, looking for him. He did hope Boris *was* neither unconscious nor dead, as Mr Fisher would certainly go completely berserk if that was the case.

"Do you have a requirement for a ride?" said Flic.

"A what?" asked Antholian, confused.

"I have a vehicle, parked up just along from this establishment," she explained.

"I'm sorry," he said, "I don't enter vehicles that burn fossil fuels!"

"It doesn't burn fossil fuels, it burns *gas*. It's a *car*!" said Flic, explaining carefully, as one might to a child.

"Chemistry *not* her strongest subject," said Walls in Antholian's ear. "She's quite ecological really!" He had just astutely ascertained that he had a flicker of hope, when all seemed lost. A sudden faint possibility of rescue from the awful fate of marriage. He did not want Tony to be put off Flic in any way!

Antholian looked at the clock again.

"I don't have any *choice*. It's that or Mr Fisher rampaging through the back door! He might attack an innocent passer-by because he thinks they are a murdering burglar! I think, to *save life*, I must waive my principles *just this once*!"

"Did you say you *did* want a ride?" asked Flic, who was finding him very hard to follow. "Or *not*?"

"Yes, yes, yes, please!" said Antholian. "But we must go *immediately*!"

"Nothing to keep *me* here!" said Flic. "Sebastian and I have completed the business that brought me here! I'll email you all the details, dearest!"

She put her loaded plate thankfully down, leaving the contents to congeal on the settee, and climbed out over the gym equipment herself.

She turned to Walls. "I have witnesses here! The date is April tenth! Write it down! I don't want you to forget it!"

"It's written on my *heart*, dearest!" he said to her and blew her a kiss.

"Make sure it doesn't bleed off it then! See you in April, honey!" said Flic, equally casually, and blew him a light kiss back from the very tip of one of her fingers.

She turned to Antholian.

"Shall we hit the road?"

They left.

Chapter 10

Walls opened the window as soon as they had gone and craned through it, stretching to see up the road as far as he could.

"A *Roller*!" he said. "It *would* be! Naturally!"

At these words Priscilla went so far as to rush to the front door, open it and lean out to wave goodbye. She was satisfyingly *just in time* to see her frugal and abstemious nephew being ushered into a huge golden Rolls Royce by Flic's uniformed driver. What a shame that she had not grabbed her mobile in time to take a snapshot!

"I *must* tell Elodea! Tony will *never, never* live this down!" she crowed.

"*No!*" said Walls. "*Don't!*" He was about to add "Don't spoil things by letting Elodea tease Tony! Can't you see the potential in this situation?" but thought better of it and actually said, "Poor old Tony; it's Boris and Mr Fisher he's worried about. Leave him *alone!*"

"I suppose you are right," said Priscilla, but she added a sigh as she thought what hilarity recounting this incident would have caused in the rest of the Smith family. Then she had a comforting thought: she could tell Elodea anyway and swear her to secrecy. Then she realised that explaining why Tony was in her house at this hour would be extremely difficult. Marathon running, that was it! Walls and Tony doing marathon running!

"Coming to bed?" she asked Walls.

Then, remembering that he had kissed her on the cheek, added, in case he had *any* ideas of gaining *comfort* with a *mature woman*, "To *separate* beds that is, for *sleep*, you know, not, er…"

She trailed off in complete confusion.

415

"*You* go to bed!" he said, his lips curling upwards. As if he would ever consider anything of that sort with her! Especially in her current state of dishevelment: hair awry, skirt crumpled, maple syrup dripped liberally over her face and blouse.

Then Walls thought that his last statement might have been a bit abrupt, even possibly unkind, and since he was feeling very pleased with himself and the world and in need of kissing someone, *anyone*, he kissed her on the cheek again

"You see," he continued, "I'm not going to bed at all! I'll take Pippy for a short walk and then I'm going for my early morning run! Flic's *found* me and, you know what that means? It means I'm *free* now! I don't have to wear that wig! I can go where I like, any time of day!"

He vanished into the lounge in search of Pippy.

Priscilla found herself tripping up the stairs lightly. Her cheek seemed to be glowing, she burst into song, "Ecco ridente in cielo…" from *The Barber of Seville*.

Walls should *not* be left alone with females, even when they were her age and married, she reflected.

Pippy had uncurled from a small furry coil on the lounge floor but, instead of bouncing gladly outside with Walls, she staggered out of the lounge and stood coughing loudly and pathetically. A fearsome sloshing noise accompanied the cough. It did not seem so much as to be *emanating* from Pippy but to *be* Pippy. The small dog had turned into a distressed, swooshing, gasping lump of fur. Priscilla, hearing the noise even from above, turned and rushed back down the stairs. Walls was standing, rooted to the spot, gaping at the terrible sight.

Her usual owners would have treated her rather as one would treat a burning saucepan, omitting the part where you cover it with a saucepan lid or damp cloth. Knowing too well what was about to happen next, they would have picked her up, held her at arm's length, and dashed towards the garden. Priscilla and Walls did not know what was going to happen or what to do. They were horrified and baffled. They clutched each other's hands and looked on wide-eyed. Pippy must be *dying* of some terrible complaint! *Right now*! She was going to collapse and fall *dead* on the carpet! How perfectly awful!

Pippy's sides heaved. She looked unable to breathe in, yet she continued to cough and the coughs became louder and more hacking. There was a final enormous cough and a sound like a drain emptying. Pippy vomited a huge pile of debris onto the hall carpet. She promptly revived miraculously. She ran around, yapping happily, wagging her tail and licking whichever bits of them she could reach.

Walls and Priscilla looked at the pile of vomit. This, they both felt, was the final catastrophe of the night, and neither of them were able to cope with it.

"You wouldn't think her stomach was *that* big, would you?" said Walls, at last.

"Toss you for the cleaning job?" said Priscilla, very dolefully, without much hope of his agreeing, let alone herself managing to win the toss.

"It's even worse than we think!" said Walls, as the liquid began to flow away from the solids and run in small streams across the Wilton. "Do you see what I see?"

"Oh no!" said Priscilla.

The pile was almost entirely composed of blood diamonds covered with slimy mucus.

They both sat down on the bottom steps of the stairs and stared at it.

"I'd forgotten that she stole that packet earlier," said Walls.

Priscilla opened her mouth to say something, shut it, opened and shut it again, and finally managed, in a weak voice, "Do you think *possessing* them is a criminal offence?"

"No idea of the *actual* legality but if you are asking my *opinion*, I would say, *yes*! Almost certainly! Kind of like stolen goods, don't you think?" replied Walls.

"Can we get hold of Flipper again? Or one of his little friends?" asked Priscilla.

Walls was about to say that he could find Finn at Flipper's funeral, when he remembered that he wasn't supposed to know what Finn did for his day job.

"I think we are meant to have forgotten he's been here," he replied.

"But not under these circumstances, surely?" said Priscilla. "I mean what if he *knows* how *many* there should be? So he knows there are *some* missing from the buddha? The only people who could have stolen them would be me or you or Tony!"

"Or, as it happens, *Pippy!*" added Walls. "The *dog* can hardly be subject to criminal proceedings!"

"But *I could!*" squeaked Priscilla.

"Not *your* dog. How about we claim Elodea is a jewel thief who has trained the dog as an accomplice!" suggested Walls, facetiously.

"*Walls!*" said Priscilla. "What a *terrible* suggestion!"

"Well what can we do?" said Walls. "We can hardly ring 999 and ask to speak to a *secret agent*! Or can we? Do they ask you if you want Fire, Police, Ambulance, Coastguard or MI5 or 6? Never rung them myself to find out! I've got a simpler idea. Why don't we just *put them in the trash can?*"

"Not the Coastguard; not in *Oxfordshire*? Or is it? Do they patrol the Thames?" wondered Priscilla. "Anyway, that's beside the point! You are distracting me! The *dustbin* is a stupid suggestion! We can't put them in the *dustbin* and have them *burst out* on the rubbish tip or something and find that we have half of Thames Valley police trying to trace us!"

"It's not very likely!" said Walls. "Why would they burst out? If we tie them up in several layers of plastic bags, surely they will just be buried safely under the heap of trash?"

"I'm *not* risking it!" said Priscilla. "But, of course, the carpet! If the carpet is replaced we could just leave them here for the carpet replacing people to find?"

She looked at Walls' face.

"I suppose *not!*" she sighed. "They might think we had concealed them in the dog on purpose! Or swallowed them ourselves even! People *do* swallow illegal things on purpose themselves, don't they? But they'd be able to tell that they'd been *in a dog* if they tested them! Doggy body fluids must be different. I suppose you don't think that doing nothing might be *simplest?*"

She looked at Walls' face again.

"No! OK, we must think of something else!" she finished.

Then she had what *she* considered to be a very bright idea!

"Can you get hold of a rowing boat at this time of day?"

"I suppose I could get a *pair* out," said Walls. "The boathouse keeper knows me and the coach won't mind me having a bit of practice out of term. It'll be open for practice by now. Can you row?"

"Of course not!" replied Priscilla. "I could pretend though!"

"*Pretend*! You can't *pretend* to row in a Kings pair!" said Walls. "Coxed singles don't exist, so you can't pretend to be a cox if *I* row, either!"

He looked at her shape dubiously. He wasn't at all sure she would fit in a seat, whether rowing or coxing!

"Why do you want to go rowing anyway?" he said.

"The *river*!" said Priscilla, with significant emphasis. "Haven't you got that? The *river*! For *disposal*, you know! I was hoping to get out there early, before anyone else was around."

"Brilliant!" said Walls.

Much later they could only both conclude that this cunning plan *appeared* sensible because they were suffering from a great deal of excitement and no sleep. But now that the river disposal idea had taken root in both their brains, they continued with it and never questioned its wisdom further.

"But I think we would be fine if we just took a hired wide bottomed rowing boat later on in the day, from Folly Bridge, say?" suggested Walls.

"Yes. That would be easier than me learning to row before we leave the house! *Later* then!" said Priscilla. "Or we could borrow the Coromandel Fellows punt instead?"

"Not a *punt!*" objected Walls. "A rowing boat. I'm better at rowing! Don't want to attract attention by my lack of finesse! Or look a complete idiot! There might be *girls* around!"

They giggled conspiratorially.

Priscilla looked at the disgusting pile of slime and diamonds. She now felt fired up by their subversive plans. She could tackle anything. She spoke bracingly.

"Come on. We will have to sacrifice my colander! We need to get a bucket, hot water, detergent, disinfectant, plastic gloves and the colander, and let's get out in the garden before the neighbours wake up!"

She wondered, idly, if she *had* a colander in the kitchen. She believed her kitchen was fully equipped; she remembered Elodea helping her to choose the requisite items in Boswells when she had bought the house.

"Just a minute!" said Walls. "There was a whole bagful of those freaking things! Are you sure that's all of them?"

He went into the lounge and crawled around the floor, hunting under the settee, under the chairs, under all the equipment.

"Crikey!" he exclaimed. "Pippy must have eaten the lot! There's nothing left but these two torn-up plastic bags! I thought she only had one of them! No wonder she was so sick!"

"Quick!" said Priscilla. "Gather *every shred* of the plastic up, take it outside, and set fire to it!"

"I've had another awful thought!" said Walls. "Er, she did have a *little accident*, earlier, you know!"

"I," said Priscilla, with dignified aplomb, "am going to manage somehow to get this pile of vomited diamonds into my colander and retrieve them. In my opinion the indigestibility of diamonds will have prevented any going *beyond* her stomach. However, *you* are going to go and find the earlier disaster in the wheelie bin and prod it with a stick to check it out. If it should appear to contain anything suspicious you are going to investigate the matter further!" She finished with a crafty final sentence: "It's a fair deal. I am *guaranteed* to have to deal with the *vomit*, whereas you may have nothing to do."

Walls groaned, loudly. What a finish to the night! Although he was impressed that she even knew she had a kitchen sieve, or knew what it was called, he had never seen her use *any* of the kitchen equipment apart from that involved with preparing and imbibing either coffee or alcohol.

Priscilla was beginning to feel less gung-ho and enthusiastic as she studied the task that she had set herself. She had another good idea.

"We should ring *Tony*!" said Priscilla. "Do you have his number? He can jolly well cycle back and give us a hand!"

"No, no!" said Walls. "Not a good idea. Tony's busy, you know!"

"Busy with *what*? He can leave his shop closed for a while; it's not *that* overflowing with customers! He's the closest available member of Pippy's family, and even if the others were closer we couldn't tell them about the diamonds. He can come and help us!"

By which she meant: he can come and clear up this vomit for me!

Walls did not want to disturb Tony, or Flic. He did not want anything to interfere with the scheme that he was hoping to achieve.

"I'm sure Tony has quite enough dog problems with Boris, and he has to deal with Mr Fisher, who will also be very disturbed after last night. It's not fair to get him back for this as well!"

That sounded *convincing*, he felt, even *kind hearted*. Then he thought of something else.

"Do you think she has got any diamonds left inside her stomach?" asked Walls.

"I sincerely hope not. I am, as you very well know, not a vet, so I have no idea about dogs' digestive systems! I am going to *assume* that she has *evacuated* them all," Priscilla pronounced.

But even as she spoke Pippy began to choke and gasp and slosh again, and deposited *another* pile on the kitchen floor.

"There's the answer! Surely she must have regurgitated them all now!" cried Priscilla despairingly.

Pippy responded by delivering one final evacuation in the doorway between the kitchen and the hall. This time she looked even more delighted, as if she finally felt *completely* better! She bounced around looking entirely pleased with herself, and was only prevented from jumping around on her earlier work on the carpet by Walls grabbing her.

"It's like a horror film!" cried Priscilla. "Did Agatha Christie ever have diamonds eaten by a dog? The Dog Who Ate the Diamonds! It's a good title!" she added dreamily. "Goethe would like Pippy. He would approve of a dog that vomited up diamonds!"

"Not if she *ate* the diamonds first though," objected Walls. "She would have to eat *broken glass* first to satisfy Goethe. You know what Groucho Marx said? 'Outside of a dog a book is man's best friend. Inside of a dog it's too dark to read.'"

In their current state this struck them both as the funniest thing they had *ever* heard. Priscilla had to collapse on the stairs whooping with laughter. Walls, still managing to hold on to the furiously wriggling and wagging Pippy, leant on the wall in hysterics.

"My stomach! My stomach!" gasped Priscilla, as she finally ceased to roll around with laughter.

Walls pulled himself together and sighed.

"Come on. I'll fasten the little horror in the lounge. No good having her trotting around the garden chucking more diamonds up *outside*. We'll gather *all* the output and then *both* go sieving and prodding! Only don't get rid of the equipment or clean yourself up when we finish until we have checked what she has been up to in the lounge!"

It took a surprisingly long time to complete Operation Cleanup. They were both clumsy with lack of sleep and at one stage finished up crawling around on the lawn hunting for a dropped diamond between the blades of grass. Finally they returned to the house, discovered Pippy blissfully fast asleep and apparently completely restored to health, and sat down gloomily in the kitchen.

Priscilla, despite Walls' disapproving stare, made herself a reviving coffee enhanced with a large slug of cherry brandy. Walls knocked back a can of Red Bull. The morning sun shone softly on the house. Outside the sky was blue.

"Do you think it's too late for sleep now?" asked Priscilla.

"Probably!" said Walls. "But I'm prepared to risk the experiment!"

"Where shall we put the you-know-whats?" asked Priscilla. "What if the carpet replacers break in and catch us red handed with them?"

"How about in your fish tank?" said Walls. "I saw that in some film once, I think. Maybe several films. It's the sort of place you could hide those easily!"

"But I don't *have* a fish tank!" objected Priscilla.

It was too much. Although Priscilla's statement was not at all funny in any objective sense, they both experienced another stomach twisting bout of hysterical laughter.

"I have another idea!" said Walls. "We could just *sell* them. They must be worth a bomb!"

"I will *ignore* that suggestion, which I do *trust* was a joke!" said Priscilla. "I will conceal the bag beneath my pillow while I am asleep, and worry about it later. If we leave doing anything till tomorrow that will give Flipper and his friends time to come back and collect them if they have noticed they are missing, and it will also give Pippy time to evacuate any others that she might have tucked in her insides."

"She'd better *not* have any more left! I really couldn't stomach doing that again, *ever*!" said Walls, from the top of the stairs. He then continued, "Pray excuse that allusion to stomachs! It caused me to have a most unpleasant vision myself. When you said 'tomorrow' did you mean today or tomorrow! Don't reply! I don't care! Goodnight! Or rather, good morning! Or something!"

Half an hour later the whole house was wrapped in a profound silence, as exhausted dog, man and woman all slept off their over-stimulating nights.

The following afternoon found Walls rowing a lady courteously up the Cherwell in a wide bottomed rowing boat. They had decided on the Cherwell rather than the Isis as Walls felt he was less likely to meet other rowers that he knew. He was dressed in the very traditional boating gear of a striped blazer, smart shirt and straw bowler hat. Priscilla was wearing a long flowing floral robe and an elegant straw hat with long flowing ribbons. Priscilla had originally worn something much more suitable for an outing in which she was likely to be in contact with river water but when he appeared wearing full Edwardian garb she had held up the entire expedition in order to change into a suitable matching outfit.

He felt rowing a broad bottomed tub was lowering to his self esteem, unless he was accompanied by a lady who was a stunning beauty. He had the Edwardian garb especially for such occasions. It never failed to impress the opposite sex. However, despite her charming outfit, there was no disguising the fact that the member of the opposite sex who was his companion today was both overweight and elderly. He had thus begun the outing in a somewhat sulky mood, but the lovely weather and pleasant river breezes had soon cheered him up. Priscilla herself, oblivious to his bad mood, had not been rowed on the Cherwell by a 'beau' for many years, and was thoroughly enjoying herself.

As they travelled elegantly onwards Priscilla trailed one hand in the water in a casual way. She and Walls began by indulging in standard casual small talk about nothing at all. But after a couple of minutes discussing the weather Walls remembered something funny that he had been meaning to share with her.

"I completely forgot to tell you, by the way," said Walls. "Buffy rang you up with a hoax phone call yesterday when I was up and you were still asleep! I pretended to be you and he gave up when he realised I wasn't riled or bothered. I must tell him it was me when he gets back."

"Barnabus made a hoax phone call? To *me*?" asked Priscilla.

"Yes," said Walls. "Perhaps he'd had an overdose of sun? Or maybe Angel thought it would be funny? He said he was from the BBC. Claimed you had applied

434

to be on some kind of quiz programme and they just wanted to check it was OK with you before they confirmed your place. I knew that you would *never* have applied to be on a BBC quiz show! So I knew it had to be Buffy, even though he was using a different voice. He gave himself away because he went and said that you and Elodea had applied to be on it together! So I agreed with him, of course. Said you would be *delighted* to be on it! He must have been expecting you to be cross. Took the wind right out of his sails, I should think! But he didn't admit it was him, even then! He must be planning to tell you the truth about it when he gets back!"

Priscilla laughed. "I must remember to tease him thoroughly when they get back!"

Odd though. She had an uneasy feeling, somewhere, deep inside her memory. Elodea, a television programme... No, it was *gone*! Then something else occurred to her, distracting her entirely from any references to television shows.

"Surely Barnabus would have known it was *you* answering the phone and not *me*?" she demanded.

"Bad line to the Pyrenees! Probably could only just hear me!" said Walls, slightly too hastily.

Priscilla looked at him rather searchingly. He quaked. He had been entertaining some of his friends with 'Priscilla impressions' recently and had, indeed, also been answering her house phone with an imitation of *her* voice to save having to explain his presence in the house to puzzled callers. Priscilla was so absent-minded that she would never remember whether she had actually spoken to people herself or not, and he always left her a message giving all the necessary information from the phone conversation. Unless the caller was a 'cold caller' or Barnabus playing the fool, naturally! In fact he was of the opinion that the callers were better off with him rather than the real Priscilla, as he at least listened properly to what they were saying to him.

"Just look at those ducks!" he cried, in a voice that suggested this was a sight not to be missed.

"Which ducks? Where?" asked Priscilla, turning in her seat and looking all around her.

There were, as usual, a large number of possible ducks to which he *could* have been referring.

"Didn't you *see* them?" asked Walls. "Hilarious! Such a shame you missed it! Er, while I think about it, we must remember *what* we are *here for*, you know."

"*I* haven't forgotten! It was not me who wandered off into funny stories!" retorted Priscilla, now diverting her entire concentration to her original task.

"Ducks, you know, fascinating birds, although rather more interesting was the Duck that was a USA-made amphibious vehicle, used in the Second World War. Surprisingly, this name was derived from their acronym D, U, K, W and not from the fact they were amphibious or that the body looked rather like that of a duck. Furthermore, many people think the acronym was a military acronym but it was actually one produced using the naming convention of General Motors, who designed them in partnership with Sparkman and Stevens. Thus D merely meant a vehicle designed in 1942…"

His monologue had the effect he wanted. Priscilla entirely forgot about the story of the phone call and also ceased to listen to anything else he was saying. She was exerting her full efforts on achieving her goal, merely saying "Yes?" or "Fancy!" if he paused for breath.

Walls continued rowing slowly while delivering a brilliant and informative lecture on the subject of DUKWs. Naturally Priscilla did not hear any of his erudite and interesting information as she was uninterested in that subject and was consequently humming Beethoven's *Pastoral Symphony*, while concentrating on her own absorbing task. Regrettably, subjects in which she had no interest included nearly every topic that lay outside her own specialism, the main exceptions to this rule being food or drink.

After she had triumphantly finished he entire first movement of the *Pastoral Symphony* and her other little task, Priscilla looked all around to check that they were out of earshot of any other boats.

"That was the *last one*. This should surprise *archaeologists* one day!" she said in a triumphant stage whisper.

"Indeed it should!" replied Walls. "Our little deposits may yet feature in a glass case in the Ashmolean."

They were blissfully unaware that their little deposits were destined to achieve notoriety rather earlier than that.

"Shall we turn back?" asked Priscilla.

"No. We hired the boat for longer. We'll carry on up to the Vicky Arms and you can have alcohol and I can have Evian water!" said Walls, much relieved to be finally safely rid of the blood diamonds. "We might as well enjoy ourselves!"

Priscilla was more than happy to agree with this suggestion. Walls might have been less inclined to suggest it if he had realised that she was going to move on from completing a quiet rendition of the *Pastoral Symphony* while travelling upstream, to singing Verdi arias, fortissimo, all the way downstream back to the boathouse.

****

Two days later Walls was sitting at his laptop in Angel's bedroom, with Priscilla leaning anxiously over his shoulder.

He could have moved out of Priscilla's house again now that Flic had discovered him but he and Priscilla had never discussed this issue, both feeling it was perfectly satisfactory for him to remain in Angel's room until Angel returned.

"Bound to be lots online; eBay must have one if nowhere else does! You can get one-day delivery from most sites if you pay enough. I'll just try Googling it... Straight away, see! Here's one!" said Walls. "Small, antique, silver, laughing buddha! Express delivery 1 day! ... We've got time! ... But it's really expensive! Look at the price!"

"Never mind! This is an emergency. I have the funds!" said Priscilla. "Charles is due here the day after tomorrow! I *must* have it here by then. Is it a *reputable* source?"

"Hard to say! It *looks* OK! Should be fine! I buy a lot of stuff online, all perfectly above board and genuine. Some of these sites can be dodgy though. They write their own reviews from pleased customers, see, so you can't tell! When the goods don't turn up it's all too late – they've changed the web site name or disappeared! But I don't think we have much choice really! Would cost you an *absolute fortune* for a silver one from a UK retail outlet!" said Walls blithely.

"Let me see it!" said Priscilla. "The light's shining too much on the screen from this angle."

He obligingly moved the laptop towards her.

Priscilla craned over the screen and was pleased with what she saw.

"You know, it does look *exactly* the same as the one Charles sent to me!" she burbled happily. "I only saw it for a few seconds, of course, before it got blown up, but from what I can remember it was identical! See, when I enlarge the image... Yes, I am pretty sure that's definitely the same hallmark. I remember it because I had just seen that there was a little pig on the first symbol of the hallmark when Barnabus rang the doorbell. Yes, yes, it's all coming back to me!"

"*Perfect* then! It must be *genuine* too!" said Walls. "Lucky you spotted that because I don't know anything about hallmarks! Shall I go ahead?"

"Yes, yes. Quick then! Just order it," said Priscilla. "Do you need my credit card?"

"No," said Walls. "I'll use mine and get it delivered by the fastest method possible! You can pay me back when it turns up. I feel partly responsible! I washed the second one up, after all!"

"Cash or cheque?" said Priscilla.

Walls was about to say that the expense would be *his pleasure* since he felt vaguely responsible for the whole crisis, although he wasn't quite sure why it should be his fault, apart from drying the second buddha after Priscilla put it in the washing-up, which was her fault! However, this much money would be a very minor expense to him and he had the feeling that it would be a major item for Priscilla! But Priscilla forestalled him.

"No, I *insist* on paying!" said Priscilla, looking at his face and speaking before he could do so. "Can't have *you* getting vulcanized as well!"

Walls looked puzzled so Priscilla added, helpfully, "Smith'ed. Vulcan, Roman god, a blacksmith himself!"

"I don't mind *how* you pay me then," said Walls, "if you really *must* pay! You have been so kind with all this free hospitality!"

"Think nothing of it!" said Priscilla, trying to sound casual about the cost, although she was inwardly sighing over the dent the buddha would make in her bank account. "I can always sell it on eBay myself after Charles has left! I wouldn't have sold his *real* present but this isn't the *original* one, so I can!"

"I am a very rich man, you know!" reminded Walls.

"Keep it. You might need it!" said Priscilla, adding very naughtily, "Expensive wedding coming up, remember!"

Walls groaned!

"Not if *I* can help it! I just have to make sure *she* decides to marry *someone else* and then *she* can break it off and *I* can sue *her*! Instead of *her* suing *me*, you see, and also no repercussions from the seniors for *me*, allowance-wise! Just for *her*!"

"Brilliantly *evil*," said Priscilla, "but who could she *possibly* prefer to you!"

"It's hard to believe that she could prefer anyone else but didn't you notice?" said Walls, deciding to let her into his plot, "I was thinking of..."

He whispered the name into her ear.

Priscilla laughed. "Ridiculous! They're poles apart!"

"*Are* they, then? I happen to have heard that a certain *non-fossil fuel user* has accepted an *invitation* to go and see the fall leaves in *New England*! I believe he has been invited to fly over there on somebody's private jet! Good for meditating under, apparently! Falling leaves, that is, not private jets! You will also be surprised to hear that a certain socialite returned home with a whole suitcase full of alternative remedies purchased from a certain Cowley Road shop!"

"*Never!*" said Priscilla. "My goodness! Elodea will never, ever, believe this one!"

"Well, he may have rejected the idea of travelling on a *private jet*, when I think about it, but a trip to New England is certainly in the pipeline. I believe the journey involved cycling to a port and then taking a private cabin on a cargo ship," said Walls, feeling he had better be honest, even if this was rather less sensational.

"*Can* you travel on cargo ships?" asked Priscilla.

"If you don't mind the length of the journey, the lack of luxury and the fact that there aren't that many berths available so you can't be fussy about when you go. Wouldn't suit many travellers! I agree with you though: the whole affair is entirely unbelievable! Can't think how it came to happen!" continued Walls, looking very innocent.

"Oh, but I think she might like him because he doesn't care about her wealth, or how she dresses or anything like that. She might find that refreshing, don't you see? He wouldn't care if she lost her allowance! And he would love her for the underneath as well as the wrapping! He might think she's pretty but he wouldn't even notice the clothes and make-up and jewellery and things. In fact he will supply her with *exactly what you lack!*" explained Priscilla, amazed at her own insights into the human condition.

"What values do I lack that she wants?" asked Walls, affronted.

"*Sincerity*, for a start! At least in your attitude to her!" retorted Priscilla.

"Oh, well, *that!*" said Walls, not at all abashed. "*You* think this relationship might be a *runner* as well then! Not likely to scratch before the big day? Wow! Liberty beckons! Celebrations! I feared I might just be imagining it!"

Priscilla was thinking how good this would be for both Tony and Flic. Flic might persuade him to make his life a little less austere; and he would convert her to Buddhism so that she thought of other things than fashion, and she might find great happiness in giving all her money away to a good cause. The girl had studied Classics. Perhaps she would like to make a large *donation* to a *university classics department*. Surely her father would not really cut her off without any money? She must be able to wind her father round her finger! Although if he did that would not matter either to Tony as he would much rather that she didn't have any and... and just then, while floating in her happy daydream of young love, something occurred to Priscilla. She began to wonder if Walls had made the whole thing up to see if she believed his ridiculous story. He might be about to fall around the room laughing because she had believed him. She looked at him narrowly. W*as* he telling the truth?

Then Priscilla had an even more terrible thought. If he *was* telling the truth he might be guilty of something worse than playing a joke on her. He might have been putting his own oar in and promoting this affair purely to gain his own ends, encouraging Tony to believe he was in love when he wasn't, not caring whether the relationship would be happy for either Tony or Flic.

Walls, watching her face, put on his most guileless face and added his most dazzling smile to it. There was, in his experience, only one way to silence females with suspicious minds who might try to put a spanner in your plans if they delved into them any further! Maybe not the *lips* in Priscilla's case though!

He kissed her on the cheek. This strategy was, to his surprise, not entirely successful. She *still* looked suspicious. She was getting rather wise to his kissing tactics by now!

"How do you *know* all this about Tony and Flic?" she asked. "I didn't think you were such close friends with Tony!"

"Because Flipper went off with Tony's tracksuit and he feels it would be sinful to buy another suit of clothing unnecessarily, wasting world resources, when there is nothing wrong with the Kings lycra suit. But he feels so conspicuous running around after Boris wearing tight-fitting Kings lycra that he has taken to going for his doggy runs with *me* for company as well. Two of us wearing Kings lycra look so much less remarkable than one. In any case, naturally, when the two of us are together no one wastes time looking at him, as they are all admiring *me*!"

Priscilla still looked as if she was about to cross-examine Walls' motivation for friendship with Tony when he was literally saved by the bell. The doorbell rang.

Walls hung out of the sash window to see who it was.

"Well, well, speak of angels and you hear the flutter of their wings! The man himself is at the door!" he pronounced.

Priscilla dashed downstairs to let Tony in.

Antholian bounced in, waving a newspaper. He shut the door hastily and firmly behind him.

"Have you seen this?" he demanded.

"Goodness," said Priscilla, taking it out of Tony's hand. "Flipper's made the headlines in the *Oxford Times*: Kings' Graduate Blows Himself Up!"

"Have you read this bit?" asked Walls, craning over her shoulder. "A gas board official said he would like to emphasise that gas appliances were very safe but only if all work was carried out by properly qualified gas engineers. He then added that having an Oxford degree in PPE was undoubtedly splendid but sadly did not qualify you to fit gas cookers. Although an investigation was still in progress it appeared that there may have been fundamental errors in the way the cooker had been installed and these appeared to

450

have, very tragically, caused the death of a young man and the destruction of an entire shop. He urged anyone else who might not have employed a qualified fitter to install their gas appliances to have them checked and refitted immediately."

"Not *that* article!" said Antholian. "*The other one*; the one at the bottom. I have a terrible suspicion that somehow, though I don't see how, it might have some kind of connection with *you two*!"

"No, *absolutely not*! Nothing whatsoever to do with me!" said Priscilla, automatically, without even looking at the article. A few years ago, she thought to herself, I could have said that with perfect and truthful confidence, unless one of my books or papers had just been published, and even then I was unlikely to feature in the *popular* press. But these days I seem to lurch from appearing in one sensational news scoop to appearing in another! Vulcanized! That's the cause of it all. I really do not want to know what it says this time!

"Why?" asked Walls. "What is it about?"

He took the paper into his own hands and searched further down the page.

"*Definitely not!*" he said after looking at it.

He handed it to Priscilla.

"Most definitely nothing to do with either of us!" agreed Priscilla, having glanced at the headline.

"*Liars!*" said Antholian, but in a friendly way. "I don't suppose they'll ever trace it back to you, and I'm sure Flipper will cover for you, but didn't you think about the *fish*? And why had you still got any of them?"

"We hadn't!" said Walls. "Why would we have? As you said!"

Priscilla found her reading glasses and perused the whole article.

"FISHY OR WHAT? UNCUT DIAMOND FOUND IN PIKE'S STOMACH", read the headline. The article continued:

A fisherman on the River Cherwell got more than he bargained for when he caught a fifteen-pound pike. Its stomach contained several lumps of shiny material which he thought were glass. He showed them to another fisherman, who sent him to the jewellers to have them checked. They were revealed to be uncut diamonds worth...

"Worth *how much?*" said Priscilla. "What a shame we didn't take a fishing rod ourselves when," she added, taking pity on Tony. "We went for that row on the Cherwell a few days ago."

"It also says that the police are investigating the matter and are going to dredge that piece of river in case someone has dropped a stolen hoard of jewels into it," said Antholian. "What if *they are* traceable? Flipper will have a giddy fit – at least he would if he wasn't dead!"

"Traceable to *where?*" said Priscilla. "Sadly Flipper died before I ever met him! If these diamonds should happen to be something illegal, blood diamonds say, and they can trace the diamonds back to the original mine, then it must mean the smugglers are operating

453

in this country! I, myself, think it must be an ancient Anglo-Saxon hoard!"

"How far do pike swim?" asked Walls. "It was probably nowhere near the spot where they were originally, er, thrown in, by whoever might have thrown them! I don't see how you would find anything that small by dredging!" He looked at the article again. He gulped. "I see what you mean about the *value*! Just think how much a few more of them would have been worth – say, two little bags full?"

"Illegal diamonds!" said Priscilla. "You couldn't *think* of selling them! They have cost lives! Whoever sold them would be cursed by the blood of the innocent!"

"This fisherman guy, though, he doesn't know that about the innocent blood, so that's OK, I guess," sighed Walls. Then he brightened. "I have had a great moneymaking idea! I am going to buy a wholesale set of cheap fishing rods and advertise *one* fishing rod for sale in *Daily Info*, so it doesn't look like I am selling so many, and I can pretend they are more expensive than they are! Bound to be a lot of demand! I could make a mint. This incident is going to popularise fishing on the Cherwell for weeks!"

"Anyway, they are *nothing* to do with us and nobody would ever be able to prove who put them there. No CCTV on the river!" said Priscilla, with absolute confidence.

"I do hope you're right," said Walls, giving up all hope of pretence, "because otherwise if Flipper can't stop them investigating further, and if they *should* make the error of putting Audrey back onto the case, she might shoot us *both,* on *purpose*, this time. Very fierce lady, Audrey! And your family," he added to Tony, "ought to train your dogs only to eat dog food!"

"Ah ha!" said Antholian, feeling the mystery had been cleared up. He then continued, "I thought Audrey was rather sweet. She is a lot like her *sister* in that aspect!"

He smiled, as if at a cherished memory.

Walls tried to keep a straight face but gave up and collapsed against the wall, whooping with laughter.

Priscilla was having difficulties in trying to keep a straight face herself. She made a muffled snorting sound, which she covered by blowing her nose. She was fond of Tony and did not want to hurt his feelings. She had also decided that a romance between Tony and Flic might be very good for both of them, irrespective of Walls' personal interest in the matter. Flic could bend Tony's rigid adherence to principles and make his austere life more comfortable, and he could teach her more worthwhile life values! Perhaps she might return to academia herself, finish her Classics degree! Use her undoubtedly brilliant brain for something useful! Such a waste!

Priscilla produced a brilliant idea to explain Walls' behaviour and prevent him upsetting Tony.

"Walls is only laughing because of a sentence we were translating into Latin this morning! I'm tutoring Walls in Latin and we happen to have just *translated that very sentence* into Latin. You know, *the sentence you just said*!"

Priscilla felt that Elodea would be very impressed with her brilliant insight into the human condition and her amazing solution to Walls' appalling behaviour! Even if she couldn't remember what it was that Tony had just said.

She glared at Walls, still full of hilarity, and added, "Walls is having *another* Latin tutorial for the whole of this evening. *A bove majori discit arare minor*!"

The thought that Priscilla might carry out this threat sobered Walls up. He had a date that evening, which he did not intend to miss!

"But I've made very good progress with studying Latin so far today!" Walls exclaimed. "Listen to this! *Puella bonam est, comme sa soeur*! So, as you can see, I don't need this evening's lesson; I can wait till tomorrow for my next lesson!"

Priscilla's jaw had dropped in horror at this muddled multilingual sentence but Walls, thinking she was impressed with his knowledge rather than horrified, continued, in a pleased way, applying a broad Boston twang to the pronunciation of each word:

"Mensa, mensa, mensam, mensae, mensae, mensa, amo, amas, amat, amamis, amatis, amant! Oh, hang it; I forgot a bit! *Mensae, mensae, mensas, mensarum, mensis, mensis!"*

Priscilla's jaw dropped further. Tony, feeling guilty about interrupting their studies and thinking he should encourage Walls' studious efforts to learn Latin, joined in, helpfully.

"Have you reached the *second* declension yet?" Tony shut his eyes to remember better himself. "You know: *dominus, dominus, dominum, domini, domino, domino, domini, domini, dominos, dominorum, dominis, dominis!"*

Walls took the opportunity of Tony's recital to whisper in Priscilla's ear, "Found your old school *Kennedy's Shorter Latin Primer* on the bookshelves. Read it while I was using the exercise bike! Quick learner or what! I'll bet you were impressed!"

Walls then added, out loud, "The second? I even know some of the *third*!" and continued with a flourish, *"Rex, rex, regem, regis, regi, rege, reges,*

reges, reges, regum, regibus, regibus! Funny how they ran out of ideas for different endings in the plural bits. A lot of repetition, don't you think?"

Priscilla decided she must curtail Walls' and Tony's classical language demonstration as fast as possible. She felt that her entire digestive system might be wrecked if she heard anything further!

"Green tea?" she proposed, hopefully, to Tony, and whisked him out to the kitchen.

Walls, who was bubbling over with giggles again, this time because of the horrified expressions that had been passing across Priscilla's face, sat down on the stairs to laugh properly. Pippy, delighted that he had sat down so close to the ground and become such an accessible human, bounced out from the lounge and sprang onto his stomach. She had the first page of the *First Latin Primer* in her mouth. She dropped the page onto his chest with the air of the Queen bestowing a knighthood.

"You little *horror*!" whispered Walls, grabbing the page, folding it carefully and hiding it hastily in his breast pocket. "We will have to stick that back into the book when your Aunty Priscilla isn't looking, or you will be an *ex-dog*! And I will probably be an *ex-human* if she discovers that I accidentally left the book open on the floor where you could reach it! Let us hope she *never* opens that book these days! Probably safe! I should think she is well past first primer standard, wouldn't you?"

Pippy climbed up his chest and licked his face lovingly. She knew how to get forgiveness from *any* human.

"It doesn't work on me!" said Walls, capitulating anyway. "I use that one too often myself!"

Postscript

"Goodness, you've transformed this room. I didn't know you were so keen on exercise these days!" said Charles, momentarily staggered by the new-look lounge. "Splendid. It'll save me trying to find a gym to use while I'm here."

"Yes, it's all the very best quality!" said Priscilla. This seemed a safe reply. She was sure that anything Walls used would be top-of-the-range equipment, and this reply neither suggested untruthfully that she did exercise nor admitted that she didn't.

"I see you've kept all the books and ornaments in here with the gym equipment! Splendid! You need something to look at while you exercise, eh?"

Charles sounded slightly puzzled by the whole arrangement but he was coping admirably. He clambered over the bench press and picked up the

461

little silver buddha from its shelf, where it was shining in a bright and eye catching way.

"Ah! You kept the little buddha then?" he asked.

"Of course!" said Priscilla. "It was a gift from you!"

"You had its head fixed back on securely too! Or did you glue it yourself? Pretty good job if you did it. What sort of glue did you use? I thought you would like my unusual wrapping idea. Brilliant way to keep the jewellery safely concealed on the journey. Can't trust these foreign postal systems. Could have got stolen en route, but there it was, all ready for you when you took the thing's head off! I know you, you see. I knew you would fiddle with its head when you found it was loose and, there you are! Jewellery in your hand! But anyone who took the lid off the box to see if there was anything worth stealing would just see a very cheap buddha statuette and not look any further! I knew that would keep it all safe on the journey! Never got round to asking you about it before. We've both been so busy these last few months!"

Priscilla's brain was reeling.

"Yes, *very* entertaining! It was a *delightful surprise!*" she managed to say, even if rather faintly.

"I knew you would like that jade jewellery! Not to everyone's taste these days but you always like real bits of antiquity! Wear it tonight when we go out to dinner!"

"Er, *perhaps!*" said Priscilla, wondering if a quick trip to the Ashmolean museum shop might rescue her in any way. *"Such a lovely design!"*

She entertained a sneaking hope that he would describe the jewellery further if she encouraged him to talk about it.

"Not often you see a neck collar quite like that, with the bracelet, earrings, all coordinated!" continued Charles, sounding very pleased with himself. "And a *particularly* intricate and unusual design!"

"Yes, yes!" purred Priscilla. "All quite, quite wonderful!" Not much chance of finding a replacement for that lot then! Not only unique but any approximation to that would cause her already bruised and dented bank account to receive a fatal blow. Perhaps if she dipped into her *savings*? No, no use. However much she spent, how on earth could she find a substitute for a very intricate and unusual design when she didn't know what it looked like!

"But," she added, as desperation produced inspiration, "I thought I would wear the pearls you sent me for our anniversary this evening!"

The disaster sunk further into her brain. Jade! Antique jade! A full set of beautiful and unusual jade jewellery! *Blown up by Paris and Barnabus*! She had barely had the buddha in her hands at all. She had unwrapped it, noticed the head was loose, and then Barnabus had burst in upon her before she could look any further Worse, it was just a *cheap* little buddha, although it probably didn't play temple bells or wink. It was just 'wrapping', with her real present inside it. Could she make an excuse and go and hide in the bathroom and wail for a few minutes?

"I'm surprised you liked the buddha itself enough to keep it!" persisted Charles, accidentally turning the tip of the dagger in her wound. "It's a bit, er, well, I know it's a traditional design and meaningful to the devout but I don't like these laughing designs at all! I prefer the meditating ones myself! And it's only mass-produced tat! I really thought you would consign it to the bin. Or the charity shop!"

Could things *get* any worse?

"Oh, I couldn't have done that with a present from *you*, darling! Even if it was only the wrapping on the real present!" said Priscilla hastily. "However fake! Of course the fact it's a fake is *obvious*!"

Her voice sounded surprisingly controlled and calm. She felt as if the floor was rocking under her feet. She had been vulcanized again, and not a Smith in sight right now on whom to take her revenge! Of course, this whole affair originated with *all* the Smiths, except Elizabeth and John. All four of the others! They were *all* guilty. Barnabus had decided her buddha was a bomb, Paris had blown it up, Barnabus had bought her a frightful replacement, and Tony had failed to supply

465

her with an adequate replacement and got her muddled up with those damn diamonds! Even Elodea was to blame since it was *her* bomb that made Barnabus think that there were explosives in Priscilla's buddha! Elodea should have known better than to get involved with mentally disturbed down-and-outs! Yes, undoubtedly, *vulcanized again*! She did hope Charles would say that *this* buddha *wasn't* too obviously a fake. Maybe she could resell it on the Internet to another gullible person?

"Not immediately obvious to *many* people!" said Charles, loftily. "You would be surprised at how many people are *fooled* by these pieces of rubbish! Many people get taken in by the weight, the appearance and the faked hallmarks."

Thank goodness, thought Priscilla. Still some hope of reselling it to one of the many available idiots then!

Charles continued, "But there's no question if you look closely. Getting the weight right by putting a base layer of iron fools a lot of people. But the top coating doesn't have the right appearance and the fake hallmarks are a *real* giveaway. That first pig symbol, nicely done but clearly not a genuine hallmark! I don't know why they don't fake *actual* hallmarks…"

Charles went on and on. It was always hard to stop him from showing off his knowledge, even if he thought you already knew everything he was saying.

Priscilla sat down on the settee, rather quickly. It did not look as if resale would be a possibility. This was not just a little bit fake. If it had been really made from silver but with a false hallmark just to make it seem to be an antique, she *might* have tried to resell it herself, admitting to the fake hallmark. But reselling this at the price she had bought it would be total fraud! A large sum of money depicted in enormous, flashing red letters arose in front of her eyes.

She decided to attempt a change of subject. Distraction! That was it!

"I know you aren't here for very long but I'm so busy with all these proofs for the new edition of my book! I have really got behind, what with one thing and another! I wondered if you could possibly spend a few hours today double-checking them for me?" she said.

She was absolutely confident about the effect that *this* speech would have! The thought of sitting reading proofs of a classical text should get him to suggest a wonderful outing somewhere *outside* her house. Otherwise, if she stayed *inside* her own house much longer she feared that Charles might witness her picking the buddha up and hurling it through her own front window!

"You know what *I* was thinking?" he said. "I know you *should* be proofreading but the publishers *will* wait! They'll *have* to! Forget all about these proofs for a while! You need a break. You can start again afterwards with a clear mind, and then you'll get them all checked in no time at all. What we *should* do is take the Eurostar, go to that little hotel in Paris again? The one we stayed in last time we went to Paris? We could carry on to Switzerland, down to Italy and then maybe even carry on to Greece? A little Mediterranean cruise, say? What do you think?"

"Do you know?" said Priscilla, smiling at him, "I think that is a *wonderful* plan!"

Elodea would get back from Japan and find that she, Priscilla, had been swept off her feet by her *own* husband and taken on her *own* exciting trip. How satisfactory! Walls could look after Pippy! He *owed* her, especially after that buddha! She *would leave him a note*!

"Let's get your stuff packed then!" cried Charles, picking her up in a King Kong lift and carrying her up the stairs.

Did Anyone Die? - the first **Little Wychwell Mystery**

Executive Synopsis
Some are born detectives, some achieve detectiveship and some have detectiveship thrust upon them. Dog sitting can be dangerous.

Synopsis
A missing wheelie bin, a gunfight with no bodies, and a carrier bagful of groceries are the ingredients that make up this very English murder mystery tale. Our heroes are two old college friends, each equally eccentric in their own way, a pseudo-posh student and a barking mad terrier. Together they must solve the mystery of the events in Little Wychwell, in between coffee mornings, rowing practice and the imminent arrival of a bouncing baby.

A Very Quiet Guest - the second Little Wychwell Mystery

Executive Synopsis

Most murdered people knew their killers, but none of our heroes seem to have remembered this fact. Also... would you rather be a duck or a jackdaw?

Synopsis

Following the events in 'Did Anyone Die?' Elodea, Barnabus and Priscilla are launched on another crime trail together. Also dragged into this mystery are Barnabus' new girlfriend, Angel, and her musical hamster Isambard and Barnabus' smooth operating friend, Walls. Elodea is in danger from an unknown assassin. Who can it be and why would anyone try to kill Elodea? Is it Ustin, back from the dead? This book is the sequel to 'Did Anyone Die?

About the Author

Stella Stafford lives in an Oxfordshire village but not in Little Wychwell itself as that particular village only exists in her novels. She has an Oxford M.A. although she did not attend either Kings or Coromandel Colleges as these colleges are entirely fictional. The human characters in her books, however delightful, do not resemble any person that she has ever met, living or dead. However Pippy is real, although fortunately he can't read and thus has never discovered that he has been fictionalised as a female, and so is Isambard the hamster. She is married and has children.

Stella Stafford writes

MYSTERY THRILLERS: the Little Wychwell Mysteries. *Did Anyone Die*, *A Very Quiet Guest* and *All that Glisters is not Silver* are published in paperback and are also available on Kindle. Two further titles will be available shortly.

SCIENCE FICTION/FANTASY: Short stories and the full length novels, the Demeter Chronicles. *And then it...* (short stories) and *Hunting the Thingle* are available on Kindle, *The Battle for Demeter* will be available on Kindle shortly.

NON-FICTION: usually written under a different authorial name

Stella Stafford twitters as @stellastafford

www.stellas-home.co.uk is the author's website and has further information about the author and her books, including reviews. Reviews can be found on Amazon and on various other online review sites.

Made in the USA
Charleston, SC
22 December 2012